DANGER

A GOOD GUYS NOVEL

JAMIE SCHLOSSER

Cover Design: Oh So Novel
Formatting: Champagne Book Design
Editing: Wordsmith Proofreading Services

DEDICATION

To my own little caterpillar pig-fish,
I love you super lightning eight one zero eight!

DEDICATION

To my own little caterpillar pig-fish,
I love you super lightning eight one zero eight!

Brielle

Technically, I'm not a stripper. As a cage dancer, I don't take all my clothes off and no one gets to touch me. I'm just the eye candy.

And I can feel their eyes on me. I know they're watching, but I don't do this for them.

This is my time.

My life may not have turned out the way I thought it would, but I'm not complaining. From 9pm to 1am several days a week I get paid to feel sexy, to feel desired, to do what I love.

I always knew I wanted to be a dancer—I just didn't realize I'd be doing it in a cage.

Colton

Erectile dysfunction—two words that can cause a collective cringe from men everywhere. The doctors can call it 'performance anxiety' all they want, but that's just a fancy way of saying my dick doesn't work.

Just when I start to think there's no hope for me, I see her. She's gorgeous, sexy, and goofy as f*ck. She also looks really familiar, but I can't put my finger on it.

When I find out who she really is, my world is turned upside down and everything seems to fall into place.

She's not gonna make it easy for me, but I've never been one to back down from a challenge. She's convinced I won't stick around.

I'll prove her wrong.

I'll show her I'm one of the good guys.

PROLOGUE

Fifteen Years Ago

Brielle

Seven Years Old

"**E**ight, nine, ten! Ready or not, here I come," I sang.

Skipping across the lawn, I headed to the backyard shed first, pretending to be clueless about where Colton was hiding.

I liked to let him think he had me stumped, even though I always knew where to find him. My mom said we were like the last two pieces of a jigsaw puzzle. I agreed with her because Colton was my other half. From the first moment I saw him, I knew we belonged together.

After confirming that he wasn't in the shed, I tiptoed around to the front of the house, being careful not to step on Mom's freshly planted marigolds.

As I approached the white porch, I heard quiet snickering underneath the wooden boards. I shook my head and smiled because he was so bad at this game.

"Gotcha!" I poked my head through the place where the lattice was missing.

Colton grinned at me, showing missing teeth on top and crooked teeth on the bottom. I loved his crooked teeth. I crawled under the porch and sat next to him in the dirt.

"Do you think they won't find us?" he asked. "Maybe we

could just stay here forever."

"No, they'll find us. That's why I brought the backup plan," I said proudly, pulling a pair of handcuffs from the back pocket of my jean shorts.

He gave me that smile again. After clasping it on himself, he carefully wrapped the metal around my wrist, making sure it wasn't too tight.

"Look." He pointed to one of the boards above my head. "I stole my dad's pocket knife."

I couldn't stop the goofy smile on my face when I saw what he carved in the wood.

Colt + Ellie 4ever

It even had a heart drawn around the words.

Early summer sunlight filtered through the boards above us as we sat shoulder to shoulder, and I tried to soak up these last minutes together.

"I wish you didn't have to move away," I said, fighting against the lump in my throat. Colton didn't like it when I cried. Said it made him sad, and I didn't want to make him sadder than he already was.

"Me too," he replied quietly.

"Is it because your mom…" *died*. I didn't want to say the last word and I didn't need to. Like true best friends, we could finish each other's sentences.

Colton nodded. "Dad says we need a 'new beginning'," he said, putting air quotes around the words. "He wants to start his own auto shop and he got a good deal on some shitty garage."

I gasped.

"Colton, don't say shitty," I whisper-yelled.

"Well, it is." He angrily picked at the dried dirt on the bottom of his shoe.

"You're gonna get your mouth washed out with soap

again," I warned.

"I don't care." He scowled. "If he wanted to have a shop so bad, I don't know why he couldn't just do it here."

"But you'll write to me?" I asked hopefully while anxiously rubbing at the knuckle of my thumb—it was my nervous habit.

"Of course, Ellie." Colton put his hand over mine, stilling my actions. "Don't do that. You're gonna give yourself a blister again."

He was right. If I kept it up, my skin would get red and raw-looking. I clenched my left hand into a fist, tucking my thumb inside.

I lifted my right hand, causing Colton's left to come up with it since we were shackled together. "Thumb war?"

He rolled his eyes because he knew I would beat him, but he put his hand in mine anyway.

Our thumbs danced together as we both chanted the words, "One, two, three, four, I declare a thumb war."

Grunting with a determined look on his face, Colton gave it his best effort. It was a little more difficult with the handcuffs on, but I managed to pin him in under a minute.

I smiled. He huffed.

"I want a rematch," he grumped.

He always wanted a rematch. And I always won.

"It's just because I'm older than you," I taunted.

"By a couple months!" he said incredulously.

"Five months," I corrected. "That's a long time in kid-years. Better luck next time." Unable to resist, I patted him on the shoulder and gave him a sympathetic look, knowing he hated it when I did that.

With a half-hearted glare, he gave me the side-eye.

I smiled cheekily at him. "You know what? We should get a house someday. A yellow house in the middle of nowhere.

Just you and me. We could decorate it however we wanted. And it would have to have a barn for the horse."

"Why a horse?" he asked, looking amused.

Shrugging, I continued my dream scenario. "I've always wanted a horse. Every girl wants one. His name will be Barnaby. And we'll have to get one of those huge trampolines because you've always wanted one of those."

With a half-smile on his face, Colton just sat back and listened. Some people thought I talked too much, but Colton? He just let me ramble until I ran out of things to say. It was one of the things I loved about him. It was also something I would miss after he was gone.

He slipped his hand into mine and linked our fingers together. We sat there in the cool dirt for several minutes in silence until my dad's legs came into view. Colton's fingers tightened around mine and I held my breath, hoping we wouldn't be found.

"Brielle, come on out. It's time for Colton to go," my dad said.

Dang. Apparently my dad was pretty good at hide-and-seek, too.

We reluctantly crawled out from under the porch, wearing defiant expressions as we proudly wore the handcuffs that tethered us together. I liked to pretend it meant we were inseparable, but my parents had figured out this trick a long time ago. My dad pulled the key from his pocket and unlocked our wrists.

"Time to say goodbye, son," Colton's dad called from the moving truck, barely looking our way.

Hank hadn't been the same since Jill died. He used to be cheerful, funny, and happy. When Jill got sick, it was the first time I ever heard the word *cancer*. And I hated that word more than any other word in the world. It took away Colton's mom, and now Colton was being taken away from me.

Maybe a new beginning really would help them move on, but that thought was only a small comfort as I looked at my best friend. The selfish part of me wondered how Colton could possibly be better off without me.

He needed me, right? Or maybe I was the one who needed him.

I threw my arms around Colton's neck and he held me tight.

"I don't want you to go," I whispered.

"I know," he said, sounding choked up.

Colton almost never cried, even when he got hurt. In fact, the only time I'd ever seen him do it was after his mom died, but when I pulled back to look at his face I was sure I saw his eyes watering.

"Promise me we'll always be best friends," I begged, my voice wavering.

"I promise." He tried to give me a smile and ruffled my ponytail, causing some of the brown strands to come loose. "Forever, remember?"

Tucking my hair behind my ear, I nodded and started our goodbye routine—the same one we said almost every time we had to part ways.

"Three," I started the countdown.

"Two," he responded as he backed away.

"One," I said, my eyes filling with tears.

"Bye." We both said the word at the same time.

Chin wobbling, I tried not to cry as he climbed into the passenger side of the giant truck then peered back at me through the glass.

As soon as it turned the corner, I let the tears fall. Overwhelming dread formed in the pit of my stomach, because I couldn't help feeling like it was the last time I would xii | JAMIE SCHLOSSER

ever see him.

"It'll be okay, Brielle." My dad patted me on the head. "He's only moving a couple hours away, not halfway around the world."

"How many miles?" I asked, curious about the distance. I knew the closest Walmart was twenty miles away and sometimes that trip seemed to take forever.

"About 130."

"One hundred and thirty miles?!" I shrieked.

That might as well have been halfway around the world.

Dad gave me a sympathetic look.

"Come here," he said, walking over to our van. He opened the passenger door, popped open the glove compartment, and pulled out a book. "This is a map of Illinois." Unfolding it, he pointed to a spot on the paper. "Can you read that?"

"Hemswell," I said, naming our town.

"Good job." He smiled, then his finger followed a long red line. "If we drove on this highway, it would take us about an hour and a half to get to Champaign." He pointed to the dot, then he peered closer to the map, turning it this way and that. "Well, I can't find Tolson, but it's somewhere around here." After gesturing to a blank area, he folded it back up. "Maybe we can visit them sometime."

I nodded, and he gave me one more pat on the head before going back into the house.

Sniffling, I wiped my face with the back of my dirt-stained hand then went to sit back under the porch. I hoped the days would go by fast because the only thing I looked forward to was getting the first letter from Colton.

Gazing up at the carving he made, I held onto the hope that I would hear from him soon as I traced over the deep grooves with my finger.

Colt + Ellie 4ever.

CHAPTER 1

Present Day

Colton

I t was four o'clock in the afternoon, but that wasn't too early for a beer. Not today. My 22nd birthday was tomorrow, but the last thing I felt like doing was celebrating.

After walking through the door to my apartment, I kicked off my boots and went straight to the fridge. Without bothering to remove my coat or wash my hands, I popped the cap off the cold beverage and took a long drink. Usually, the first thing I did when I got home from work was get out of my dirty auto shop coveralls and take a shower, but that would just have to wait.

I made my way into the living room and closed the blinds on the windows. I was about to do some serious brooding, and I needed it to be dark and quiet for that. After sinking down onto the couch, I spent the next several minutes enjoying the silence.

I wasn't an alcoholic—I just wanted to forget my problems for a few hours. I was tired of pretending everything was okay. Tired of putting on a happy face for everyone. People expected me to be the happy-go-lucky, laidback guy they'd always known.

But I wasn't that guy anymore.

Swirling the beer bottle in my hand, I realized I was

getting low. I finished it off in one gulp and got another from the fridge. Just as I sat back down on the couch, my roommate came through the front door, wearing an identical grease-covered uniform.

Travis stopped dead in his tracks when he saw me. Heaving out a big sigh, he threw his keys on the table, then flopped down into the chair by the couch.

"Alright. What the fuck, Colt?"

"What?" I demanded grumpily.

He sighed again. "I didn't want to say anything because I thought you needed time to get over the breakup with Tara, but I come home to find you drinking before five o'clock, in the dark. By yourself. That's some serious shit. It's fucking creepy, man."

I didn't have a response, so I just took another long drink of my beer.

"You were in a shitty mood at work today. In fact, you haven't been the same for a while," Travis stated. "Is that what this is about? The breakup?"

I was already shaking my head because he was way off base. "No. It's not that."

"Then what is it? Come on, we've been friends since we were seven years old. There isn't one thing we don't know about each other."

He was wrong. There was something he didn't know about me. Something I'd kept a secret.

But I knew Travis. He would keep coming at me with questions until I talked, so I tried a different tactic—changing the subject.

"Where's Angel?" I asked. After all, she was his favorite thing to talk about these days.

"Shopping with my mom." He grinned, his green eyes practically sparkling with happiness. "We just got engaged and they're already wedding-planning."

He'd proposed to his girlfriend recently, and I couldn't have been happier for them. They were perfect for each other in a disgustingly cute sort of way. I didn't even mind that Angel had moved in with us several months ago. She pitched in with the bills and the cleaning, and it didn't hurt that she was one hell of a cook. Travis was like a brother to me so, technically, that made her family.

"You guys set a date yet?" I asked.

"Not yet, but she wants a summer wedding. Maybe July," he replied.

The conversation stalled. I didn't know anything about wedding shit. I would've kept him talking if I'd known what to ask.

Travis ran a hand through his hair and the brown mass fell over his eyes.

"You need a haircut," I told him, once again trying to distract him from talking about me. "You should just do what I do and buzz it off."

"Angel likes it long on top. Gives her something to hold onto." He smirked.

"Dude." I barked out a laugh. "There's such a thing as too much information."

"And there's such a thing as trying to change the subject," he shot back, giving me a pointed look.

Deciding to get it over with, I took a deep breath. With my elbows on my knees and my head in my hands, I confessed my deepest secret.

"I've got a problem with my dick," I blurted out, grimacing at how blunt I was.

"Shit," Travis breathed out. "Did Tara give you something? Is that why you broke up?"

"No!" I practically shouted, lifting my head. "Hell no. I got tested for everything after we broke up. Clean bill of health." I held up my hands. "Tara was into drugs. The hard stuff, too. I didn't even know it for most of our relationship. I don't know how she hid that shit from me, but she did."

"You guys didn't exactly spend a lot of time together," he supplied.

I nodded because it was true. Honestly, I never enjoyed Tara's company all that much. If anything I just stayed with her out of convenience, which hadn't been fair to either of us.

"So, what's the problem?" Travis asked, reminding me of my confession.

"It's like—" I paused, trying to think of a way to explain it. "It's like whiskey dick, but I haven't been drinking. I can't keep it up. Fuck, sometimes I can't even get it up in the first place."

Realization dawned on his face. "The arguments. I heard her yelling about stuff a few times," he said. "What she said didn't make sense at the time, but it does now."

"Yeah, she wasn't exactly understanding about it. It only made it worse." I took another swig of my beer as I remembered the way Tara berated me.

What's wrong with you?!

Don't you think I'm sexy?

Are you gay or something?

"We didn't even have sex for, like, the last two months of our relationship," I said. "I got tired of trying. And failing."

"Did you ever think maybe you just didn't like her? I mean, maybe your dick knew better than you," he joked, making light of the situation.

I shook my head. "I had the problem in high school a few times. You remember Katie? Of course you do." I chuckled because Travis hated her. She could be a total bitch, but she was hot. Back then, that was all I cared about. "Anyway, it happened with her a few times, too. I'd been drinking those times, though, so I thought it was because of that…"

"What about since Tara? You guys broke up months ago."

"I tried to go home with a girl from a bar one night." I cringed, thinking about my desperate attempt to prove to myself that my cock wasn't broken. "I got to her place and we started to mess around. I couldn't even get half-mast. I ended up making some lame excuse and leaving." The shame and embarrassment weighed down on me. You'd think talking to my best friend would make me feel better, but it didn't. I'd already told him this much, so I thought I might as well spill everything. "I went to see a doctor about it earlier today," I admitted, looking up at Travis to find him listening intently.

"And?" he prodded.

"He gave me a prescription for Viagra. Fucking Viagra!" I removed the orange bottle of blue pills from the pocket of my Carhartt jacket and set it on the coffee table. "I'm twenty-two years old and they tell me I have erectile dysfunction."

I finished off the second beer and got up to get another one.

"Wanna grab me one, too?" Travis called from the living room.

I got two beers from the fridge, handed one to him, then sat back down.

"Aren't you a little young to be experiencing that kind of issue?" Travis asked skeptically. "Maybe the doctors were wrong."

"They said it's probably just in my head. Called it 'performance anxiety'." I made a sound of frustration. "I don't know how to fix that. But they said the pills might give me more confidence."

"Have you talked to Hank about it?" he asked.

My face twisted up in a horrified expression. "I'm not talking to my dad about my dick problems," I said

6 | JAMIE SCHLOSSER

incredulously. "Anyway, he'd just tell me there's nothing wrong with me and say some shit like 'if it ain't broke, don't fix it'."

Travis nodded because he knew my dad as well as I did. "Or he'd tell you that line about the broken clock."

Then at the same time, we both said, "Even a broken clock is right twice a day."

Chuckling, I cracked the first real smile I'd had in a long time.

Travis cleared his throat. "What about when you're... by yourself?" he asked.

"It's better then, unless I think about it too much," I admitted.

"You want to know what I think?" he asked, and I nodded. "I think your dick is smarter than you." I huffed out a laugh and he continued. "I'm serious. I think you just haven't found the right girl yet."

CHAPTER 2

Colton

"**W**hat the hell are you doing?"

I glanced up to see Travis standing in the living room, arms crossed over his chest as he looked at me as if I'd grown two heads.

"What does it look like I'm doing?" I held up my beer and gestured toward the TV. I laughed out loud at the funny home-video show. They were doing a special segment on dogs biting people on the ass. That shit never got old. The screen suddenly went black. "Hey!" I glared at Travis. "I was watching that."

"Go get ready. We're going out," he announced, tossing the remote onto the chair.

"I don't feel like going out. I'm comfy," I grumbled and pointed down at my favorite sweatpants.

He shot me a look. "It's your birthday. Angel's getting home any minute and she volunteered to be our designated driver for the night."

I sighed and ran a hand over my face. "Where are we going? She's not even old enough to get into any bars."

"She can get into Caged. They're 18 and up," he replied.

My eyebrows went up. "Angel wants to go to a strip club?"

"It's not a strip club. They have, like, go-go dancers or whatever, but they're not naked."

I just grunted and sat back into the cushions.

"Plus," he continued. "It's the only dance club she can get into and she wants you to have a good birthday. It would mean a lot to her if you came out."

I groaned. "You're really gonna play the guilt card?"

"I'll say whatever I can to get your ass off that couch." He grinned. "Cheer up. Get some clothes on. It's a dance club and you love dancing."

"Fine." I sighed, knowing I wasn't going to get out of this.

Travis wasn't wrong—I used to love dancing. I used to love a lot of things, but having a non-functioning dick had done some serious damage to my self-esteem.

Trying to shake off the depression I felt, I went to my room and put on worn jeans and a gray long-sleeve Henley T-shirt. I opened the top drawer of my dresser and saw the little orange bottle of pills staring back at me.

Mocking me.

After grabbing a clean pair of socks, I slammed the drawer shut a little harder than necessary. I slumped down onto the side of my bed and put my head in my hands as I tried to snap myself out of the funk I was in.

Get yourself together. It's not the end of the world if you can't get a boner.

I let out humorless laugh. Because it *was* the end of the fucking world. What good was I if one of the most important parts of my body wouldn't function?

How was I ever supposed to have a healthy relationship? Marriage? Kids?

Maybe I didn't want those things right now, but I definitely wanted them someday.

The first few times I had problems with performance anxiety I wrote it off as a fluke, but over the past few years it happened again and again. The more it happened, the more it fueled my anxiety. And the worse my anxiety got, the more it fueled the problem. It was a vicious cycle I couldn't seem to break.

I heard the front door open and shut, followed by the sound of Angel's voice. I didn't want her or Travis to worry about me. In all honesty, I appreciated the fact that they cared enough to not let me sit at home alone tonight.

Standing up, I took a deep breath and tried to put a convincing smile on my face.

It was time to go out there and pretend I was having the best birthday ever.

∽

The drive to the club was about twenty minutes long, so my buzz had started to wear off by the time we got there. Angel looked proud of herself as she successfully parallel parked on the street a block away from Caged.

I still couldn't believe Travis let her drive his '72 Chevy pickup truck. That thing was his baby. Hell, he wouldn't even let me drive it.

"You did real good, baby," he praised, and she beamed back at him.

Then he kissed her and when they pulled apart, she giggled as she lovingly poked at the dimples in his cheeks.

I had to look away. I might've been happy for them but that didn't mean I wasn't envious of what they had. Travis and Angel were proof that soulmates existed, that fate was a real thing. They were each other's one and only.

For twenty-one years, Travis held onto his V-card, patiently waiting until he was in love. And he fell for Angel, hard and fast. Of course, I thought they were crazy at the time, but if they were happy that was all that mattered.

"Well," I said, breaking up their love-fest. "I'm ready for another drink."

Angel happily clapped her hands. "Let's go, birthday boy!"

The snowfall from Christmas Day was mostly just melted mush on the ground, but the night air was cold. Our breath came out in visible puffs and the short walk to the club entrance was enough to make me wish I'd just stayed inside where it was warm.

However, once we got past the doorman, I was instantly hit with a wall of warm, stuffy air that only resulted from too many bodies being packed into a room. The inside of the nightclub smelled like alcohol, too much perfume, and bad decisions.

Maybe tonight wouldn't be so bad after all.

After we found an open table, Travis turned to me. "What do you want to drink? It's on me tonight."

I'd already had a few beers and switching to something stronger sounded like a good idea.

"Whiskey and Coke," I replied.

He raised his eyebrows and smiled, probably because he knew that was my 'get crazy' drink of choice.

"7-Up and grenadine for me. With a cherry on top, please," Angel piped up.

I laughed. "A kiddie cocktail?"

"It's delicious," she huffed defensively. "And don't call it that. Adults can enjoy a cherry-flavored beverage, too."

Chuckling and shaking his head, Travis left the table to head up to the bar. I leaned back, enjoying the '80s monster ballad booming through the club.

That hair-raising feeling of being watched came over me and I looked over at Angel to find her staring.

"What?" I asked self-consciously.

As far as I knew Travis hadn't told her about my issues, and

I appreciated his ability to keep it between us. Angel wasn't one to beat around the bush. If she suspected my problem, I had a feeling she'd come right out and say it. The last thing I wanted to do was talk about my penis with a girl I thought of as my sister.

"It's just…" she started. "If you ever have anything you want to talk about, you know you can tell me, right?"

"Yeah, of course," I said, shifting uncomfortably under her scrutiny.

"Especially if it had something to do with me," she continued quickly. "I know it was just you and Travis for a long time and when I moved in, it was so sudden—"

"Wait a second," I interrupted, leaning forward to put my elbows on the table. "You think I'm upset because you moved in with us?"

She shrugged and looked down, picking at an imaginary piece of lint on her purple sweater. "Things with Travis and me happened really fast. And I never knew if you were okay with me intruding."

I shook my head. "Angel, you couldn't be more wrong. Yeah, I'm having a hard time right now, but it has nothing to do with you. I'm glad you moved in. Honestly, I love you like family."

Her blue eyes shot up to mine and I could see tears glistening there. "That means a lot to me." She swallowed hard. "You're like family to me, too."

Reaching across the table I ruffled her blonde hair, and she smiled as she smoothed it back down. Suddenly, I felt bad for not making sure Angel knew that I cared. She'd had a hard time of it over the last year.

When she came to Tolson several months ago, she had nothing but a backpack. No family. No friends. After the death of her aunt, she'd been hitchhiking across the country. Angel was one of the sweetest people I'd ever met and she deserved way better than the hand she'd been dealt. At first, I was shocked when Travis brought her home. He'd left on a long haul for our trucking company, then returned three days later with Angel in tow.

"You and Travis are pretty lucky to have found each other," I told her. "It's not every day the trucker falls in love with the hitchhiker."

She giggled. "Yeah, that's pretty weird, huh? You'll get lucky someday, too," she said with more certainty than I felt.

My drink appeared in front of me, saving me from having to respond, and Travis sat back down with us. I took a sip and enjoyed the way the alcohol burned on the way down while my eyes roamed around the club.

The bartender polished the already-gleaming black granite bar top. Booths upholstered in red leather, like the one we were sitting in, lined the walls and free-standing tables were scattered around the perimeter of the dance floor. A bachelorette party crowded the bar and ordered a round of shots while they loudly encouraged their already inebriated friend to drink more.

Caged was way bigger than I thought it would be, and it was a nice place. A lot fancier than the small-town taverns I was used to. The inside had high ceilings with industrial beams running the length of the room. Multi-colored flashing lights hung down over the dance floor and all the walls were painted black, giving it a rave-type feel.

The large dance floor was shaped like a triangle, and at every corner there was an elevated circular cage. Each one had a dancer inside. The girls weren't wearing much, but they weren't naked.

I'd never been here but I had heard about it. The way people talked made it sound like a strip club, but now I realized that wasn't true at all.

The cage closest to our table had a busty blonde dancing around in a skimpy outfit made out of neon pink spandex, keeping with the '80s theme of the night. Bending over, she rubbed one of the metal bars between her ass cheeks.

I waited to feel something. Just one dick twitch. Anything.

Nothing.

Tipping up my glass, I swallowed the rest of the drink in one gulp. The dance floor was filled with writhing bodies, and if I got a few more drinks in me I just might join them.

At least dancing doesn't require an erection.

My attention was snagged by a girl in the cage on the opposite side of the room because a guy had approached her. He tried to stick his hand through the bars, obviously intent on copping a feel. A bouncer quickly intervened, steering the intoxicated man over to a less crowded area.

Through body language and hand gestures, I could tell the bulky security guard was explaining that touching the girls was against the rules.

Drunk Dude huffed, gave the dancer one last lingering look, then staggered over to the bar.

My eyes trailed back over to the girl who was still moving around as though nothing happened and, suddenly, I couldn't look away. I was captivated.

Not because she was hot—and she was hot—but because she was smiling. A big, genuine smile.

Her movements kept in time with the peppy beat of 'Vacation' by the Go-Go's as she started hopping around.

Her big '80s-styled hair flew through the air as she spastically tilted her head from side to side. The long chocolate strands whipped around the confines of the cage and I swear I could see her laughing.

She was having fun. She loved this.

The jean shorts she had on were so short that I could see her ass cheeks hanging out of the bottom and my eyes traveled down her toned legs, then back up. Her waist was tiny and she had an hourglass shape with full breasts, which were jiggling with her every move.

This was entertainment.

Not only was this girl gorgeous and sexy—she was also goofy as fuck. She did some sort of head-banging move before twirling around like a ballerina.

She was still grinning and her chest shook with giggles. I could almost imagine what it would sound like to hear her laugh.

And as I watched, I found myself laughing along.

I felt a familiar tightness in my jeans and was beyond shocked when I glanced down to find myself stiff as a board.

I looked back up toward the dancer with my jaw hanging open.

She was fully facing me now, but the fog machine near her started going nuts, blocking her from my view. I sat up straighter, waiting for the air to clear, and when it did I almost felt like I couldn't breathe.

She was so fucking beautiful.

Flashing lights lit up her features. Full red lips. High cheek bones. A slight cleft in her chin. Her eyes were closed as she tilted her head back and she brought her hands up to her hair. The action made her body arch, pushing her breasts out. Her wide smile was still in place and her white teeth stood out in the black lights as she wiggled her hips.

Something about her was familiar but I couldn't put my finger on it. She definitely wasn't from Tolson. It was possible she was from another surrounding town or from the college in Champaign.

"Hey," Travis said over the table, interrupting my ogling. "Angel and I are gonna go dance. You want to come with us?"

I absentmindedly shook my head without looking his way. "No, you guys go have fun."

"You sure?" he asked, sounding reluctant to leave me by myself.

Nodding, I made a shooing motion with my hand.

I was preoccupied.

Over the next few hours, I couldn't take my eyes off the dancer. During 'Girls Just Want to Have Fun', she really went wild. I'm talking ass-shaking, hands-in-the-air, I-don't-give-a-fuck *wild*.

When she did some sexy version of 'the lawn mower', I ended up laughing while trying to take a sip of my Coors Light, which resulted in the liquid going down the wrong pipe. Coughing and wheezing, I couldn't wipe the huge grin off my face as her ridiculous dance move morphed into 'the sprinkler.'

"Hey, can I get you another whiskey and Coke?" the waitress asked while clearing the empty glasses from our table.

"No, thanks," I replied, barely glancing at her. "A water would be great, though."

Since I didn't want to get too drunk to remember tonight, I'd switched back to beer. I hadn't even moved from my seat yet, but this had already been the best birthday I'd had in a long time.

Angel and Travis alternated between hanging out at the table with me and going out to the dance floor. I tried to engage in conversation with them, but I was having trouble concentrating on anything other than the fact that I had a massive boner in my pants.

My balls felt heavy and my dick was chafed from being pressed up against my zipper for so long. I didn't even care.

I felt great. I felt alive.

I had to know who this girl was.

CHAPTER 3

Brielle

T he heavy bass pulsed through the club as I seductively swayed my hips to the beat of 'Thunderstruck'. Lights flashed and fog filled the air. I smiled to myself because I was totally in my element. Eighties night was my favorite.

Raising my arms up, I grasped the metal bars of the cage surrounding me while I arched my back and shook my ass. It was what the customers wanted and I needed to give them a good show.

Technically, I wasn't a stripper. As a cage dancer, I didn't take all my clothes off and no one was allowed to touch me. I was just the eye-candy. And I could feel their eyes on me. I knew they were watching but I didn't do this for them. I did it for me.

This was my time.

To go along with the '80s theme, I had on tiny jean shorts and a gray off-the-shoulder sweatshirt that had been cut and cropped to show my stomach and cleavage.

See? All the important parts were covered. My least favorite part of the outfit were the hot pink heels. I swore I could feel a bunion forming on my big toe and I made a mental note to Google 'bunion treatment' later. Or maybe I would just wrap it in a Band-Aid with some ointment and call it a day.

Closing my eyes, I leaned my head back and enjoyed the

moment while reminding myself that thinking about toe deformities wasn't sexy.

And this was supposed to be my sexy time.

From 9pm to 1am four days a week, I got paid to feel desired. To be young and free.

For a few hours, I wasn't a 22-year-old single mother.

I was just a dancer.

There was a little girl at home who loved me, who looked at me like I was the most important person in the world. Ava had my whole heart. I lived and breathed for her giggles and her sweet words. But, while the title of 'mom' was my favorite, sometimes it was nice to just be me.

Getting lost in the music was my own kind of therapy. Plus, it doubled as a workout and the pay was great. Being a dancer at Caged had allowed me to make enough money to be a stay at home mom while saving up for school—something I wouldn't have been able to do with a normal day job.

I also had to give some of the credit to my parents because I still lived with them, which was a huge help financially, and they watched Ava while I worked so I didn't have to hire a babysitter.

They knew what I did for my job—it wasn't a secret. Even Ava knew. There was no shame in my family, no judgment. I was extremely lucky in that department.

I liked to think having a great family was the universe's way of paying me back for getting knocked up by an asshole my senior year of high school.

It helped make up for my non-existent lovelife, too.

In the past few years, I'd been on exactly three first dates and exactly zero second dates. Funny thing was, men in their early twenties had a tendency to get freaked out about dating a woman with a kid.

It was their loss. Ava was the best person I'd ever met. She amazed me every day. For only being three years old, she was emotionally mature. Her ability to empathize with others, combined with her selfless nature, made her the kind of person I'd always strived to be.

Maybe I wasn't meant to be with anyone in the romantic sense—maybe Ava was the love of my life. And if that was the case, I considered myself one of the luckiest people in the world.

In the cage across the dance floor, I saw Chloe giving me our signal. I tried to keep moving while I watched her through the bars.

After motioning a 'you and me' gesture with her finger, then pointing at her wrist, she bent over and wiggled her ass at me. I laughed.

She was asking me if I wanted to dance later. I nodded and gave her a discreet 'thumbs up' sign.

Normally, I didn't stick around after a shift but tonight was Chloe's last night working at Caged, so there was no way I would miss hanging out with her one more time.

In a word, Chloe was gorgeous. Tall and lean, with light brown skin. Her eyes were light green and her dark hair fell around her shoulders in a mass of tight ringlets.

When I started working here three years ago, she'd taken me under her wing and I was grateful for her friendship. The other dancers who worked here weren't always nice. It wasn't a surprise to me. I knew just how catty girls could be.

Speaking of catty, I spied Tasha in the third cage doing her signature move—rubbing her ass up and down the bars.

I cringed.

Sure, guys might've found it sexy, but it just made me want to whip out the sanitizing wipes I always kept in my purse.

The song switched to another '80s favorite and I went back to getting into the zone.

When my shift was finally over, I was tired and thirsty. I climbed down from the cage and headed straight to the bar. After chugging a glass of ice water, I met Chloe in the dressing room.

"I can't believe we won't be working together anymore," I told her as I slipped on skinny jeans and a white shirt. "It won't be the same around here without you. But I'm really excited for you, *Nurse* Chloe." I put emphasis on the title, knowing how proud she was of her accomplishment.

"Hey, we'll be working side by side again in no time. You're starting classes soon, right?" she asked, pulling on a bright green tank top and black leggings.

"Yeah, in just a few weeks," I said, sighing at how good it felt to slip my feet into the comfy knee-high boots.

After Chloe entered the nursing program at the community college, she'd convinced me to apply. Nurses were in high demand and they got paid well.

Besides, I couldn't work at Caged forever. Once Ava went to kindergarten, I would prefer to have a day job. With the two-year program, the timing should work out perfectly.

As much as I would miss working with her, I couldn't be more proud of my friend. Nursing school was tough. Over the past two years, I'd watched Chloe stress and struggle over clinicals and tests. Her recent graduation and job offer were a result of her hard work and dedication.

While attempting to comb out my messy hair, the brush caught on some of the over-teased strands by my scalp.

"Ouch." I winced. "I might've gone a little heavy on the hairspray."

Chloe let out a laugh, took me by the shoulders, and guided me to a chair. "Give it here." She took the brush from my hands and started to work through all the knots on my head.

Blinking, I stared at my reflection in the large lighted

mirror. My eyelashes felt weighed down by several coats of mascara and the dark red lipstick made my mouth look bigger than it really was.

"I can only stay for another half-hour," I told Chloe as she made my hair semi-normal again.

"Well, we'd better make the most of it then," she said, finishing up in record time and handing me a baby wipe. We both scrubbed over our faces and around our eyes to remove the excess makeup.

After shoving her purse back into the locker, Chloe stood up straight and turned toward me.

Uh-oh. She had her serious face on.

"You need to live a little, Bree. Have some fun."

"I hang out with a three-year-old all day. Fun is what I do," I quipped, giving her the same response I always did.

It wasn't the first time we'd had this conversation and probably wouldn't be the last. No matter how many times I explained it, Chloe couldn't seem to understand that I liked my life the way it was.

Her face softened. "You know what I mean."

I sighed.

"I do know. But I don't feel like I'm missing out on anything. And by the time Ava's old enough to take care of herself, I'll be ready to party," I told her. "After all, they say 30 is the new 20."

She rolled her eyes. "I'm going to hold you to that."

We left the dressing room and she linked her arm with mine, practically dragging me out into the middle of the club.

Toward the end of the night, the DJ usually started to switch the music up more. As much as I loved the '80s, after a several hours of Van Halen and Def Leppard it was nice to hear something new.

Rihanna's 'S&M' came on as Chloe and I found an open

spot under one of the strobe lights hanging down from the ceiling. Even though I was tired from dancing all night, the beat of the music and the energy from all the people surrounding us encouraged my body to move.

Tilting my head back and closing my eyes, I enjoyed the moment. The bright flashes of light could still be seen through my eyelids, and the bass was so strong I could feel the vibrations through my feet.

Several bodies brushed against mine, but that was inevitable with how crowded the club was tonight.

A lot of people came here to meet someone—a hook-up, a relationship, or a fling. In fact, a couple of the dancers had met their significant other at Caged, but that wasn't the norm. Most men didn't actually want to date the girls here. The very nature of the job seemed to make it difficult to be seen as relationship material.

I understood the allure of finding someone random to rub up on. I also understood Chloe's desire to see me happy. However, I always preferred to dance alone.

Getting pawed by some sweaty pervert wasn't my idea of a good time.

Just as I was about to ask Chloe if she wanted to find a less crowded spot, I felt someone come up behind me.

Hands lightly grasped my upper arms and I stiffened. I was about to turn around and tell whoever it was to go away when a husky voice spoke next to my ear.

"Can I dance with you?" he asked, the feel of his breath against my neck causing goosebumps to spread over my skin.

I don't know why I said yes.

Maybe it was because he asked permission. Most guys just assumed if I was on the dance floor alone, it was an open invitation to hump my ass.

Or maybe it was the tingle that shot through me when his

hands ran over my shoulders.

Either way, I found myself nodding and felt his palms slide down to my body, leaving a trail of more tingles in their wake.

Turning my head to the side, I caught a glimpse of a clean-shaven face and chiseled jaw out of the corner of my eye. I glanced down to see muscular forearms encasing my body, and the sight of his strong hands on my stomach caused me to feel something I hadn't felt in a long time—longing.

Longing to be touched.

There was a difference between knowing men wanted me and actually *feeling* it.

And suddenly, I wanted to feel it.

He gently gripped my hips and pressed my back to his front as we started grinding to the rhythm of the music.

The span of his hands was so wide that his pinky fingers ran over my hip bones while his thumbs skimmed the undersides of my breasts.

We rocked together and every place where his body touched mine felt alive.

Maybe a little pawing isn't so bad after all.

Even though we were separated by at least two layers of fabric, I could feel the heat from his skin on my back. His palms scorched my abdomen as his hands traveled lower.

I also felt an unmistakable hardness poking at my backside and I bit my lip, surprised by the fact that it turned me on.

Although I hadn't seen his face yet, I could tell his shoulders were broad and, judging by the way my body fit against his, he was probably close to six feet tall.

At 5'4", I was average height for a girl. It didn't take much for a guy to make me feel petite. But with this guy, petite wasn't the right word for what I was feeling.

Consumed was more like it.

Something about his touch was hard, yet gentle.

When dancing, there's always a leader and a follower. Somehow, he made me feel like I was doing both. We moved in perfect rhythm together, as though we were one person.

So this is why people like coming here to dance.

I'd almost forgotten what it was like to be turned on. The feelings slamming through my body were so unexpected.

Arousing and erotic.

Wetness pooled between my thighs as places of my body awakened and came to life—places that were long forgotten and neglected.

My nipples stiffened to the point of being painful and I could feel my pulse in my clit.

I hadn't been affected by a guy like this in a long time. Maybe not ever.

I relaxed into his hard chest and let my head fall back against his shoulder while closing my eyes. My heartbeat sped up and I suddenly felt light-headed.

I didn't know this guy but, honestly, it didn't matter anyway. By this time in the night, most people at Caged were drunk out of their minds. Chances were, my mystery man wouldn't even remember me tomorrow.

The song changed to 'Don't Let Me Down' by The Chainsmokers and the DJ slowed the tempo and increased the bass, giving it a more sensual beat.

Arching my back, I rubbed the stranger harder with my ass as my hand came up to grip the back of his neck. His fingers dug into the dips of my waist and his body curled around mine.

Knowing how much I was affecting him gave me a sense of power. In the back of my mind I knew what I was doing was crazy, but the euphoria of the moment caused all sanity to flee.

He buried his face into the back of my neck and I felt him inhale.

Was he smelling me? It probably should have creeped me out, but it didn't—it only turned me on more.

As I felt him exhale against my skin, I tilted my head to the side, exposing my neck, offering a taste.

He didn't disappoint.

His lips closed over the skin at my pulse point and he gently sucked. He and I both moaned at the same time. I couldn't hear it over the music, but I felt it—felt the vibrations from his mouth.

His hands continued to caress and grip my hips and stomach. He pushed a leg between mine and as we rocked together, the seam of my jeans rubbed against my center. I felt a fluttering in my belly and a tightening in my core.

I knew that feeling.

But the truth was I'd never experienced it with anyone else. I may have had sex before, but all my orgasms had been self-induced.

I was both horrified and amazed to realize I was extremely close to getting off with a complete stranger and in a public place, no less.

Maybe that's what happened when you went years without being touched.

That had to be it. I was so sex-deprived that I'd been reduced to humping a random guy at my place of employment.

My eyes snapped open and I searched for Chloe—who probably just witnessed my inappropriate hump-a-thon—but she was nowhere in sight. I guess I couldn't blame her for not wanting to watch, but at least I'd be able to tell her that I did, in fact, 'live a little' tonight.

A slow song came on—'She's Like the Wind'—and all the couples around us started to pair up. *Dirty Dancing* was one of my favorite movies and I'd always wanted to slow dance to this song.

Deciding I should probably introduce myself to the guy who just almost rocked my world, I turned in his arms. But instead of looking up at his face like I'd intended, I let my cheek rest against his hard chest and I linked my arms around his neck.

I wanted to keep the mystery for a little bit longer. For some reason, I was afraid that if I saw his face the good time I was having would be ruined.

As we slowly swayed back and forth together, he enfolded me in his arms and it felt so good to be held by someone.

I was the perfect height to nuzzle my nose into the side of his neck and noted there was a hint of masculine-smelling cologne lingering on his skin. I thought about tasting him the way he did to me, but before I could his hand came up to thread his fingers through my hair and he lightly tugged my head back.

Apparently, he was ready for introductions. Sighing, I lifted my gaze to meet my mystery man.

My eyes landed on his face and a gasp left my mouth.

What I saw—who I saw—had me stumbling backwards and he caught me around the waist before I could fall.

My shock wasn't because he was extremely attractive, but because I knew him.

Or at least, I used to.

I was probably looking at him like I'd seen a ghost, but I couldn't help it. Staring back at me was a face I hadn't seen in fifteen years. You would think after all this time I wouldn't recognize him, but I did. Instantly.

His dirty-blond hair was buzzed short—exactly how it had been when we were kids. The scar over his left eyebrow was barely noticeable, but I saw it. I knew that scar because I'd been the one to give it to him when we were playing baseball in his back yard. A line-drive straight to his face had ended with him needing four stitches.

His eyes, though… That was the ultimate give-away. They weren't just blue. The color was so light it was almost silver. And the gray shirt he was wearing only made the unique color stand out more.

Colton Evans had grown up.

His shirt clung to the sculpted muscles of his arms and chest. The baby face I remembered now had a square jaw, straight nose and full, yet masculine, lips. I'd always imagined he would end up good-looking, but seeing the reality in front of me was breathtaking.

I waited to see the same recognition on his face, but he didn't seem to know who I was. We stared at each other for a couple seconds before he smiled.

"Hi," he said, leaning in close. "I'm Colton."

He held out his hand to me, still grinning. I sucked in a breath when I caught sight of his crooked bottom teeth. One of the teeth sat slightly back behind the others. Colton used to call it his 'shy tooth'. I had loved that tooth. In fact, I'd even threatened him with bodily harm if he ever got braces to fix it.

His hand was still stretched out toward me and I placed my palm in his. I tried to ignore the electric zing that shot up my arm at the contact. Maybe he felt it, too, because when I looked back up at his face, desire was evident in his eyes.

He pulled a little so my body was back up against his. We were front to front, and I felt a hard bulge against my stomach. The feeling of him pressed against me, knowing how much he wanted me, almost made me moan.

Removing his hand from mine, he slid his arm around my waist and put his face by my ear.

"Are you gonna tell me your name?" he asked, and my breath whooshed from my lungs. I hadn't even realized I'd been holding it, but now I felt dizzy from the lack of oxygen.

Suddenly, I was too overwhelmed by his presence and a feeling of irrational panic flooded my system.

Colton probably never realized it, but he'd been the cause of my first real heartbreak. When we were kids, my innocent heart had been convinced we belonged together.

And now he was here, in front of me. Touching me. He kissed my neck.

I almost had an orgasm.

"I have to go," I said abruptly before pulling away.

Turning from him, I fled into the mass of people, ducking and dodging around bodies until I saw the exit sign. Completely forgetting about Chloe, I ran straight to the dressing room, grabbed my purse, and left the club.

CHAPTER 4

Colton

By the time 1am rolled around I'd sobered up, and the way I'd been staring at the dancer all night was starting to make me feel like a creep. My stalking tendencies only got worse when I saw her hop down from the cage and disappear into the crowd.

I followed.

She stepped up to the bar and leaned over to say something to the bartender before he handed her a glass of ice water. Seeing her heart-shaped ass bent over like that had me groaning out loud.

I told myself that I just wanted to know her name. That I'd be satisfied just to talk to her. But, honestly, I wasn't sure if that was true. Still, I wanted to find out.

I started to walk toward her, planning to start up a conversation, but I didn't get the chance.

After quickly finishing her drink, she darted to an exit door at the back of the club. Before it swung shut, I could see it led to a dark hallway. I walked closer to the door, not really sure if I planned to open it or not.

The decision was made for me when the same bouncer I'd seen earlier stopped me several feet away.

"Employees only," he said gruffly.

I nodded because I understood. Actually, I was glad he was

there looking out for the dancers, but it still sucked.

I went back over to the bar to sulk while trying to think of what to do next.

Obviously, I knew where to find her if I wanted to hunt her down, but I didn't want it to come to that. Plus, patience had never been a virtue of mine and I wanted her. Now.

Fortunately, I didn't have to think about it for too long because she reappeared with one of the other dancers and headed straight for the dance floor.

Fuck yeah.

It was the perfect opportunity. I snaked my way through the writhing bodies until I found her.

As I watched her body move, my erection roared to life once again.

She had changed out of her previous outfit and the skin-tight jeans hugged her shape perfectly. With the long-sleeve shirt she was wearing, you'd never know she was just up in one of those cages. Even her hair had been smoothed down a little.

I stood behind the dancer for several long seconds, trying to figure out how to approach her.

Her friend, who was facing my direction, noticed me. More specifically, she noticed that I'd noticed her friend.

She raised her eyebrows and a grin appeared on her face as she looked back and forth between us. She must've approved of me because she nodded and pointed toward the goofy girl, who was oblivious to my presence, before backing away.

I walked up behind her and stopped when I was a couple feet away. My dick was painfully hard and I briefly wondered if it was unhealthy to have a hard-on for this long.

I don't even care.

This girl made me feel hungry. Out of control. It was a feeling I wasn't familiar with.

Just as I was about to tap her on the shoulder, she flipped her hair and it smacked me in the face. I laughed.

I placed my hands on her shoulders to get her to stop moving for a second and she flinched.

Shit.

I didn't mean to scare her.

"Can I dance with you?" I leaned down to ask, praying she'd say yes.

She paused, seeming to think about it for a second.

When she nodded her head, it took everything I had not to fist-pump the air. And when I pulled her body against mine, she melted into me.

As we moved together, I got a very vivid idea of what it would be like to be with this girl. To have her naked beneath me. It did nothing to help the state of my erection, which was pressed up against her ass.

I didn't even pay attention to the music. I had no idea what songs were playing and it didn't matter to me as long as I could keep touching her.

I got a whiff of her hair and it smelled fruity and tropical. Like strawberries and coconuts. My cock throbbed and my mouth watered.

When she tilted her head to the side, I couldn't stop myself from kissing the skin on her neck. She tasted slightly salty, probably from working up a sweat all night. Dancing for that long had to be one hell of a workout.

As my lips left her skin, she arched into me. Her hand came up to grasp my neck, like she didn't want me to stop.

This was, by far, the hottest experience of my life. I wanted more. So much more.

A slow song came on and she turned in my arms. Instead of looking up at me, she buried her face in my chest and wrapped her arms around my neck.

Something about the way she clung to me made warmth spread through my chest. It felt like she needed me. Or maybe she just needed a hug and I wanted to be the one to give it to her.

My dick definitely liked her, but as I held onto her I realized I'd never had this kind of emotional reaction to someone before. I'd already seen so many sides to this girl tonight. Sexy. Goofy. Funny. Vulnerable.

And I didn't even know her name.

I needed to know her name.

What color were her eyes? What would it be like to see her smile at me? What would it feel like to run my thumb over that cute indent on her chin?

Tilting her head back with my hand, I silently begged her to look at me. When she finally did, I noticed two things.

First, her eyes were brown. The outer part of the iris was the color of chocolate and it got lighter around the pupil, reminding me of honey.

Second, the expression on her face wasn't what I was expecting. She looked horrified. I tried not to be offended, but damn.

Deciding to play it cool, I introduced myself and pulled her close to me, hoping she would tell me her name and keep dancing with me. Much to my disappointment, that wasn't what happened.

Not only did I not get her name, but she also ran away from me. Fast.

She had the advantage of being smaller and more agile, so she was able to quickly make it off the dance floor and out of sight.

Some people got pretty pissed off as I pushed through trying to catch up to her. I quickly mumbled a random "sorry" and "excuse me" as I made my way through the crowd.

By the time I made it to an open area where I could search for her, she was gone.

~

"I met someone tonight," I told Travis as we drove home from Caged. We were both completely sober now, and Angel slept between us on the bench seat, her head leaning against Travis's shoulder.

"No shit?" he asked. "What's her name?"

I frowned. "I don't know."

"You forgot her name? You weren't that drunk, were you?" He chuckled.

"No," I told him grumpily before admitting the truth. "She wouldn't tell me."

Travis threw his head back and laughed, causing Angel to stir a little. He lowered his laugh to a quiet snicker. "That's classic, dude."

"It's not funny," I grunted. "I don't understand what happened. We were having a really good time, then she just took off."

"Maybe she needed to puke. Just be glad she didn't do it on your shoes."

"She wasn't drinking." I shook my head. "She was one of the cage dancers."

Travis smirked at me and shrugged. "Well, at least you know where she works."

I grinned, determination kicking in. "That's exactly what I was thinking."

Persistence was a trait I came by honestly. My dad was the same way. It was the main reason he was able to keep his business from going under in a small town that couldn't even support a grocery store.

Tolson, Illinois was many things—quiet, friendly, and un-believably tiny. So small, it didn't even show up on most maps. It was my hometown and I was proud to live there. But the fact was, it was a place where small businesses went to die, and Hank's Auto Shop was no exception.

Growing up, I'd spent many nights watching my dad sift through the mounting bills, his eyebrows furrowed and his lips thinned as he knew the incoming money didn't add up to the cost of keeping his life's work afloat.

Even with the cards stacked against him, he wouldn't give up.

After my mom lost her battle with breast cancer at the young age of 30, my dad tried his best to provide for me while being a great parent. And he succeeded.

Wanting to help any way I could, I started on at the shop when I was fifteen, and Travis wasn't far behind. At the time, Dad insisted we didn't need to—that we should be off hav-ing fun with our friends or playing sports. But I could see his shoulders sag with relief when we told him there was nowhere else we'd rather be. And I swear I saw my old man's eyes get misty when Travis said he thought of him as family. I knew my dad returned the sentiment.

Dad had clapped his hands together as a huge smile broke out on his face because he'd have help from not one, but two people he trusted. He'd said we were going to be an unstoppa-ble team and started spouting off all the plans he had for the business.

His big ideas paid off.

Not only did he expand the auto shop by adding a truck testing lane, he also decided to start a moving company. Hank and Sons Transport was the ultimate key to his success—and mine. When he'd asked Travis and me to be co-owners of the business, I was ecstatic.

We got our CDL and my dad bought the rig. It'd been a big investment, but the risk was worth it. Hank and Sons had clients calling even before we were officially open for business.

I loved the idea of truck driving, but I didn't like being away from home for days at a time. That's where Travis came in. My best friend was born to drive, and he insisted on taking the long hauls. Local deliveries took me a day, tops.

My thoughts wandered back to the events of tonight and I was shocked as hell to realize I was still half-mast. Grinning, I discreetly adjusted my cock.

I'd never been happier about having blue balls.

I recalled Travis's words from the day before and had to admit that maybe he was right—maybe there wasn't anything wrong with me.

Maybe I just needed the right girl, and now I knew where to find her.

CHAPTER 5

Brielle

When I got home, the first thing I did was go upstairs to check on Ava. Sleeping peacefully, her face was squished up as she drooled on her Sofia the First pillowcase. I placed a light kiss on her cheek, then I haphazardly threw my hair up into a messy bun before I went to the bathroom to brush my teeth and wash my face.

After changing into gray yoga pants and a worn high school softball tee, I sat down on the edge of my bed, still reeling from the encounter with Colton. The fluffy white down comforter looked inviting, but I still felt so wound up.

I should've been tired. I should've gone straight to sleep.

Instead, I went to my closet and dug out an old box of childhood keepsakes. Dust flew up into the air as I lifted the cardboard lid. Coughing, I waved my hand at the air before digging through the old memories.

On top were a bunch of high school book reports and art projects my mom insisted on keeping. I set them on the hardwood floor beside me.

My sparkly dance team pom-poms were next, and the feelings they brought up were bittersweet. It reminded me of a different time. A time when my aspirations for the future included going to college and living it up with my friends.

I felt a slightly painful twinge in my chest as I took out

the folded up letter from the state university. The black and white letters stated that not only did I get accepted, but I also received a dance scholarship. I remembered opening it with shaky hands, then running around the house waving it and cheering at the top of my lungs.

A few weeks later I found out I was pregnant, causing all my plans to shift.

These were modern times we lived in. People got knocked up all the time, but getting pregnant out of wedlock caused quite the scandal in my old small town. I might as well have been walking around with a scarlet letter on my chest.

If it wasn't for the support and love of my parents, I don't know what I would've done. When it was clear that staying in Hemswell wasn't the best option, they took action and moved us all to a city where they got new jobs.

They bought a house big enough for the four of us, I got hired at Caged, and the rest was history.

I loved the way my life turned out and wouldn't change it for the world.

I would've traded in a *thousand* dreams to have Ava.

But the truth was, my present wasn't the future I'd imagined for myself back then.

Sighing, I continued digging until I reached the bottom where I knew I'd find a wooden box. It contained memories I hadn't thought about in years.

The music box had been a gift from Colton on my sixth birthday and I'd used it to store everything that reminded me of him. I thought I'd never have a reason to open it again and I hesitated, afraid of the emotions it might conjure up.

Taking a breath, I lifted the lid and the tinkling melody of 'You Light Up My Life' filled the room. There was a wrinkled letter on top and I unfolded it to read what it said. In child's writing, the letters weren't perfect, but they were legible.

Dear Ellie,

I miss you. I don't like our new house. My neighbor came over to play today. I don't want a new best friend so I punched him in the face.

Love, Colton

Smiling, I folded it back up. There were several pictures and a Christmas card, but the shiny object underneath was what caught my attention. Metal clanked against metal as I picked up the handcuffs.

I laughed lightly as they dangled from my fingers. We'd had many inside jokes but the handcuffs had been 'our thing'. I remembered how we would cuff ourselves together in hopes that our parents wouldn't be able to separate us.

It never worked.

I had only been five years old when I knew I was in love with Colton. People might argue that someone so young couldn't possibly know what real love was—but it was real to me. So innocent and pure.

It was the most genuine love I'd ever experienced with someone who wasn't a member of my family. Plus, what I felt for him was a different kind of love—the kind that made my heart pitter-patter and my palms sweat.

The kind that made me dream of *someday* and *forever*.

But that love—along with my young, sensitive heart—shattered when the letters stopped coming mere months after he moved away. There was no explanation and no goodbye. At one point I had freaked out, telling my parents something must've happened to Colton. I couldn't believe that he would just forget about me. They'd looked at me with sympathetic expressions and told me Colton was fine. That he was happy in his new town. He'd moved on to a new life.

And I was crushed.

Looking over at the clock, I realized it was 3am. Ava was an early riser. In a few short hours, she would come bounding in to wake me up.

I packed everything back into the box and shoved it into my closet, certain it was the last time I would ever have a reason to open it.

But as I drifted off to sleep that night, I couldn't stop thinking about the boy I used to know.

CHAPTER 6

Colton

"What can I get for you?" the bartender yelled my way. I almost didn't hear him over the noise of the club. It was New Year's Eve and Caged was packed from wall to wall. With it being a holiday and the fact that it was Saturday night, the place was a madhouse.

"Coors Light, bottle," I told him and he nodded.

His head was shaved and the black T-shirt he wore, which was probably two sizes too small, stretched over muscles big enough to suggest that he was either really into weight-lifting or he was on 'roids. Maybe both. With the bald head, tight shirt, and the hoop earring in his left ear, he looked a lot like Mr. Clean.

As I waited for my drink, I looked around the club and spied my dancer in one of the cages. I smiled.

My dancer.

She was the reason I was here tonight. Alone.

I wasn't in the habit of going to bars by myself, but Travis and Angel had a delivery down in Florida. They'd decided to make a vacation out of it and stay a few extra days.

So, I was flying solo tonight. It was probably for the best because I wouldn't have been great company.

I didn't want to talk. I didn't want to dance.

I just wanted to *watch*—which I could admit was creepy

as hell.

When the bartender set my drink in front of me, I put five dollars on the bar and slid it his way.

"Hey," I said, catching his attention before he could walk away. I pointed toward the brunette. "What's that girl's name?"

He shook his head. "Sorry. We're not supposed to give out that information."

Disappointment weighed down on me and I frowned. "It's just that she looks really familiar and I can't put my finger on it," I explained, hoping he would let her name slip.

"She gets that a lot. She's a dead-ringer for that Kelly Kapowski chick on that old show, 'Saved by the Bell'."

Cocking my head to the side, I studied her and I had to admit he was right. Maybe that was it. I turned back toward the bar.

"I just want to know her name." I held up a twenty-dollar bill and set it in front of him, wondering if he would take the bait.

He looked at it for a beat before grabbing it and stuffing it into the back pocket of his jeans. "Her name's Bree."

Bree.

I smiled and nodded my thanks, but also glared at him as he walked away. While I was satisfied that I got her name, I was also a little pissed that it was so easy to get the bartender to give me information about her.

I found a high-top table that wasn't too far from Bree's cage and sat down to nurse my beer.

This time I knew where she would be headed after she got out of that cage.

When the time came, I made my move. Like a total stalker, I waited by the wall with the door to the hallway. Right on the dot, a couple minutes after 1am she walked in my direction.

I moved toward her, intending to meet her before she was out of sight but the bouncer must've seen me coming. His large body appeared in front of me and his meaty hand landed on my chest, stopping me from going any further. I had to crane my neck to look up at the face of the brute who stood in my way. He had at least six inches of height on me and I wasn't stupid enough to try to get around him.

I caught a flash of brown hair and tan skin as the dancer passed by. She was less than ten feet from me but getting farther away with every step. The thought of not getting to talk to her caused me to panic.

"Bree!" I shouted out of complete desperation.

Yeah, she didn't really know me and there was a chance she would just flip me off and keep walking.

But it was a risk I was willing to take.

When she turned my way, her gaze collided with mine. Her eyes got so wide, they looked like they were in danger of popping out of her head.

Damn.

That wasn't the reaction I'd been hoping for. I wanted to see a smile—not the shock that was clearly written all over her face. Just like the other night, I tried not to feel offended. To my relief, she slowly walked over to where I was standing.

"It's okay, Carl." She nodded her permission at the security guard and he reluctantly backed away while giving me a look that said 'I'm watching you'.

"Bree," I breathed out, grinning wide. Now that I had her in front of me, I didn't know what to say. I went with the lamest approach possible. "Hi."

Her lips tilted up. "Hey."

"Listen, I know you don't know me, but—"

"How did you know my name?" she interrupted, her eyes narrowing suspiciously.

"Ah, I kinda paid the bartender for the info," I said guiltily.

She huffed and muttered something that sounded like *that jackass*. Her brown eyes swung up to mine. "How much did he charge you?"

"Gave him twenty bucks," I said and she huffed again. I shrugged. "I would've paid more."

Her small smile returned and she glanced down, almost as if she was shy. It was amazing to me how someone as sexy as her could be timid.

Tonight she had on some kind of black boy-shorts with a lace trim. The black corset top matched, and my eyes followed the light purple ribbons woven up the sides. A tiny purple bow was strategically placed in the trim, smack dab in the middle of her ample cleavage.

Now that she wasn't in the cage anymore, I had the urge to cover her and as I looked around, I noticed the leers she was getting from all the men. I took my Carhartt jacket and draped it over her shoulders.

She looked up at me in surprise. "What are you doing?"

"Trying to hold a conversation with you when you look like that is distracting," I joked so she wouldn't be offended by my sudden possessiveness. "But really... I wanted to ask you what you're doing after you get off work tonight."

"Oh," she said, looking surprised again. "Well, I usually go straight home. It's late..." She shrugged while pulling my jacket more snugly around her shoulders, almost as if she was wrapping herself in a hug.

"It's New Year's Eve. We had a good time the other night, right?" I didn't wait for her to answer the question. "I just want to spend time with you. Hang out and talk," I told her with complete honesty.

Yeah, my dick liked her now—the stiffy I was sporting was evidence of that. But once the pressure was on? I had no idea what would happen. I didn't want my issue to be a disappointment to her or me.

Hanging out was good. Talking was safe. No pressure.

Don't say no. Please, don't say no.

"Okay," she said reluctantly, after thinking about it for a few seconds. I let out a breath I didn't realize I was holding and smiled at her. "But just for a little while. I have to get up early in the morning," she added.

I nodded, unable to contain my excitement over the fact that she actually agreed. "My place or yours? Or do you want to go get something to eat?"

"Not my place," she blurted out. "Where do you live?"

"Tolson. It's about 20 minutes from here."

"I have an idea of where that is, but I've never been there. I can just follow you, if that's okay."

"Yeah, that's perfect," I said, still grinning a mile wide. She started to shrug off my jacket and I put out a hand to stop her. "You can wear it."

She shook her head. "It's cold out there. I'll meet you outside around back. Wouldn't want you to freeze your tushy off."

I laughed because she said *tushy*.

"Fine," I relented and took the coat from her.

As she walked away I couldn't stop myself from staring at her ass until she disappeared into the hallway.

CHAPTER 7

Brielle

What I was doing was bad. Very, very bad.

I never went home with strangers. I never went home with anyone, period. And I never would have agreed to go home with Colton if I didn't know who he was, but he didn't know that.

As I drove through the darkness, I followed Colton's truck and stared at the red taillights while scolding myself for making such a reckless decision.

At first, when I saw him at the club again, I thought maybe he'd had some kind of epiphany and realized who I was.

Then he kept calling me *Bree*. Colton had never called me that.

Despite my initial protest when we were kids, he'd affectionately given me the nickname Ellie. I hated it, but every time I told him not to call me that, he'd just grin and my insides would turn to mush. Eventually, I learned to love it.

I should've fessed up and told him who I was before agreeing to go back to his place. It would have been the right thing to do.

But I didn't want him to stop looking at me the way he was—like he wanted me.

I was afraid that if he found out who I was, the desire in his eyes would go away. That I would go from someone sexy and mysterious to just being his long-lost friend.

Colton said he just wanted to hang out and talk. Once I got comfortable, I could tell him the truth. It might be awkward at first, but then we'd probably laugh about it.

Then I'd be placed in the friend zone and life would make sense again.

After driving for twenty minutes and only seeing empty fields and a few farmhouses, I started to wonder where the hell I was. But then a little green sign that said 'Welcome to Tolson, Illinois' came into view. As I passed it, I saw it said 'Population 320'.

Wow. Small town.

I passed a few blocks of quaint little houses and two lively taverns before following Colton's truck into a parking lot next to a small apartment complex. Just a block away, I saw a big sign hanging over a garage that said 'Hank's Auto Shop'.

It was surreal seeing the place Colton had lived for the past fifteen years. I'd often wondered what Tolson was like and if he was happy here.

After parking my car next to his truck, I took a deep breath, readying myself for the uncomfortable conversation that was about to take place.

I'd spent the whole drive trying to figure out what to say once I got to his place, and I had it scripted in my mind.

However, once I got there the words wouldn't come out.

After Colton opened his apartment door, I followed him inside. He flipped on the light and I looked around at what was a small, but clean, living room and kitchen. The floorplan was open, but a breakfast bar separated the galley kitchen from the dining area, which held a tiny card table and three chairs. A newer-looking brown couch and chair lined the walls of the living room and there was a large flat-screen TV mounted to the wall.

"It isn't much, but it's home," he shrugged, and took off his jacket.

"Hey, at least you don't still live with your parents," I told him and inwardly cringed for opening up with that information. I wasn't embarrassed by my parents, but the fact was that most people my age had their own place.

"Ah, so that's why you didn't want to go back to your house." He smiled. "Do you want something to drink?" he asked, heading toward the fridge. After opening it, he frowned and glanced my way. "Well, we only have beer and water, so, not many choices."

He nervously tapped his fingers on his jeans as he waited for my answer.

"Water is fine," I said, enjoying the way he seemed to be so flustered around me.

He grabbed two bottles of water then handed one to me on his way over to the couch. After sitting down next to him, an awkward silence ensued.

"So," I started, "the Tolson sign on the way in said 320 people. That's pretty small."

"That sign is outdated. It might be closer to 325 now." He chuckled. "It's nice and quiet. Except for when the taverns get busy, like tonight. You'd be surprised how many people in this town like to party."

"So that's it? Just some houses and a couple taverns?" I asked, trying to keep the conversation light.

"There's a church, too," Colton added. "And the auto shop down the street. I work there. Hank's my dad."

I know.

Taking a deep breath, I tried to muster up the courage to tell Colton my name—my full name. Instead, nonsensical rambling spewed from my mouth.

"Is this microfiber?" I asked, running my hands back and

forth over the smooth material of the couch cushion. "I've always thought microfiber is way better than real suede. It's easier to clean and way cheaper. Your apartment smells good. A lot better than I thought it would. Not that you look like you're stinky or anything..."

Stop stalling. Tell him.

Just as I was about to open my mouth, he spoke.

"Bree," he said quietly.

Just one word.

Somehow he made my name sound like a plea and I turned to look at his face. I'd never seen anyone look at me that way. His silver eyes held lust and desire, but also a hint of pain.

His expression was so raw it took my breath away.

"Colton." My voice cracked.

Before I knew what was happening, his lips were on mine. I wasn't even sure who made the first move, but I didn't care.

I opened my lips and our tongues met at exactly the same time. Slowly.

I moaned into his mouth as we matched each other stroke for stroke. Colton kissed like he danced—in control, yet somehow letting me take the lead. He wasn't dominating our kiss and neither was I.

So much for small talk.

Colton's hands came up to grasp my face. When he pulled back enough to break our kiss, I made a sound of protest. He looked at me with wonder and awe while shaking his head.

"Fuck," he muttered quietly before diving back in.

His teeth scraped over my bottom lip before he bit down lightly and tugged. When I sucked on his tongue, a moan reverberated in his throat and the sexy sound sent a jolt of lust straight to my core.

My mouth left his to trail kisses down his jaw and when

I got to his neck I sucked lightly at a place under his ear. His hands, which were fisted in my hair, tightened and the slightly painful pull on my scalp only turned me on more.

My hands traveled down his chest and when my fingernails scraped over his nipples, he let out a half-gasp, half-moan.

Interesting. Was it weird to think a guy's nipples were sexy?

Wanting to see if I could push him further, I did it again, scraping in a circular motion over the fabric of his shirt. He moaned again.

I guess he felt it was his turn because his hands left my hair and he ran his thumbs back and forth over my breasts. My nipples were already painfully hard, and every swipe had me biting back a whimper.

His mouth attacked my neck and I literally started panting.

My fingers fisted in his shirt and I pulled his face back up to mine. I fell back against the arm of the couch and Colton came over me. The position was awkward because my legs were still hanging off the front and I squirmed, wanting my body closer to his.

"Bedroom?" Colton asked, breathing hard.

"Yes."

He placed his hands under my ass, then picked me up. Winding my legs around his waist, I let out an unattractive squeal as he practically sprinted down the hallway.

After shutting the door to his room, he leaned back against it with me still fully attached to his body.

"We probably shouldn't have sex," he said, causing the lust-fog my mind was in to clear a little. "We don't know each other that well. Or at all." He huffed out a laugh.

"I don't normally do this," I told him honestly as I ran my hand over his short hair. "Actually, I *never* do this."

"Neither do I," he admitted, and I felt relief at the fact that he wasn't in the habit of taking girls home, not that it was any of my business.

I had no claim on Colton. Not tonight and not fifteen years ago.

But just for one night I wanted to be selfish. I wanted to pretend that he desired me, that he loved me.

And it was in that moment I made the very selfish decision not to tell him who I was.

Living in the moment wasn't a luxury I was accustomed to. I hadn't felt loved by a man in so long, and not just in the physical sense. My very limited experience with the opposite sex had taught me one thing—that they only wanted one thing.

And once they got it, they were gone.

I'd had offers for the occasional one-night stand, but casual hook-ups had never been something I was interested in. For the past few years, I'd denied men and, in doing so, I'd also denied myself.

So tonight I decided to pretend. To live in the moment. To put myself first, even if it meant doing the wrong thing.

One way or another, Colton would get what he wanted, and in the morning I would leave knowing I got what I wanted, too—even if it was just for one night.

CHAPTER 8

Colton

I pushed off the door and carried Bree over to my bed. Since we'd agreed we shouldn't have sex, the pressure was off.

Mental pressure, that is.

The other kind of pressure I was experiencing in my jeans was a different story. I wanted this girl. Badly.

However, I was still afraid I might not be able to perform when the time came, so I settled for touching her. Kissing her.

Everywhere.

Not having sex didn't mean we couldn't do other things.

I didn't know why I was so drawn to Bree or why I felt so comfortable around her. Even before I ever talked to her, I felt some kind of connection.

And I couldn't believe she'd agreed to come home with me, but I wasn't going to question it. I just wanted to let it be what it was—which was fucking awesome.

Once I put Bree down, I settled on top of her, my elbows on either side of her head. The feeling of her soft, warm body beneath mine was heaven. It'd been so long since I'd been physically close to someone.

Too long.

In the grand scheme of things, six months without sex wasn't that big of a deal. But I was a 22-year old guy. So, yeah, it seemed like it'd been forever.

Warm eyes gazed up at me as I lowered my mouth to hers. Her lips parted for me instantly and I pushed my tongue inside. Her tongue pushed back.

Our mouths melded together perfectly and I brought my hand up to her face, finally doing something I'd thought about way too much over the past couple days—I ran my thumb over the cleft in her chin. Then I pulled down, opening her mouth wider, giving me more access.

As we kissed she slipped her hand underneath my shirt to feel my stomach, and my muscles quivered at her touch. Her hand went higher, fingernails grazing my skin.

A strangled sound escaped me when she brought her fingers up to my nipple and pinched. Hard.

It kinda fucking hurt. It also turned me the fuck on. Lifting my head, I looked down at her.

Playful. Mischievous. Naughty. That was the kind of smile she gave me.

I had no idea what kind of kinky shit this girl was into, but I was game. Honestly, I'd never been into nipple play before. This girl was pushing buttons I never even knew I had.

I shifted lower down her body until my face hovered over her right breast. With heated eyes, she watched me as I brought my mouth to where I knew her nipple would be and bit down.

She moaned and arched her back. Suddenly, I had the un-controllable need to get her naked. I wanted to tease her, drive her wild, see how far I could push the limits—her limits and mine.

"Can I take this off?" I asked, tugging at her shirt. I want-ed to do what I just did without fabric in the way.

After sitting up, she pulled the shirt over her head and without even having to ask, she unsnapped her bra and tossed both off to the side.

The darkness of the room made it difficult to see her, but there was just enough moonlight shining through the window to see dark pink nipples on the best tits I'd ever laid eyes on. Without even touching them, I knew they would feel heavy in my hands.

My cock throbbed painfully in the confines of my jeans as I reached out with both hands and cupped her full breasts. Her breaths started coming faster as I brushed my thumbs back and forth over her stiff peaks.

Just thinking about sucking on them made my mouth water. Lowering my face down to her right breast, I sucked as much of it into my mouth as I could. As I pulled back, I let my teeth scrape over the hardened bud and she let out a loud whimper.

I looked up at her face to make sure what I just did was okay.

"Colton." She made an impatient noise before turning her body slightly and arching up, offering her other breast.

I smiled. It was a little difficult to keep the suction I needed to get the job done while grinning like an idiot, but I did the best I could.

Bree started clawing at my shirt and I chuckled because of how impatient she was. I guess it was only fair that I took mine off, too. After tossing it to the side, she practically tackled me.

Laughing, I fell back onto the bed as she started kissing her way down my stomach. When she made it to the waist of my pants, she paused before pulling the fabric down so she could kiss lower. When she pushed her tongue under the waistband of my boxers, the wet warmth flicked over the tip of my cock.

Groaning, my hips involuntarily jerked forward.

Pre-cum leaked from me and, for a second, I thought there was a chance I might blow my load without even getting my pants off.

Bree tugged a little on the button of my jeans and raised her eyebrows in question. All I could do was nod enthusiastically, and she eagerly snapped it open before pulling down my zipper.

In a flurry of motion, clothes were shed between gasps and giggles and moans until both of us were completely naked.

I sat back against the headboard and she straddled my lap. Her pussy wasn't even touching me but I could feel the heat coming off her center.

"Oh my God," Bree gasped as she wrapped her hand around the base of my cock and looked down between us. "You're so thick."

Definitely something a guy likes to hear.

It was too dark to see very well so I put my hand over hers, noticing that her fingers barely made it all the way around the circumference.

She made another sound like she was impressed and she stroked her hand up and down my length.

"You have a really nice dick," she whispered.

Fuuuck. I'd never been one to shoot off early, but it was a real possibility right now. Fingernails lightly scraped over my sensitive skin and she moved down to cup my sac. My body tensed as she explored me and I tried not to come all over her hand.

Before I could embarrass myself, she stopped what she was doing and looped her arms around my neck.

"Hi," Bree said softly, her face so close to mine that I felt her breath against my cheek.

For some reason, it made me smile. "Hi."

I brought my hand up to her face and playfully tweaked her chin, wishing the lights were on so I could see her face better.

When she leaned in to kiss me, her wet slit slid over my cock. I groaned as my head fell back to hit the headboard with an audible thud.

I brought my hand up between her thighs, confirming what I already knew—that she was very wet and also completely bare down there. No hair at all. She either shaved or waxed, both of which I found sexy as fuck.

Her skin was smooth and so slick. Swiping my fingers over her bundle of nerves, I gave her clit a little pinch. She gasped and rocked her hips forward.

Grabbing her ample ass with my hands, I dragged her smooth flesh over mine again. That time we both gasped together and her forehead came to rest on mine.

"Colton?" she whispered through quick breaths. "I know you said we shouldn't have sex…" She made a frustrated sound. "But what if you just put it in a little…?"

Once her words registered, I threw my head back and laughed. Loud.

"Did you seriously just suggest that we play a game of 'just the tip'?"

Bree covered her face with her hands. "Oh my God. I totally did." Her voice came out muffled. She pulled back, shaking her head and looking embarrassed. "I can't believe I just did that."

I didn't want distance between us, so my hand went up to tuck some hair behind her ear then I ran my thumb over the cleft in her chin again.

That cute fucking indent was going to be the death of me.

"Maybe I should put a condom on, just in case," I suggested, realizing how close we were to actually having sex.

"Yeah, just in case. It's totally possible it could just fall in," she teased while eagerly nodding her head.

Chuckling, I reached over into the nightstand and grabbed

one of the condoms I hadn't been sure I'd ever need again.

After rolling it on, we went back to kissing. She started moving her hips over mine, rubbing her pussy on my dick. With one hand on her ass and the other on her breast, my mouth went to her neck. I sucked at the same sensitive spot I found the other night on the dance floor and she started panting.

She continued rubbing herself over my cock. Back and forth. Back and forth.

Overpowering desire slammed through me and that out-of-control feeling from the other night returned. It felt like my mind was in a fog and my vision went blurry. All I could think about was getting my dick inside this girl.

Just as she raised her hips, I shifted slightly and the tip slid in a little.

I gasped and Bree whimpered. It felt so fucking good. We both froze, realizing that this was it—this was really happening.

"Can I?" she whispered by my ear, her voice thick with need. "Please? Please, Colton…"

Hearing her beg almost had me coming on the spot, and any hesitation I had vanished.

"Fuck, yes," I replied automatically.

She didn't waste any time. As soon as I gave my permission she sank down while letting out a raspy moan.

Ecstasy.

So warm and wet. Her snug walls squeezed around me and I moaned into her neck, the feeling of her tight heat around my cock overwhelming.

My fingers dug into the skin on her back as I held her. Any anxiety I had about not being able to keep my erection flew out the window.

For at least a minute we sat together, connected fully and

completely still. Holding onto each other. Breathing together.

With every rise and fall of her chest, I felt her nipples rub against me.

Burying my face in Bree's hair, I inhaled her scent again, ready to do anything—*anything*—she asked me to. I was completely at her mercy.

Her body shuddered, and I noticed she was gripping my shoulders a little tight.

"You okay?" I asked, concerned.

"Uh-huh." The quiet confirmation left her mouth and her breath tickled my neck. The side of her face slid against mine as she pulled back to look me in the eye.

In that moment something passed between us. Something I'd never felt before. I had no idea what it was or what it meant, but it was intense—it felt like something bigger than just a physical connection.

"Where the hell did you come from?" I whispered, and her eyes widened a fraction.

Instead of answering me, Bree raised up then sank back down.

"Oh, fuck," I groaned, my eyes slamming shut. "Don't stop."

In a circular motion, she started moving her hips over me.

Leaning back against the headboard, I looked down at the place where we were joined. There was just enough light coming through the window to see her body—the way her tits jiggled with every movement, the way her head tilted back and her lips parted.

As she slid up and down on my cock, I realized I'd never enjoyed sex this much. It'd never felt this good, been this fun. There was something about her that put me at ease. I couldn't explain it, but all the anxiety I'd experienced in the past was gone in her presence.

I palmed her breast with one hand while rubbing her clit with the other and her motions sped up. Her tits started to bounce faster and I leaned forward, sucking one of her nipples into my mouth.

Bree's hands went to my head, holding me in place as her fingernails scraped over my scalp.

"Oh my God," she whimpered. "I think I'm gonna come. I've never..." Bree sounded surprised as she trailed off and her walls started fluttering around my dick.

It almost sounded like she was going to say she'd never come before, but that couldn't be right, could it?

Without slowing down, she locked eyes with me and it felt like an electrical current ran through my entire body.

"Colton," she pleaded, looking a little lost, and it felt like she needed something from me. Reassurance maybe.

"I've got you," I told her while I continued to rub circles over her clit. "I've got you."

"Oh... Fuck. Shit. *Fuck*." Her voice came out in a hoarse whisper as the bucking rhythm of her hips sped up.

With a gasp, her breath caught in her throat.

Watching Bree in those few seconds right as she was about to come was the sexiest thing I'd ever seen. Head tilted back. Mouth open. Eyes shut.

And I fucking loved her dirty mouth.

Her body trembled and she dug her fingernails into my shoulder blades.

As her walls clamped down on me, she connected her lips with mine and I swallowed her loud moans. After several seconds, her rocking motions slowed and her whimpers subsided.

Letting out a satisfied sigh, her body became more languid and she let go of the death grip she had on me.

Running my hands up her thighs, I grabbed fistfuls of her

ass before moving up her sides, over her breasts, and down her arms.

I wanted to touch every inch of her body.

I hoped she wasn't ready to stop yet because I was far from being done. I felt like a kid in a candy store. Looking around the room, I tried to decide what I wanted to do next.

Keeping my cock inside her, I started scooting off the bed.

Laughing, Bree wrapped her arms around my neck in an attempt to hold on while I stood up. "What are you doing?"

"I want to fuck you on every surface of this room," I said, carrying her over to the dresser. I set her down. "Is that okay with you?"

"You don't hear me complaining, do you?" she quipped.

I chuckled before slipping out of her.

"Turn around and bend over," I ordered softly.

She cocked an eyebrow but did as I said. Bree lowered her body, resting her elbows on the wooden surface, then turned her head to look at me.

The expression on her face took my breath away. Something about it made me want to fuck her and make love to her at the same time.

Heavy lidded eyes. Messy hair. Lips swollen and red from kissing.

Desire and vulnerability.

And trust.

Why did she trust me?

Maybe I should've questioned it, but all the blood in my body was currently occupying my lower half.

I ran my hand down the smooth skin of her back before stepping up behind her. Guiding my cock to her opening, I pushed inside, moaning at how good she felt. As I pumped my hips, Bree threw her head back and gasped.

Any control I was holding onto snapped.

Bracing one hand beside her and wrapping my other arm around her stomach, I started thrusting into her hard and fast. Every movement caused the dresser to bang against the wall.

Letting out a squeal, Bree collapsed, laying her face on the top of the dresser while her fingernails scraped at the wooden surface.

The new angle caused me to go deeper, and she whimpered. I slowed, thinking I was being too rough with her, but she pushed her ass back against me.

"Please don't stop," she breathed out.

Fuck. Yes.

Grabbing onto her hips, I pushed into her over and over again, feeling her tight walls stretch around me until I knew I was about to come.

Forcing myself to stop, I pulled my cock out of her and helped her stand back up.

"What are you doing? Why did you stop?" she complained breathlessly, making me chuckle.

"Oh, I'm not done yet," I reassured her.

Gripping her around the waist, I picked her up and she automatically wrapped her legs around me. I moved us over to the wall, put her back against it, then drove up into her again. Tilting her head back, she moaned while hanging onto my neck.

I wanted to make her come a second time and I needed to see her face when it happened.

I started a steady rhythm with my hips while I began rubbing her clit with one hand and grabbing her ass with the other.

"Colton," she gasped. "Oh my God."

"Kiss me," I demanded, needing to feel her lips against mine, needing to be more connected to her than I already was.

"Harder," she begged into my mouth.

Bree's tongue swept past my lips as I gave her what she wanted.

A minute later, her pussy clenched around me and her mouth fell open as she let out a half-gasp, half-sob.

I was glad Bree came when she did because I wasn't going to last much longer. Grabbing her ass with both hands, I started thrusting myself up into her with so much force I thought we might make a dent in the wall.

My balls tightened and ripples of pleasure shot through my entire body as I felt my release building. My vision blurred and my hands tightened on her flesh, probably hard enough to leave bruises.

With a roar, I came inside her, emptying myself into the condom. Trying to catch my breath, I groaned into the skin on her neck while inhaling her scent.

Strawberries. Coconuts. *Her.*

Ruined. This girl had just completely ruined me for life.

CHAPTER 9

Brielle

olton cupped my jaw, kissing me slowly. It was sweet and wonderful—so different than the rough, almost frantic sex we'd just had. Before tonight, I never knew sex could be like that and I loved every second of it.

But this—the way Colton was being so gentle—allowed me to stay in the fantasy for a little longer as he kept me pressed up against the wall with his body.

With a grin, he gave my ass one last squeeze before lifting me off him so he could get rid of the condom. After tossing it in the trash he hopped back onto the bed, and I immediately missed his warmth.

I wasn't sure what to do next. Awkwardly shifting from one foot to the other, I wondered if I should get dressed and leave. Colton made the decision for me when he grinned and patted the mattress. I sat down next to him.

Without hesitation, he scooped me into his arms and held me against his chest.

"So I have to ask," he started, and there was a playful note in his voice. "Was that as good for you as it was for me?"

I giggled, still on some kind of post-sex high. "Yeah. I'd say it was pretty great. I can't believe I actually came. Twice."

Immediately, I wished I could take the words back. I couldn't believe I just told him that. The only logical explanation I could come up with was that Colton had fucked me senseless.

"Do you mean to tell me you've never had an orgasm before?" he asked, sounding shocked.

"I mean…I have… I've just never been able to with someone else… I thought maybe there was something wrong with me." I looked away, embarrassed. If the lights had been on, he would have seen my cheeks burning from the confession.

Since I'd never been able to get to the grand finale during sex, I never saw what the big fuss was about.

I could definitely see it now.

"So I gave you something no one else ever has?" His cocky tone had me glancing at him and, even in the dark, I could see the familiar confident smirk on his face.

That was the Colton I remembered, and it made me smile.

A loud crash and yelling from the other side of the wall snapped me out of the sex-stupor I was in.

"What was that?" I asked, alarmed and suddenly alert.

Colton chuckled. "That's Champ. He lives in apartment 3 and we share a wall." He pointed behind the headboard.

"LARRY!" the voice shouted, followed by a loud thud. "Goddammit, Larry!"

Worried, I started to sit up. "It's not like a domestic violence situation or anything, is it?"

Barking out another laugh, Colton put his hand on my shoulder to pull me back down next to him. "Champ lives alone. There is no Larry."

I raised my eyebrows. "What do you mean 'there is no Larry'?"

"I mean, Larry doesn't exist. Champ is… Well, he's not quite right in the head. He'd never harm a fly, but sometimes when he drinks he sees things that aren't there. My guess is, he just got back from the tavern."

Champ's agitated voice came through the wall again, closer this time. "Larry, you're a very arrogant little man with very little to be arrogant about."

"You tell him, Champ!" Colton yelled and banged his fist on the wall. "I'm on your side!"

A quieter, muffled reply came through the wall. "Thanks, Colton."

I couldn't help it—I laughed. And laughed. And when I thought I was done laughing, I would lock eyes with Colton and it would start all over again.

Somewhere in between taking breaths and wiping the tears from my eyes, I realized he was laughing, too. Lying on his back, his head was tipped back and his eyes were screwed shut as his chest shook. His grin stretched wide and he held a hand to his stomach while we completely lost our shit.

It felt so good because for a second, it felt like I had my friend back. How was it possible that fifteen years passed, but things still felt the same?

Then I remembered he had no idea who I really was. If anything could end my giggling fit, it was that sobering thought.

We weren't seven years old anymore. Life was a lot more complicated now.

Colton had grown up into a handsome man. If anyone knew how dangerous to the heart handsome men could be, it was me. Girls like me didn't nab guys like him. No one wanted to settle down with the cage dancer. No one wanted to date the single mother.

Tonight was all I could have and I needed to be okay with that.

Our laughter faded and he smiled down at me as I rested my chin on his chest.

The guilt of knowing I'd deceived him caused me to look

away. If he found out who I was now, after everything that happened, he'd probably hate me forever.

"Can you stay the night?" he asked quietly. "I really meant it when I said I wanted to hang out."

I glanced over at the clock. It was already after 3am.

"I can stay for a little while," I told him, not wanting our time to end yet.

Before leaving the club, I'd sent a text to my parents letting them know I would be going out after work—something they encouraged me to do from time to time. They wanted me to be able to experience young, carefree life once in a while, and that was something I was so grateful for.

However, they were also big believers in natural consequences, so any hangover or exhaustion from pulling an all-nighter was completely on me if they weren't available to help. Taking care of a little kid all day with zero sleep sucked, but I was willing to make the sacrifice this time.

"So how long have you been working at Caged?" Colton asked while rubbing his hand up and down my arm. I was snuggled into his side and, although his body heat kept me warm, goosebumps broke out over my entire body at his touch.

I shivered.

Without even asking if I was cold, Colton pulled the dark green blanket up to cover my shoulders.

"About three years," I answered, trying not to read into how sweet he was being. "What about you? You said you work at the shop down the street."

Maybe if I kept the conversation about him, I wouldn't be in danger of giving too much away about myself.

"Yeah. I've worked there since I was a teenager. We also have a moving company called Hank and Sons Transport, so I drive a semi to make deliveries a couple times a month."

"Sons? You have a brother?" I asked, shocked by the idea that his dad might have had more children after they moved away. It never occurred to me that Colton might have siblings now.

He shook his head. "Travis is my roommate. He works at the shop, too, and he does all the long hauls for the company. He's been my best friend since we were seven." He shrugged. "Might as well be my brother."

My heart clenched painfully as I realized this Travis guy must have been my replacement. I told myself it was ridiculous to feel jealousy over that fact, that it was a good thing Colton and his dad were able to move on. After all, that had been the whole point of them starting over.

I tried to picture Colton under the hood of a car or behind the wheel of a semi, and I had to admit it was pretty sexy.

Just like me Colton had a good life, a great family. When he talked about his dad and best friend, it was obvious there was a strong bond between them. Honestly, I was glad to know things worked out for him. Maybe this was meant to be my closure on the friendship that had been lost. I would never have to wonder about Colton again. He was happy, successful, and really good in bed.

Eventually he would find the woman of his dreams, and I would just be the exotic dancer he had a one-night stand with.

Not wanting to talk anymore, I propped myself up on my elbow and looked down at Colton before bringing my lips to his. He responded to the kiss by threading his fingers through my hair and rolling us so he was on top.

He playfully nipped at my chin with his teeth.

"Did you just—" I brought my hand up to my face. "*Bite my chin?*"

"Yup." He grinned and did it again. And again.

I laughed and squirmed as he continued to assault me with his mouth. My knees parted and I felt his hard length slide against my clit.

I gasped.

He looked down, and when his eyes came back up there was a hint of disbelief on his face.

"I want you again," he breathed out.

"I want you, too."

He quickly reached over to his nightstand to grab another condom. After rolling it on, he slid into me and we both moaned. The way his thickness stretched and filled me felt unbelievably good.

This time the sex was different.

Colton thrust in and out at a torturously slow pace. Every time he pulled back, his cock slid all the way out, then he pushed into me again. It was like he was savoring it, enjoying every sensation.

Cupping my face, he caressed my cheeks and my chin. Between ragged breaths he kissed me, and I was able to lose myself in the fantasy once again.

It was so easy to pretend that this wasn't just one night with a stranger because the way he was looking at me, the way he was moving inside me, felt a lot like making love.

Although I didn't come again, I enjoyed every breath, every gasp, every moan. I memorized the way his body felt over mine. The slide of skin on skin. The brush of his lips on the side of my neck.

When Colton found his release again, he looked into my eyes and rasped, "Bree."

And when he wrapped his arms around me and asked me to stay, I couldn't find it in myself to say no.

I knew—without a doubt—that after tonight I would never be the same.

∽

Worn out and completely satisfied, I started to drift off in Colton's arms, but the clock on the nightstand said it was nearing 5am, which meant I needed to get my butt home.

As quietly as I could, I slipped out from under Colton's arm and tried to find my clothes in the dark room. Using the light on my phone, I found my jeans and panties on the floor by the end of the bed. Next, I found my shirt on the other side of the room by the closet. I almost thought I would have to leave without my bra when I spotted the white material peeking out from under the bed.

I snatched it up, happy I was able to find it. The bra was plain white cotton. Not sexy at all. But it was my favorite bra and I would've hated to leave it behind.

As I got dressed, I noted a pleasant soreness between my legs and I was glad. I wanted to be able to feel what Colton and I did. Even though our time together was over, I wanted the experience to linger.

Before I walked out of the room, I paused. With my hand on the doorknob, I turned back to look at Colton. He was shirtless, lying on his back with his arm draped over his stomach. His lips were parted and his muscular chest rose and fell with every breath.

He looked so innocent while he slept—so much like the boy I used to know. I allowed myself to gaze at him for a few more seconds before quietly closing the door behind me as I left.

CHAPTER 10

Colton

The room was quiet but the curtains were drawn, letting in the bright afternoon light.

"Colton? C'mere, baby," my mom said from the hospital bed that sat in the middle of what used to be Dad's office.

The hospice nurse gave my shoulder a gentle squeeze as she passed me to leave the room. My mom patted the side of the bed and I eagerly climbed in next to her.

"So tell me about your day." Mom's voice sounded weak and tired but I knew I could cheer her up.

"Ellie and I had ketchup and mustard sandwiches for lunch."

"Mm, your favorite," she said, her blue eyes shining back at me.

Although she'd changed a lot since getting sick, her eyes always remained the same. My dad and I had blue eyes, too, but the color was so pale it almost looked gray. My mom's eyes, though... They were bright and vibrant. My dad always said it reminded him of the sky on a clear summer day.

"And we played thumb war a few times, but she beat me." I frowned.

My mom smiled. "No one can beat Brielle at thumb war. You know that."

I shrugged. "I still gotta try."

"That's right. And you keep on trying. Don't ever give up on something just because it's hard." Her face got serious. "You and

Brielle... You two have something extraordinary. Someday you'll realize just how special it is." she said as she lovingly ran a hand over the short hair on my head.

Smiling, I did the same to her, letting my fingers slip underneath her pink stocking cap. The radiation treatments had made her hair fall out but I still thought she was beautiful. My dad and I even buzzed our hair so we could all be the same.

"Ellie's my best friend," I told her, not sure what she was getting at. "I guess that's pretty special, right?"

She struggled to take a breath, her inhalation sounding wheezy. I had a feeling that what she was about to say was really important, so I leaned closer.

Suddenly, "Free Fallin" by Tom Petty started blaring through the room. It was so loud my hands went up to cover my ears. Mom's lips were moving, but I couldn't hear what she was saying.

I jackknifed up in my bed, my heart hammering in my chest. As my breathing slowed, I realized I'd been having a dream. Only it wasn't just a dream—it was a memory. Well, all except the part with the music. That was just weird.

As the chorus started again, I noticed my phone was ringing on the nightstand next to me, the cause for the strange end to the dream.

"Dad, it's too early," I answered grumpily after seeing his name flash across the screen.

He chuckled. "You know what they say—the early bird gets the worm."

I followed up with the same response I always had to those particular words of wisdom. "That might be true, but the second mouse gets the cheese."

He laughed as though it was the first time he'd ever heard it. "It's not even that early, Colton. It's after ten. Just wanted to wish you a Happy New Year."

"Happy New Year, Dad," I said as I dropped back onto

my pillow.

The scent of strawberries and coconuts wafted up from my sheets and I immediately sat back up, looking around for Bree, but there was no sign of her.

No articles of clothing anywhere. No note.

Empty, wrinkled sheets that smelled like her—that was the only evidence she'd been here, that last night was real.

That, and the fact that I wasn't wearing any clothes. I confirmed it by lifting the comforter and seeing my naked lower half.

My dad's voice cut through my thoughts, making me realize he was still on the phone. "Colton, you still there?"

"I'm sorry, what?"

"I said, do you want to come over this afternoon? I thought I could put a pizza in the oven for dinner."

"Yeah, sure. That sounds great," I said, feeling disappointed that Bree left without a word. "I'll be over in a little while."

"Ten-four." My dad ended the call the same way he always did, and I always found it amusing. Since starting the transport company, my dad tried to incorporate trucker lingo into every conversation.

After placing my phone back on the nightstand, I scrubbed a hand over my face as I thought about the night before. I should've been ecstatic. The sex had been off-the-charts awesome—the best I'd ever had. And some of my confidence had returned.

But it would've been better if I hadn't woken up alone.

Honestly, my feelings were a little hurt. She didn't even leave her phone number. Then again, I didn't ask for it.

I should have asked for it.

Idiot.

I'd just been so happy my dick was working, I couldn't think about much else. Frustrated, I fell back onto the pillows.

It's not like I didn't know where to find her. Even if it did make me feel like a complete stalker, going back to Caged was the only option.

After I rolled around in Bree's scent for longer than I cared to admit, I finally decided to get up and take a shower before heading over to my dad's.

One cup of coffee and a bagel later, I was headed out the door. I slipped my hands into my Carhartt pockets to keep them warm on the one-block walk over to my dad's place.

I caught sight of my neighbor leaning up against the side of the building next to his door and I shook my head. Pissing. He was pissing.

It wouldn't be the first or the last time Champ peed in public. His mostly-bald head was tilted down, and the red plaid shirt he was wearing was wrinkled as though he'd just rolled out of bed.

"Happy New Year, Champ," I said as I walked by.

"You too," he grunted, not bothering to look up or stop relieving himself.

As long as it wasn't in front of my apartment, I didn't care where he decided to take a leak.

My footsteps faltered as I recalled the way Bree and I laughed together the night before because of my neighbor's eccentric ways. I remembered how good it felt to be with her. So comfortable and fun.

Again, I cursed myself for not getting her number or asking her on a date.

The gravel of the parking lot crunched under my boots as I approached the back of the auto shop where my dad's apartment was. The shining sun reflected off the white brick exterior, making me squint against the bright light.

When I got to his door, I didn't bother knocking. People in this town had a habit of leaving their doors unlocked, which was one of the many things I loved about Tolson.

I walked straight into the kitchen, and the smell of baking pizza let me know I was right on time.

Heading into the living room, I found Dad where I always did—in his old brown recliner. I was convinced he spent about 90% of his free time in that thing. The TV was on ESPN. Also, not a surprise. If there was one word to describe my dad, predictable was at the top of the list.

When we first moved to Tolson he rented a small house for us, but once I moved out he didn't need the extra space. He'd spent at least a year converting the back area of the garage into a one-bedroom apartment. Living there was convenient for him, not to mention rent-free.

"Howdy," he greeted me, and I flopped down onto the cream-colored couch. "Travis and Angel are off gallivanting somewhere in Florida."

He wasn't telling me something I didn't already know, so I just said, "Yep. Lucky ducks."

"You know," he started, "you can take long hauls, too, if you want."

"Nah." I shook my head. "I'm sure the beach is great, but I like to stay put. If I want to see a body of water, I'll just go down to Elmer Lake," I said, referring to the large pond about 20 minutes away.

He nodded because he understood. "It's probably halfway frozen right now, though."

I gave an over-exaggerated shiver. "Ice fishing isn't really my thing. I'll wait a few months."

We sat in comfortable silence for a few minutes before I brought up a subject we didn't talk about often.

"Do you ever think about Mom?" I asked, and I saw the brief flicker of pain cross his face.

"Yeah. All the time," he said, then smiled a little. "It's hard not to with a hard-headed son like you. You're just like her."

Chuckling, I shook my head because he always said that, even though I was pretty sure I took after him. "Do you ever dream about her?"

"From time to time." He nodded and his face turned concerned. "Why do you ask?"

I shook my head. "It's nothing, really. I just have dreams sometimes, but they're more like memories. Things we talked about when she was sick. I was so young then... I can't remember everything she said. Every time I have this dream, I feel like maybe I'll find out what she was trying to say, but I always wake up before that happens." I shrugged, then decided to change the subject to keep things from getting too heavy. "I met a girl."

A smile lit up his face. "Oh, yeah? What's her name? Where's she from? When do I get to meet her?"

"I told you I just met her," I said, amused at his interrogation. I decided to go for aloof because I didn't want to admit that she ran away from me. Twice. "I guess I don't know that much about her yet."

"That's okay. Nothing wrong with taking things slow." The timer on the oven started going off and Dad got up from his chair. He clapped me on the shoulder as he walked by and gave me another one of his signature words of wisdom. "Slow and steady wins the race."

Inwardly, I laughed.

Slow and steady. That was the last thing Bree and I were.

CHAPTER 11

Brielle

"**D**o you like ants?" Ava asked. Sometimes she had difficulty saying the letter 'L' and it came out sounding like a 'Y'.

Do you yike ants?

The selective speech impediment was something she was getting better at all the time. While I was proud of her when she got it right, sometimes I wished she wouldn't grow up so dang fast.

"Ants are okay, I guess," I tiredly answered her 150th random question of the afternoon.

"Why?" she asked, repeating the same word I heard countless times a day.

I shrugged without opening my eyes as we cuddled on the blue sectional couch in the living room. "I don't mind them as long as they stay outside."

"Do they bite?"

"No, not usually."

"Why?"

I sighed, feeling mentally and physically drained. Ava woke up about 30 minutes after I got home from Colton's, which meant zero sleep for me.

My parents had left this morning for their annual New Year's Day getaway. Every year they went to a bed and breakfast up in northern Illinois for a night. It made me happy to see my parents still so in love after all the time they'd been together, but that meant I was on my own today.

"How about we just watch our movie," I suggested as I adjusted my arm; it was starting to fall asleep under Ava's weight.

I put on her favorite movie, *Frozen*, in hopes that she would let me rest. For breakfast, I let her have a spoonful of Nutella, half a scrambled egg, and fruit snacks. Lunch wasn't much better. I'd made 'cheesy toast' which was basically toasted pieces of bread with American cheese smashed in between.

I wasn't a perfect mom, but I loved Ava more than anything in the world. Let's just say I wasn't winning any Pinterest awards today.

To say I was tired would be an understatement. Naps were a thing of the past now. Ava started refusing them shortly after her 3rd birthday, but right now I might've done just about anything for two hours of peace and quiet.

Not only was I exhausted from not getting any sleep last night, but I was also feeling a little down. Being with Colton had left me on a high and now I was experiencing the crash and burn. I missed him, which was ridiculous. I'd gone most of my life without him in it.

One dancefloor encounter and a night of hot sex shouldn't make me feel his absence—but it did.

I also felt guilty about my lie by omission. I knew right from wrong, and what I did was all kinds of wrong. But, while I wasn't proud of what I did, I couldn't bring myself to regret it.

Ava was silent for a few seconds, but it didn't last long. "Are you frustrated?"

I finally opened my eyes to look down at her concerned face, and the bright daylight coming in from the bay window caused my head to ache. "No, bug. I'm not frustrated."

"Are you sad?"

She was too damn perceptive. Ava could always pick up on how I was feeling, even when I tried to hide it. It was something I loved about her, but sometimes it worried me. Weren't three-year-olds supposed to be self-centered?

"I'm a little sad," I admitted, and tried to vaguely explain the situation. "I saw an old friend last night, but I don't think I'll see him again for a long time. I kind of miss him."

"But maybe you could just call him," she said as she threw out her hand in a gesture that said it was the obvious solution to my problem.

I laughed lightly. "Well, I forgot to get his phone number," I told her as I ran my hand over the messy brown bun on the top of her head. It matched mine because she always wanted to be just like me. We even had matching pink princess-themed PJs on. My parents had gotten them for us for Christmas and it was one of my favorite gifts ever. Ava hadn't been as excited as I was but, then again, kids usually didn't care much for clothes.

"Oh." She sounded disappointed. Ava picked up my hand and kissed it. "There. Now you can be so happy?"

Nodding, I kissed her head. "Now I can be so happy."

I loved this age—such an innocent time where almost anything can be made better with a simple kiss.

"Can I touch your ear?" she asked.

I smiled at her weird habit. "Sure."

Her fingers came up grasp my earlobe while she ran her thumb back and forth over the skin.

"Your ear is so soft," she giggled, and my bad mood started to dissipate.

I decided I needed to stop wallowing. And drink coffee. Lots of coffee.

"Did you know today is New Year's Day?" I asked her and

she nodded.

"Grandma told me."

"Well, I think we should do something special to celebrate. How about we make brownies?"

"Yes!" She sat up and started bouncing on me, causing me to grunt. "I yuv brownies. And I yuv you! I yuv you super lightning eight one zero eight!"

"Wow, that's a lot of love," I told her seriously then sat up to wrap her in a hug. "I love you, too, Bug."

I peppered her face with kisses until we were both laughing.

A little while later the kitchen counters were a disaster, covered in brownie mix and dirty dishes. Sitting on the floor, Ava was stirring a big bowl of batter with a giant wooden spoon.

Smiling behind my coffee mug, I took in her appearance. Her pajamas were covered in smudges of chocolate and some of it even ended up in her hair. I had no idea how someone could manage to get so messy in five minutes, but she would definitely need a bath.

Ava stopped stirring and looked up at me, her blue eyes bright and happy. "I bet you'll see your friend again soon. I bet he misses you, too."

"Yeah, you might be right," I lied.

CHAPTER 12

Colton

"**B**ack again, I see?" The smug bartender from the other night laughed as he handed a tray of drinks to one of the waitresses. "Getting rejected once wasn't enough?"

I smirked and took a sip of the beer I'd just ordered. "I wasn't rejected."

I wasn't about to spill the details of the other night, but this ass-hat had no idea what he was talking about.

It was 1am and Bree had just hopped down from her cage. My plan was to get to her before she could do another disappearing act.

Was it creepy that I knew her usual routine was to go straight to the bar to get a glass of water? Yes. Yes, it was.

Did I care? Nope.

Caged wasn't very busy tonight, probably because it was a Tuesday. I preferred it this way. Fewer people for me to push aside as I chased Bree down.

Mr. Clean let out a loud huff of disbelief as he wiped down the bar in front of me. "Brielle doesn't give anyone a chance. Don't take it personally."

I sucked in a breath at the name. *Brielle.*

"What did you say?" I hissed.

"I said don't take it personally. She shoots everyone down."

"No, not that part. The part where you said her name. I thought her name was Bree."

"Short for Brielle." He was giving me a funny look, but I was too busy making the connections in my head to care.

Suddenly, I felt like I couldn't breathe. I looked across the club to where she was standing, talking with another dancer. Cocking my head to the side, I looked at her—really looked at her. I studied her face, her hair, and the way she moved.

My eyes fell to her hands where she was anxiously rubbing the skin on the knuckle of her left thumb. The action was so familiar I don't know how I didn't see it before. That one little thing. That was all it took to push me over the edge of recognition.

No. No fucking way.

A hundred memories slammed into me all at once.

Unending giggles. Scraped knees. Bee stings. Ketchup and mustard sandwiches. Catching fireflies in my backyard. Thumb war.

Sleepovers. The innocent kind, where it didn't matter that I woke up next to a girl because she was my best friend.

The realization was so staggering that I had to hold onto the bar to steady myself. I slept with my best friend.

I *slept* with my best friend.

And I didn't even know it was her.

Did she know? As I watched her, seeing her through new eyes, I saw the way her eyes nervously darted over to me. She looked guilty and turned away from me, like she was about ready to run.

Oh, hell no.

I definitely wasn't letting her get away now.

CHAPTER 13

Brielle

I could feel Colton's eyes on me before I even spotted him in the club. I don't know how my body could be so aware of his presence but I knew he was watching me. My hair stood on end, my heart rate sped up, and certain parts of my body revved to life.

While moving my hips to the music, I slowly spun a 360 in the cage and searched for him. Standing over by the bar, he leaned back casually, his silver eyes watching me.

Why was he here again? Was he here for me?

Panic overwhelmed me; I wondered if he'd realized who I was. Maybe he was here to confront me about it. Because I was a coward, avoiding him was the best option I could come up with.

When my shift was over I got down from the cage, but I didn't go over to the bar like usual. Instead, I sucked up my pride and asked a favor from someone I really didn't want to owe anything to.

"Tasha?" I didn't waste any time getting straight to the point. "I need a favor."

She raised her blonde, perfectly plucked eyebrows while rubbing a bright red fingernail over her hot pink bra strap. "Oh, yeah?"

Tasha and I weren't friends, but we weren't enemies either.

It was obvious we didn't care for each other, and we'd come to some unspoken agreement not to interact if we didn't have to. But, desperate times and all that jazz.

"Can you go over to the bar and get me a glass of water? Then meet me in the dressing room?" I swallowed hard. Pride was a tough pill. "Please?"

"Why?" She narrowed her eyes suspiciously.

I fidgeted anxiously. "Because there's a guy over there that I don't want to talk to right now."

Her eyes lit up with interest and she started to crane her neck to see around me. "Who?"

"Just an old friend." I said impatiently, waving my hands to regain her attention before adding, "Please?"

"Is your old friend really hot?" she asked breathlessly, and I rolled my eyes. Then she continued. "Because there's a hot guy headed this way."

Crap.

Who needed water anyway? I was about to make a bee-line for the back of the club when Colton's voice stopped me.

"Hello, Bri*elle*," he said beside me, putting emphasis on the last part of my name.

I glanced at him and, from the way he was looking at me, I could tell that he knew who I was. And even worse, he knew that I knew who he was.

He looked pissed, and rightly so.

Tasha shrugged as if to say 'Oops' and walked away.

I closed my eyes and took a deep breath before facing him. "I'm sorry."

It was a such lame thing to say. How could two words make up for what I'd done?

"For which part?" he replied, his expression hard to read.

"What?" I asked, confused, because I didn't realize I had more than one thing to apologize for.

"Why are you sorry? For leaving without a word the other morning? Or for not telling me who you were?"

A group of obnoxious frat guys started chanting about taking shots at a nearby table. Needing clarification and a better place to talk, I grabbed Colton's hand and dragged him across the club, trying to ignore the tingle where our skin touched. There was a door that led to a hallway with an emergency exit. I opened it and pulled him inside. The music was still loud but it was muffled enough that we wouldn't have to shout at each other.

I let out a resigned sigh. My secret was out.

"How did you know?" I asked, feeling extremely exposed in my dark purple boy shorts and cropped top. My sense of anonymity was gone—I wasn't just some random girl anymore. "I mean, after what we did… When did you figure it out?"

"That." Colton pointed down to my left thumb which was close to forming a blister from all the rubbing I'd done. I hadn't even realized I'd been doing it. He remembered my bad habit. Shaking out my hands, I curled my fingers around my thumb so I would stop. Then he added, "Also, Mr. Clean might've let your full name slip tonight."

"Who?" I felt my face scrunch up in confusion.

"The bartender. He sort of looks like Mr. Clean, don't you think?" he asked, tilting his head to the side.

Despite the seriousness of the situation, a nervous laugh burst from my mouth because Colton was totally right about that. Jerry, aka Mr. Clean, took his time in the gym way too seriously and wore his T-shirts a little too tight. Also, he'd been banging Tasha for the last few months and that made her think she could get away with murder around here. And now, apparently, he was taking bribes from customers and giving out personal information. Needless to say, I wasn't his biggest fan.

The humor immediately left me as I glanced at Colton's

face. He looked hurt. Maybe even a little disappointed, and that was way worse than angry.

"I'm sorry, okay?" My voice was heavy with remorse. "Yes, I knew who you were that first night. I should've told you."

Shame over my lie caused me to look down, and my chest tightened when I wondered if Colton would hate me after what I'd done. If I'd been honest with him from the start maybe we could've rekindled our friendship, but it was too late for that now.

"Why didn't you?" he asked and, instead of sounding angry like I expected him to, his voice came out soft.

I looked up at his face again and found curiosity, confusion, and shock. But not anger or bitterness. I had nothing left to lose at this point, so I just went for the truth.

"I had a really big crush on you when we were kids. In fact, I thought I was in love with you. And now you're so... so... *hot*." I waved my hands wildly as the word-vomit spewed from my mouth. "I know it sounds stupid, but when you looked at me the way you did the other night... I just wanted to experience that. Just one time. And then I thought you'd just get what you wanted and I'd never see you again." I shrugged.

"And what was it that I wanted?"

I let out an exasperated noise because the answer was obvious. "To sleep with me."

He stared at me for a few seconds then nodded. "Okay. Yeah. I did want that. But that's not all I want."

"It's not?" I asked, baffled.

Colton brought his hand up to my face and he ran his thumb over my chin. His expression turned tender.

"Ellie." He spoke so quietly I couldn't hear it over the music, but I could read his lips.

He was looking at me like I meant something to him. Like I wasn't just a hook-up. Like I wasn't just his long-lost friend.

"No one calls me that anymore," I told him. Because it was true. I was so heartbroken after he moved away I wouldn't let anyone call me by that name.

"You'll always be Ellie to me," he said gruffly, before closing the distance between us.

CHAPTER 14

Colton

I picked Ellie up, causing her to squeal with surprise, and she wound her legs around my waist. I placed her back against the dark wall of the hallway. Anchoring her there with my body, I pushed myself against her so she could feel my hardness.

I wanted Ellie to know how much I wanted her, that finding out who she was didn't change how I felt about her.

Was I shocked? Fuck yeah.

But learning who she really was made me like her more. A lot more. I didn't think it was possible to be more attracted to her, but now it made complete sense why I was so comfortable around her, why I'd even been drawn to her in the first place.

It almost felt too good to be true.

"Are you mad at me?" she asked, and suddenly I was transported back in time as I looked into her familiar eyes.

How did I not recognize her? I wanted to blame my over-eager dick for this oversight.

Then again, the Ellie I remembered was a bit of a tomboy. Knobby knees, ripped up jeans, and teeth that were a little too big for her face. More often than not she had dirt caked under her fingernails and almost always wore her hair in a ponytail.

And I had loved her.

She'd been my best friend, but the feelings went beyond

that. I used to think she was the most beautiful girl I'd ever seen—and even now, fifteen years later—that was still the case. Her confession that she felt the same way caused a surge of happiness to spread through my entire body.

Ellie certainly wasn't the tomboy anymore. Curves in all the right places. Smooth flawless skin. A face so perfect, it made me want to never stop kissing her. She'd grown into her body—and her teeth.

"Honestly, you shocked the hell out of me," I told her. "And I really wish you'd told me to begin with. But I'm not mad. Actually, I'm really fucking happy."

Her eyes went wide. "You are?"

I nodded, unable to stop myself from grinning. "When I came here tonight, it was for you. I already knew I wanted something with you. Something more than just sex. But now… this is like getting two for one. I get the beautiful girl and my best friend."

"You have a new best friend now," she reminded me.

"Travis is more like a brother to me. That means my best friend slot is still open," I reasoned.

She smiled a little and I could tell I was getting through to her. I didn't know why she felt the need to put up walls the way she did, but I would show her she could let me in.

Needing to feel her soft lips against mine, I leaned close and gave her a gentle kiss. After finding out her true identity, it almost felt like we were kissing for the first time. She opened her mouth for me and I savored the moment, loving the way her tongue slid against mine. Her hands pulled at the collar of my shirt, like she couldn't get me close enough.

Chuckling into her mouth, I broke the kiss and pulled back. "I thought I was totally obvious about the way I felt about you back then. How could you not know?"

"You stopped writing to me," she said, hurt lacing her

words as she fiddled with the buttons on my shirt.

It wasn't just an accusation—it was a fact. How could I possibly explain that I missed her too much? That every time I got a letter from her, it was like a punch to the gut? It was a reminder of something too far away, something I couldn't have.

Simply saying I was sorry didn't seem like enough, so instead I kissed her again. Using my thumb, I pulled down on her chin, causing her plump lower lip to jut out. Sucking it into my mouth, I swiped my tongue back and forth over the smooth flesh before biting down. Moaning, she wrapped her hands around the back of my neck while devouring my mouth.

Things were getting out of control quickly as my hips started rocking against hers. If only we didn't have clothes on. I would've loved nothing more than to fuck her up against this wall.

My confidence was back. No way in hell was my cock going down. I was quickly realizing my issue wasn't so much of an issue with Ellie.

Our heated make-out session was interrupted by a whistle and a catcall as the blonde dancer walked by. "Old friend, my ass! Get it, girl!"

Resting my forehead against hers, Ellie and I both laughed, but I didn't bother to separate our bodies.

"So where do we go from here?" she murmured against my lips.

"I think a good place to start would be to forgive each other. Start with a clean slate," I suggested. "I can try to explain why I stopped writing... But maybe right now isn't the best time."

She nodded, her nose brushing against mine. "Okay."

"Then we do the normal stuff," I said, getting one more

kiss in before pulling back. "Go on dates. Get to know each other again."

"I guess we have a lot of catching up to do, huh?" she asked, her legs still firmly wrapped around me.

"Yeah, we do. Speaking of that, what are you doing now? Want to come over?"

Her face fell. "I can't."

"You have another date or something?" I sort of meant it as a joke, but I couldn't keep the edge out of my voice at the thought of her seeing someone else.

"No." Ellie's eyebrows furrowed together the same way they always used to when I pissed her off. "It's nothing like that. I've just lost a lot of sleep lately and I'm tired." She gave me a pointed look because I was the reason for her loss of sleep.

"But will you go on a date with me? Soon?" I asked hopefully.

I didn't even try to stop myself from sounding desperate. Normally, I would've tried to play it cool. But this was Ellie. We could just skip all the bullshit.

"I have Friday night off," she told me as she lightly ran a finger over my left eyebrow.

That was only three days away. What I wanted was to spend time with her now, but I guess I'd just have to be patient.

"Friday it is, then." I grinned and took out my phone.

After exchanging numbers, I walked Ellie to her car. We made out against the driver's side door until both of us were numb from the cold and sporting chapped lips.

Before I walked away from her, I said goodbye in the best way I knew how.

"Three," I said quietly, and took a step back.

A bright smile lit up her face. "Two."

"One." I grinned because she remembered.

The whole goodbye routine had started because we could never decide who was going to say bye last. We'd spent many phone conversations arguing about who got to have the last word, so I had come up with the solution.

We looked at each other for another few seconds before we both uttered the last word at the same time. "Bye."

After I got home I took off my boots, flopped down onto the couch, and sent Travis a text. Even though it was late, he responded right away.

> **Me: I've got something tits oasis when you grab ass.**
> **Travis: Wtf?**
> **Me: Omg. Autocorrect is ducking with me again.**
> **Me: Fuck.**
> **Me: I have something to tell you when you get back. That's what I typed out, I swear.**
> **Travis: Does it have something to do with a girl?**
> **Me: Yeah. How did you know?**
> **Travis: Hank told me.**

I rolled my eyes. Of course my dad told him. That was the thing about being as close as the three of us were—there were no secrets. Most of the time, I liked it. Other times, I just wanted some damn privacy.

> **Me: My dad is a nympho gopher.**
> **Travis: Hahaha.**
> **Me: Dammit! A nosy gossip.**

Giving up on the conversation, I changed into a T-shirt and sweat pants before crawling into bed. Ellie's scent still lingered on my pillowcase and I buried my face in it, wishing she was with me.

I thought back to the other night, to the times when I felt that emotional pull.

Although I didn't know it was Ellie at the time, somehow my subconscious recognized her. That was the only explanation I could come up with for the instant connection we had.

Just thinking about having her back in my bed made me hard as a rock. I looked down at the wood I was sporting and sighed.

Friday couldn't come fast enough.

CHAPTER 15

Brielle

My phone chirped, alerting me that I had a message. Colton and I had been texting almost non-stop since the other night.

But his text would have to wait.

Scrunching my face up against the freezing wind, I put my arm around Ava and tried to shield her from the harsh weather as we approached the community college where I would be taking my classes. Snowflakes started to blow around us and I hoped this errand wouldn't take too long.

Adjusting the purse on my shoulder, I took Ava's hand when we got close to the entrance. The automatic sliding doors opened, blasting us with a wall of welcome warm air, and I looked around for a map that would direct me to the bookstore.

"What are we doing here?" Ava asked while skipping next to me.

"I have to buy some books."

"What kind? Yittle Critter books?"

I laughed.

"No. Boring books," I replied. "For my classes."

"How many?"

She twirled and almost bumped into another student. The young guy already looked a little lost, but when his eyes landed on Ava a panicked expression crossed his face and he glanced around as though he was wondering if he was in the wrong building.

"Sorry," I sent the apology his way as I took Ava's hand again. "Well, I'm taking three classes, and I need five books," I told her, looking down at the crazy outfit she was wearing.

Usually, I let Ava pick out her own clothes. As long as it was weather-appropriate and she wasn't naked, I didn't really care what she wore.

Today she picked out a poofy purple princess dress. She put up a little protest when I told her she had to wear a long-sleeve shirt and pants underneath it, but as soon as I told her we could match she gave in. She thought the black leggings, pink shirt, and brown fur-lined boots made us twins. Add to that the fact that our gray wool coats were almost identical, she was one happy girl.

The hallways of the college seemed like an unending maze, but eventually we found the bookstore.

Pausing in one of the aisles, I took out my course list. English 101, Bio 121, and Math 098. I didn't know what to expect out of these classes. I only knew two things—they were required, and my study skills were super rusty. At first, I'd been a little disappointed that I wouldn't get to dive into the medical stuff, but the class counselor told me I had to get all the prerequisites out of the way.

After locating all my books, I went up to the counter to pay. I almost choked on air when the cashier announced the total.

Holy crap. Almost $300 for five books? I'd even picked out the used ones.

Sighing, I handed over my debit card and made a mental note to ask for an extra shift at Caged next week.

As I dropped the books into my large purse, I felt a tug on my coat and glanced down at Ava's worried expression.

"Are you frustrated?" she asked as we walked toward the exit.

"No, Bug. These books were just very expensive."

She stopped me before we could get back out into the hall-way and looked up at me with teary eyes. Her chin wobbled. "We can sell my Barbies if you want."

"Oh, sweetie, no." I kneeled, dropping down to her level. "We don't have to sell any of your toys. I've got it covered."

"Okay." She gave me a watery smile.

My sweet, sensitive girl. I picked up her hand and kissed it, then she did the same to me.

We resumed our walk, trying to find our way out of the building when my phone chirped again.

Colton: Hoes your day?
Colton: HOW is your day? Autocorrect ruins my life.

I giggled, gaining Ava's attention. "What are you yaughing at?"

"Just a funny friend," I said before typing back a reply.

Me: Good. Just got the books for my classes.
Colton: Excited for our date tonight? I can't wait to sex you.
Colton: SEE you. Omg. That's what I meant.
Me: Suuuure. I think you had it right the first time though ;)

Unable to stop myself from smiling, I slipped my phone into the pocket of my coat.

"Are you so happy?" Ava asked, beaming up at me.

"Yeah, Bug," I replied, swinging our hands between us. "I'm so happy."

Ava ran to the living room as soon as we got home because I promised her she could watch Tom and Jerry while she ate her lunch. I warmed up the leftover spaghetti and meatballs from the night before, then dished it onto a Scooby-Doo plate.

Setting it next to her on the couch, I reminded her of our deal. "You have to eat it all, okay? Every bite."

"Okay," she agreed, already entranced by the TV.

My phone started ringing from the kitchen. Not many people called me these days, so I wasn't surprised to see Chloe's name flashing on the screen.

"Hey, what's up?" I answered while unloading all the books from my purse onto the counter.

"Hey." She paused, then her tone turned suspicious. "You sound cheerful. What's up with you?"

I huffed out a laugh. "What do you mean? I can't be happy to hear from a friend?"

"No, you can… But that's not it. You sound peppy. Did you get laid or something?" Taken aback by her accurate guess I hesitated, and she gasped. "You did! Oh, my God. Who was it? Fess up, Hoe Bag."

I sighed. There was no way I could deny it. "I really can't go into details right now," I said, glancing around the corner at Ava, who wasn't holding up her end of the deal. "Hang on a sec, Chloe."

Leaning down over the back of the couch, I tapped the full plate next to Ava. "You gotta eat, baby. Or else I turn off your show."

"Okay, okay." She picked up her fork and took a big bite.

Satisfied, I went back into the kitchen and realized Chloe was still talking. "What?"

"I said, it was the guy from the other night, wasn't it?"

"What guy?" I asked, wondering if the rumor mill at Caged extended to ex-employees. I wouldn't be surprised if Tasha had been gabbing.

"Don't play dumb with me," Chloe said, sounding insulted. "The guy! On the dance floor. The one I hooked you up with."

I gasped. "That was you?"

"Um, you're welcome."

"I knew him," I blurted out.

"Oh. Like you *knew* him? Or you knew him then you got to *know* him?"

Shaking my head, I smiled as I tried to decipher Chloe's code talk for sex. "Ava can't hear you. You can say it. Yes, I knew him a long time ago. Then I got to *know* him," I told her, then groaned when I had to say the worst part. "But he didn't know who I was… And I sort of didn't tell him."

"What the hell? Back it up. I'm confused."

I groaned again. "Me, too."

"So you had sex with him," she whisper-yelled, "and you didn't tell him that you knew him?"

I slapped a hand over my face, because when someone else said it back to me it sounded really bad. "Yes. But he knows now, and we have a date tonight."

She made a *tsk tsk* noise, and I could imagine her shaking her head at me in disapproval. "Okay. We're gonna talk about this. Soon." She paused. "But let's talk about the fact that you have a date tonight!"

"Don't get too excited." Glancing around the corner, I was happy to see that Ava was making progress on her lunch. "For all I know, he might just be looking for a good time." I lowered my voice. "And he doesn't know about Ava yet."

I realized my concerns went unnoticed when I heard

Chloe singing through the phone, "Bree is gonna get married, Bree is gonna get married, Bree is gonna—"

"Chloe!" I laughed.

"Is that Chloe?!" I heard Ava shout from the other room before she came barreling into the kitchen, her feet pounding on the laminate floors. "I wanna talk! I wanna talk!"

I put it on speaker phone and Chloe's voice filled the kitchen.

"Miss Ava, is that you?"

"Yeah, it's me," Ava responded much more calmly now that she had Chloe's full attention. "Where are you?"

"I'm at my house. Where are you?"

"I'm at my house, too." Ava smiled and excitedly clasped her hands under her chin. "Are you coming over?"

"Well, I wish I could, but I have to work tonight."

"Aw, man." Ava pouted, and I rubbed her chubby cheek.

"You get to hang out with Grandma and Grandpa tonight," I reminded her. "If you go finish your lunch I'll let you have an Oreo."

Those were the magic words. She scampered back into the living room.

Chloe's laugh came through the phone. "It's nice to know where I rank next to Oreos."

"Don't be offended. I'm pretty sure Oreos come before me, too."

"Listen, if you need someone to watch her don't hesitate to ask. I can help out with your classes, date nights, whatever."

"Thanks." I smiled. "I'll take you up on that and I'll even pay you."

She made a dismissive sound. "Your money's no good with me. I only accept currency in the form of dirty details about your new man."

"He's not *my* man. It's the first date."

Nervousness suddenly hit me as I realized that in a matter of hours, I was going on a date—a real date—with Colton. *Colton Evans*. The childhood version of myself would've been crapping her pants about right now.

So much had happened in the last fifteen years. There was so much he didn't know about me. What if he didn't like what he found out?

"Get out of your head," Chloe said, reading my thoughts.

"No, you get out of my head. It's creepy when you do that," I told her with a smile.

She sighed. "Have fun. Live a little. It's going to be great and you deserve this. And don't forget to tell me *everything*."

"Okay, okay," I agreed, holding my hands up in surrender.

After we ended the conversation, I tried not to think too much about the outcome of tonight. I busied myself with the dishes, then Ava helped me clean the kitchen. When I say she helped I mean she dumped an entire bottle of vinegar water on the floor, then attempted to soak it up with a roll of paper towels.

Ava smiled up at me, still mopping at the puddle, and my heart swelled with love.

I just had to hope Colton didn't tuck tail and run when I told him about her.

CHAPTER 16

Colton

Ellie: Suuuure. I think you had it right the first time though ;)

Fuck.

I felt my cock start to thicken as I read over Ellie's last text, which let me know she was up for a repeat of the other night. Having an erection at work was totally unprofessional. I set the phone down on a nearby tool box while trying to make my hard-on go away.

Friday was usually one of our busy days at the shop and I'd just gotten done fixing a loose belt on an old Cadillac. Next up was a standard tire rotation, then after that, an oil change.

"So what did you have to tell me?" Travis asked beside me, reminding me of the text I'd sent him a few nights ago.

Travis and Angel came back from their trip the day before, but I hadn't gotten a chance to talk to him yet. Now that he asked, I couldn't wait to spill the news.

"Do you remember the first day we met? When we got into a fight?" I picked up a rag to wipe the grease off my hands. I faced him as I thought about the day my dad introduced me to the boy living three houses away in our new town.

"Of course," he replied with a smirk. "That shiner I gave you lasted a week."

"Yeah, you got me good." I chuckled. "But I threw the first punch. Do you remember why?"

"We had a disagreement about some game or something. Right?"

I shook my head. "No. It was because I was pissed that we had to move and I didn't want a new best friend. I was angry and I took it out on you."

"That's why you hit me?" he asked incredulously. "Not cool, man. And all these years you let me believe it was because you were jealous of all the marbles I won. I just thought you were a sore loser."

"My dad was so mad at me. I'd never punched anyone before." I chuckled. "Do you remember that stupid shirt he put us in together?"

Travis barked out a laugh. "The get-along shirt. I wasn't very happy about that either, but you decided I wasn't so bad by the end of the day, huh?"

I nodded. "You're kind of impossible not to like."

He put a hand over his heart like he was touched. "Thanks, man."

As I thought back to that day, I remembered how mad I was. I had lost my mom, my home, and my best friend. Then my new neighbor came over, and the last thing I wanted to do was play nice.

Honestly, I needed to let out some of the anger I was holding in. When I hit Travis, it felt good. Really good.

When he hit me back? Not so much. He'd been smaller than me at the time, and I underestimated him. Seven-year-old Travis had one hell of a right hook.

Then my dad put us in that stupid over-sized T-shirt. He even went as far as taking out a Sharpie and writing 'The Get-along Shirt' on the front.

Travis and I spent the first hour giving each other the

silent treatment while I held a bag of frozen peas to my eye and he dabbed at the blood coming from his nose.

The turning point for us had been when he told me his dad had died in a car accident a few years before. That's when I realized Travis wasn't much different from me. We called a truce, and my dad and I walked him home that night.

When his mom came out to meet us, she swayed on her feet, eyes glassy and words slurred. Her brown hair was in a messy ponytail and she had a smear of what looked like spaghetti sauce down the front of her pink T-shirt. Despite her appearance being in total disarray, her face lit up when she saw Travis. She thanked us for bringing her son home, then stumbled a bit as she walked back up to the house.

Travis was right there to catch her. He put her arm around his shoulders, letting her lean on him, and guided her up to the house.

Over the years I would come to learn that Karen Hawkins was one of the sweetest people in the world, drunk or sober. But it was clear that Travis had taken on the role as man of the house, and I gained respect for him that day.

As my dad and I walked home, he told me Travis was going to need us. Grudgingly, I agreed.

But what I didn't tell my dad was that I thought maybe I needed Travis, too.

"Anyway," I said, bringing my thoughts to the present. "The girl I was best friends with before I came here… Her name is Brielle. She was the dancer from the night of my birthday."

"The one who ran away from you like you had the plague?" Travis asked, amused.

I threw the dirty rag and it hit him in the face before he could catch it. Sputtering, he pulled it off his face and glared at me.

I snickered. "That's the one. We spent some time together," I said cryptically, not wanting to give away too many private details. "I didn't have any *issues*."

"Yeah?" Travis smiled. "That's awesome. So, are you gonna see her again?"

Unable to keep myself from grinning, I nodded. "We have a date tonight."

"You better let us meet this girl soon. Angel will be stoked to have another woman around."

Whenever Travis said 'us' he was referring to both himself and Angel. They'd become a 'we' couple. Even when the other wasn't around, they still spoke as if they were right next to each other. It was sickeningly sweet. I used to find it a little nauseating, but now I could admit that I was just jealous—I wanted that for myself.

And for the first time ever, I had hope that it could happen for me.

My pleasant thoughts were interrupted when the greasy rag came flying at me and smacked me in the forehead. I wiped at my skin, probably only making it dirtier.

"You're a dick," I called after Travis as he walked away, laughing.

CHAPTER 17

Colton

Ellie's neighborhood was nice. Two-story houses, mature trees, and brick-paved streets gave the older part of town a nostalgic feel.

As I approached the light-blue colonial, I remembered Ellie said she lived with her parents. Dave and Susan Mitchell had been like second parents to me. They'd loved me and always welcomed me into their home.

I just hoped they still felt the same way now that I was here to take their daughter out. Swallowing hard, I tried to keep the nerves at bay.

I knew these people and they used to know me. What I hoped they didn't know was that Ellie and I had already been *intimate*. Parents had a sixth sense about those kinds of things.

I groaned because now I was thinking about the other night. What it felt like to have Ellie naked. Writhing and moaning. Coming on my cock.

Normally, I would've been happy to get a boner, but right now was a bad time. The last thing I needed was to show up at Ellie's parents' house rocking a massive hard-on.

I adjusted myself in my jeans and tried to think of the time I'd walked in on my grandma in the bathroom. Or spiders—I fucking hated spiders. Or those sad ASPCA commercials with all those neglected animals. Anything to get my erection to go down.

It seemed to work, so I took a deep breath and rang the doorbell. The chime I heard ringing inside the house wasn't just a simple 'ding dong'. Instead, I heard the tune of 'She'll be Coming Around the Mountain' followed by rapid stomping of feet, as though someone was literally sprinting to the door.

I started to smile, thinking Ellie must be really excited to see me, but when the door swung open I had to glance down to see my greeter. Looking back at me was a three-foot-nothing little girl with big blue eyes and long brown hair.

"Uhh... Um..." I stuttered and took a step back, thinking maybe I had the wrong house.

The door opened wider and someone came up behind the girl.

I recognized Dave immediately. In my youth, he'd seemed like a mountain of a man. Now he and I stood eye to eye because I matched him in height. His full head of once-dark hair was now peppered with gray, and his face owned a few more wrinkles than I remembered.

"Colton." He smiled and gestured for me to come inside.

Once I got past the threshold, he threw his arms around me and clapped my back in a manly hug.

"Dave, it's great to see you again," I said, looking around at the nice house. The staircase was to the left of the foyer, and off to the right there was a living room with a big blue couch. The kitchen was straight ahead and I thought I saw Susan walk by the doorway as she wiped down the counters. Original woodwork lined the baseboards and crown molding, giving the home character.

"You, too," Dave responded with a smile. "What a small world, right?" His face suddenly got serious and he crouched down next to the child, who was still staring up at me. His voice got quieter as he talked to her. "What have we told you about answering the door?"

"I'm not supposed to do it," she replied immediately.

"And what did you do?" Dave asked.

"Weeeeell," she started, drawing the word out. "Actually, I sort of did answer the door, but actually, it was okay. Yeah. Because I actually knew who it was."

I had to stifle a laugh at her explanation and her overuse of the word *actually*, which she definitely couldn't pronounce correctly.

"You know who this is?" Dave asked, pointing up at me.

She nodded. "Colton."

"And how do you know that? You've never met him before."

She let out an exasperated sigh and held out her hand. "Because you just said so."

Well, she had him there.

"We'll talk about this later." He gave her a pat on the head and I could see he was fighting back a smile. He stood up to face me. "I'll go tell Brielle you're here."

"Thanks." I watched him walk up the stairs, then realized the little squirt was still hanging around.

"Can you guess what I am?!" she asked excitedly as she waved her arms up and down while running in place.

"Uhh…" I laughed. "Are you a bug?"

It seemed like a logical conclusion because she was wearing some sort of green dress with wings attached to the back.

"No!" She burst into a fit of giggles.

She covered her mouth with one hand while pointing at me with the other, and the wild laughter continued.

Great. I was being mocked by a toddler.

I couldn't help but laugh, though. This kid was crazy.

Then it occurred to me that I had no idea who she was or what she was doing in this house. The family resemblance was there, and I tried to mentally calculate how old Dave and Susan were. I guess it wouldn't have been impossible for them to have another kid a few years ago. Unusual, but not impossible.

"What's your name?" I asked the bug, who was still hopping around and flailing her arms.

"Nope! You hafta guess what I am first."

I snapped my fingers as it came to me. "You're that fairy. The one from Peter Pan."

"No!" More giggling. More tap dancing.

"I give up." I shrugged and held my hands up in defeat.

"I'm a caterpillar pig-fish!"

"Well, I never would've guessed that in a million years," I told her honestly.

"Ava, are you entertaining my friend?" I glanced up to see Ellie coming down the stairs dressed in skinny jeans and a form-fitting long-sleeve T-shirt with horizontal black and white stripes.

She had a lot less makeup on than when she worked. Her hair was up in a loose ponytail and runaway strands fell around her face. It reminded me of the little tomboy she used to be.

Again, I was stunned by how gorgeous she was.

"Hey." My voice cracked on the word and I cleared my throat. I guess I was more nervous than I thought.

"I showed Colton I'm a caterpillar pig-fish," Ava said as she went back to skipping around.

"You're the cutest caterpillar pig-fish I've ever seen," Ellie responded, beaming down at the little girl.

Just then, Susan came around the corner. "Colton," she said with a big smile on her face as she leaned up to give me a hug. "You certainly look different than the last time I saw you."

"Well, you look exactly the same," I told her, and she made

a dismissive sound while blushing. I wasn't kidding, though—she really did look like the woman I remembered. Her dark brown hair was styled in a short bob and her eyes—the same honey brown as Ellie's—had a youthful glow.

Dave and Susan had both aged well. My guess was having another kid in their mid-forties must've kept them young.

"You kids have fun tonight," Susan said, as if we were still seven years old. Then she looked down at Ava. "I'm about to make some cookies and I think I need a helper."

"I'm a helper," she replied, her hand shooting up into the air, and they started walking to the kitchen.

"It was nice to meet you, little bug," I told Ava, unable to remember what kind of hybrid animal she'd called herself.

She waved without looking back at me.

"I love you and I'll see you tomorrow," Ellie called after her and shrugged when she didn't receive a response. "Sometimes cookies take full priority, I guess."

Chuckling, I placed my hand at the small of her back and reached for the doorknob.

"Hey!" Ava shouted, and I turned around to see her running back over to me.

She tugged on my arm until I had no other choice but to kneel, our faces level. When she smiled, I noticed a familiar indent in her chin and a warm feeling of affection filled my chest.

"How did you know my mom calls me 'Bug'?" she asked.

I glanced over at Susan, who looked amused.

"I didn't. It was just a good guess." I shrugged.

She seemed to be satisfied with that answer and, with quick, thundering footsteps, she disappeared into the kitchen.

What a funny kid.

CHAPTER 18

Brielle

Walking out to Colton's truck, I mentally rehearsed how I would tell him I was a mom. That dating me didn't mean just dating *me*.

There would be another person involved, and I had no idea how he would react to that news. I'd specifically instructed my parents not to inform Colton of who Ava was because I wanted to be the one to tell him, but now the anticipation was killing me.

We passed my beige Camry and my heart raced as Colton guided me over to the passenger side of his dark blue Ford pickup truck. Like the gentleman he was, he opened the door then gave me a grin that caused a fluttery feeling in my stomach.

Those adorable crooked teeth got me every time.

As I closed the door to the truck, I took a deep breath. I wanted to get the inevitable over with as soon as possible.

After Colton got behind the wheel, I opened my mouth to let the words come out, but he spoke first.

"Before we go out, I feel like we need to get a conversation out of the way… It's kind of awkward," he said, and I felt my heart break a little.

Here it comes.

I sat up straighter, steeling myself for the rejection I'd

encountered so many times before. "Okay."

"Do you know what performance anxiety is?" he asked, and it took me a second to comprehend his random question.

"Um, you mean like stage fright?"

"Yeah, exactly. Only it happens in," he paused, seeming to try to find the right words, "sexual situations."

"I guess I don't really understand what you're getting at," I said, pinching my eyebrows together in confusion.

He sighed and ran a hand over his jaw before looking at me. "Sometimes I have trouble getting it up. My dick, I mean."

"Really?" I asked, surprised. "You didn't seem to have any trouble the other night."

He smirked. "Nope. Come here for a sec."

I hadn't put on my seatbelt yet so I was able to scoot over to him. He took my hand and put it over the front of his jeans.

My eyes went wide when I felt the bulge beneath the fabric. "Are you seriously hard right now?"

"Yup. You seem to do that to me. I'm beginning to wonder if you're a hazard to my health," he joked, then his face got serious. "I felt like I needed to tell you in case it ever happens. I thought if I told you about it and you were okay with it, maybe I wouldn't feel so much pressure…"

His face looked tortured as he glanced away from me, and I caught a glimpse of an insecure side to him I'd never seen before. It was obvious that someone in his past hadn't been okay with it, and my protective side kicked into gear.

"Hey. You never have to feel embarrassed around me. Not about anything," I said softly and squeezed his hand. "Remember that time you peed your pants?"

Giggling, I covered my mouth and Colton's jaw went slack.

"You promised we'd never speak of that again," he said, his voice hushed as if someone might overhear. "You pinky swore."

"My point is, it doesn't get more embarrassing than that. I've already seen you at your worst."

His face turned incredulous. "There was a huge spider crawling up my leg. It was that big!" He held his thumb and forefinger in a large circle that was an exaggeration of the real thing. "And I was six. It was fucking scary."

I laughed. He huffed.

I soothingly rubbed his thigh as my voice turned patronizing. "You're right. It was a big spider. Very, very scary."

A slow smile spread over his face. "Move your hand a little higher and something cool might happen."

Quickly removing my hand, I scooted back over to my seat. "I'm not opposed to getting busy with you in your truck, but *not* in my parents' driveway."

He barked out a laugh. "Fair enough."

"Colton, wait," I said before he could put the truck in reverse. He relaxed back in his seat and gave me a lazy grin that caused more butterflies to erupt in my stomach. "Before we go out on this date I need you to know something." He raised his eyebrows and waited for me to continue. "Do you remember when you said the other night that dating me was like getting two for one?"

"Yeah." He grinned again.

"Well, you'd literally be getting two for one. Ava is my daughter."

Although I was nervous about what Colton's reaction would be, pride and happiness caused me to smile when I claimed ownership of my little girl.

Holding my breath, I watched his smile fade as shock appeared on his face, and I braced myself. I expected awkwardness, the 'let's just be friends' speech, and fear—I was always surprised by the number of young men who were totally freaked out by little kids.

Instead, the corner of his mouth quirked up.

"Wow," he breathed out. "She's like a mini-you." He shook his head, still smiling. "That's awesome, Ellie. She's awesome."

My mouth opened and closed several times, not knowing how to respond. I finally settled on a simple, "Thank you."

He let out a chuckle. "You're just full of surprises. I thought she was your sister." Glancing at the house, his eyes bounced from window to window as if he was looking for her. "Is her, uh, father still in the picture?" he asked, his face going serious as he turned toward me.

I shook my head. "No. Obviously, Ava was an accident—a happy accident. I got pregnant at the end of my senior year. At first, I was devastated," I told him truthfully. "I didn't know how to be a mom and all my plans had to change. I never even considered the possibility of not keeping her and, at the time, my ex, Josh, was supportive of that decision."

"So what happened?" Colton asked, reaching over to hold my hand. Just that little action gave me the support and courage I needed to get through this conversation.

I shrugged. "I guess he changed his mind. After we graduated, he told me he planned to get a job in our town. But over the summer, he kept partying with his friends and became more distant. Then he told me he got accepted to an out-of-state university and that he was going. He didn't even come back for the birth," I said, remembering how heartbroken I was. "And when Ava was two weeks old, he called to tell me he didn't want anything to with her. Or me."

"Anyone who would leave you like that is a grade-A asshole," he stated, his voice filled with rage. "You could've fought it, though, right? I mean, legally, he should've been responsible."

"No," I said firmly, "I didn't want that. If he didn't want to be involved, then he would've been a terrible father." I gave him a small smile. "Ava and I do pretty well for ourselves. We have a good life together."

Colton looked down at our intertwined hands and fiddled with my fingers.

"I'm hoping you'll let me be a part of that life," he said softly before glancing back up at my face. My heart skipped a beat because his words were so sincere, so honest. "Do you want to bring Ava to dinner with us?"

I paused, taken aback. "You want to take Ava on our date?"

"Sure, why not? I don't know much about kids, but I can learn. She's cool as shit." He grinned, then his face turned horrified. "I mean—shit. Crap." He shook his head and laughed at his inability to stop cussing. "I'm gonna have to learn how to watch my language."

I nodded. "She's heard me slip a few times, but I try to control myself. She's like a little sponge. Kids soak up everything they see and hear," I said. "And you have no idea how much it means to me that you want to know her. But tonight, I'd kind of like for it to just be you and me."

"Maybe next time, then?" he asked hopefully and I could tell he meant it—he really wanted to include Ava.

"Definitely." I couldn't stop the big goofy smile on my face. "So what are we doing tonight?"

"Going dancing."

CHAPTER 19

Brielle

When Colton said dancing, he meant line dancing. I had no idea this was something he liked doing, but I was up for it.

That is, until I saw him attempt the moves.

As 'Head Over Boots' played through the tavern, he looked totally lost as he watched the people around him and tried to copy their steps. I wasn't familiar with this particular dance, but years of dance classes made it easier for me to follow along.

Colton bumped into an older woman and apologized, sending her a charming grin, and I swear I saw her blush.

The small-town bar he took me to was way busier than I expected it to be. When we arrived, the gravel parking lot had been so full we had to park down the street. Aptly named The Brick House, it was exactly that—a ranch-style home with a brick exterior, metal roof, and pink shutters. The inside smelled like fried food, beer, and popcorn, and the small wooden dancefloor was packed.

"Colton." I motioned down to my feet. "Here, like this."

I took his hand and tried to show him the steps, but he was hopeless. Colton shrugged, put his hands on his hips, and literally started doing a bad imitation of River Dancing. I started laughing so hard that I doubled over with my hands on my stomach and people moved around us.

Giving up on his ridiculous display, he grabbed me around the waist, put my right hand in his left, and started spinning us around while swaying to the music.

The song changed over to 'Why Don't We Just Dance' by Josh Turner and I had an idea.

"I can teach you how to two-step," I told Colton. "It's really easy."

Keeping our hands clasped together, I put some space between our bodies so we could look down at our feet.

"Okay, so you're going to step forward with your left foot, and I'll step back with my right," I instructed and when I glanced up at his face he looked uneasy.

"I'm going to step on your toes," he warned.

"Probably." I laughed. "But it'll be fun. Now, you're going to take two quick steps, then two slow. Like this…" Colton started to follow me. "Good. You're doing good. Quick, quick—ouch!"

"Sorry," he apologized and bent down to inspect my injured foot.

Giggling, I pulled him back up. "It's okay. Let's try again."

Colton may have been good at a lot of things, but it turned out that two-stepping wasn't a talent he possessed.

But he tried. After a few songs he started to get the hang of it, but I was getting hungry so we decided to take a break.

Hand in hand, we walked off the dancefloor to go back to our table.

"You didn't do too bad," I said, and he made a scoffing sound. "Seriously. You only stepped on my feet, like, three or four times."

Just to tease him, I started doing an exaggerated limp. But my joke blew up in my face when he picked me up, tossed my body over his shoulder, and carried me to our table caveman-style. I laughed as he sat me down and my face burned with embarrassment when I realized we'd caused a scene.

"Nothing to see here, folks," Colton said with humor. "My girl really put her life on the line out there."

Someone shouted from a nearby table, "You're a brave woman, honey! Everyone knows Colton can't dance."

"Hey!" he yelled back, pretending to be offended. "I thought you guys were my friends."

Snickering, I tried not to read too much into the fact that he called me his girl. "Do you know everyone here?"

He shrugged. "Pretty much. We're only about five miles from Tolson. You know how small towns are."

I nodded because he was right—I did know. Hemswell might've been a little bigger, but the small-town mentality was still the same.

After we ordered—a burger and fries for me and a giant steak for him—we talked.

"What do you do for fun? I have to assume your hobbies have evolved from mud pies and sand castles," Colton joked before dumping half a bottle of steak sauce on his plate.

"This is going to sound totally lame." I grimaced. "But I don't really have a social life. Or hobbies. Ava's my life now." Shrugging, I continued. "I could sing all the words to most kids' songs, but I've never tweeted on Twitter. What's the past tense of tweeting? Twatting? I've never twatted before."

Colton threw his head back and laughed. "Tell me more. I want to know everything."

It was so nice to sit across from him and talk about my life, lame details and all. In a way, it felt like we'd just picked up right where we left off. Only this time we were adults and my feelings for him weren't unrequited. He was still just as good at listening as he was when we were younger.

I filled Colton in on how I loved working at Caged, but wanted to be a nurse. How Chloe had talked me into applying to the program and how nervous I was about being in school for the first time in over three years.

He told me about starting on at the shop as a teenager and how he became a certified mechanic after high school. His face lit up when he talked about Hank and Sons Transport and it was obvious that he had a passion for his career.

When he asked about Ava, I rambled on about her for a good twenty minutes. I told him everything, from her favorite shows to how she had a speech impediment. Ticking off the list on my fingers, I named her favorite foods, which included Oreos, mac n' cheese, and broccoli—in that order.

"Broccoli?" he asked, his mouth twisting in disgust. "That's kind of weird."

I laughed. "Kids are strange. She has this weird habit where she likes to rub my earlobe. Kind of like a security blanket. She's done it since she was a baby and she only does it to me and my dad."

"That's cute. Must mean she loves you a lot."

"Well, she seemed to like you," I said, remembering the way Ava was 100% herself around him. "She's usually shy around strangers. I'm surprised she was so talkative when he came over."

A cocky smirk appeared on his face. "What can I say? She's obviously a great judge of character."

"Actually, she really is. It's almost freaky how she can sense people."

Colton leaned forward, setting his elbows on the table, and I admired the way his biceps strained against the material of his blue plaid button-up. "I guess now I can understand why you still live with your parents. It must be tough raising a kid alone," he said, his eyebrows furrowing.

I nodded. "Honestly, I don't think I'd be able to do it without them. I usually put Ava to bed before I leave for work. Luckily for my parents, she's a good sleeper. I'm pretty sure most of the time she doesn't even realize I'm gone."

"So, how did you end up in Champaign?" he asked, taking a sip of his soda. "If I'd known you were so close, I might've tried to find you sooner."

I grimaced, not wanting to relive how harsh everyone in our small town had been over the scandal. "People were pretty judgmental about the fact that I ended up pregnant in high school. I stayed after graduation, planning to find a job, but no one would hire me. It's not like there were many choices anyway."

"Either the diner, the grocery store, or the antiques shop," Colton said.

"You remember." I smiled, but my grin faded as I recalled the real reason for moving away. "After Josh decided he didn't want to be involved, he spread rumors that he wasn't the father. That was the final nail in the coffin. People were rude to me. My parents heard the whispers all around town. My dad got a teaching position at the university in Champaign and Mom got a job at Hobby Lobby. Moving to a place where no one knew us seemed like a good idea."

"If I ever see this fucker..." he warned, looking seriously pissed on my behalf.

Fighting a smile, I shook my head. "I haven't seen or talked to him in over three years. It's honestly not even worth being angry about." Wanting to keep the mood light, I decided it was time to talk about something less depressing. "So how's your dad?"

Colton's shoulders relaxed. "He's great. You already know about the auto shop and the trucking business." He shrugged.

"That's all there is to tell."

"Has he ever dated at all since…" I trailed off, not wanting to bring up painful memories. But just like when we were kids, I didn't need to finish the sentence.

"Technically, no."

"Technically?" My eyebrows went up. "What does that mean?"

He huffed out a laugh. "Well, once I tried to set him up with Travis's mom, Karen, but it didn't work out. I think he was interested, but she wasn't. Travis's dad died when he was little and Karen never really got over it."

"That's sad," I said, frowning, and he nodded.

"But Dad seems happy. He's made the business his life. And he's got me," he added, leaning back in the booth and cockily spreading his arms out. It reminded me of the little boy I used to know—even at five years old, he'd been so full of himself.

I smiled. "I still remember the first time I ever saw you."

Colton grinned. "By the monkey bars. Tommy Ackerman made fun of you because he saw your underwear. I kicked his ass."

Laughing, I shook my head. "You're wrong."

"I shoved him down. In kindergarten, that's kicking someone's ass," he insisted, crossing his arms over his chest.

"I mean, you're wrong about that being the first time I saw you. That was the day we became friends, but I'd noticed you before." Colton gave me a questioning look so I continued. "It was the first day of school. The whole left side of your face was covered in scabs…" I paused and touched my cheek, thinking about how painful it had looked. "You'd fallen off your bike—hit your face on the sidewalk. At least, that's what I heard you telling people."

He groaned. "That was the worst case of road rash ever.

How do you even remember that?"

Suddenly feeling shy, I looked down and shrugged. "Even when your face looked like hamburger meat, I still thought you were the most beautiful boy I'd ever seen."

CHAPTER 20

Colton

Ellie's confession hit me straight in the chest because it reminded me again how far back her feelings for me went. It made me feel insanely happy and incredibly guilty at the same time.

Reaching across the table, I took her hand in mine.

"Will you be honest with me about something?" I asked, keeping my face expressionless. She nodded. "You really thought I was beautiful?" I cracked a teasing smile and the corners of her lips tipped up.

"I still do," she admitted quietly.

Loud laughter broke out at the bar, and I was suddenly very aware of all the people around us. The intimate nature of our conversation had me wishing we were alone.

"Do you want to get out of here?" I asked.

"Yeah," she replied with a smile. "I'm not sure my feet can take any more abuse tonight."

I just snickered because I didn't even have a witty comeback. At least I warned her about my lack of two-stepping skills beforehand.

Dropping cash on the table, I stood up and looped my arm around Ellie. As we walked out of the restaurant, I pulled her close and planted a kiss at her temple.

Sighing, she melted into me.

The drive away from the bar was quiet except for the low music on the radio. 'Middle of a Memory' by Cole Swindell was on, and it reminded me of the way Ellie ran away from me that first night on the dance floor.

It was cute that she thought she could get away from me. She was all mine now.

I enjoyed the way Ellie's hand felt in mine, and my whole body buzzed with anticipation as we left the town lights behind.

After several minutes, I pulled my truck over on a deserted country road and put it in park.

"What are we doing here?" Ellie asked, and I answered her question by waggling my eyebrows and sending her a suggestive smirk. "Oh," she breathed out and blushed.

"I think I have something to apologize for first," I told her, wanting to get any old shit out of the way. "I'm sorry I stopped writing to you."

When I looked over at Ellie, I could see the hurt that lingered in her eyes.

"Why did you?" she asked quietly.

"I missed you. A lot. Every time I got a new letter from you, it was just a reminder of something I couldn't have." Guilt weighed heavily on me as I pictured Ellie anxiously waiting for my next letter and the disappointment she experienced when it never came. We'd written back and forth a few times after I moved away, but shortly after my eighth birthday, I decided to stop responding. I'd gotten two more letters and a card from her before they stopped coming, and then I never heard from her again.

"So you thought it was just best to cut off contact?" she asked quietly, looking down at her hand and rubbing at the knuckle on her left thumb.

"I know it doesn't make sense," I said as I placed my hand

over hers. "We were just kids. I could barely write a legible sentence."

"I lived for those letters." Her confession only caused me to feel worse.

"I wonder what would've happened if we'd kept in touch," I thought out loud. "What we could've been if..." My words faded away as I thought about what it might've been like if we'd gotten together as teenagers. If Ellie could have been my one and only. Then I shook my head, chasing the what-ifs away. "I'm glad things are the way they are now," I told her honestly. "If anything had been different, there might not be an Ava, and I'd never want to change that."

When I glanced back over at Ellie, a tear balanced on her eyelashes, but she brushed it away before it could fall.

"Colton," she whispered, "you have no idea how much that means to me."

Even if it was a happy tear, I still hated seeing her cry. Reaching over, I swept my thumb under her eye before tweaking her chin, causing her to smile.

I held my hand out. "How about a game of thumb war? For old time's sake."

There was no way she could win now. My hand was almost twice the size of hers.

"You just think now that we're older you can beat me," she accused, as if she read my mind. Then she shrugged. "I guess I do owe you a rematch."

Her hand felt warm in mine and after saying the beginning chant, we went to war. Well, I guess you couldn't really call it war. It would be more accurate to say I got my ass handed to me.

"What the hell?" I frowned down at my thumb and Ellie giggled. "You have bionic thumbs. It isn't natural."

"Sore loser," she taunted.

I huffed, although I wasn't upset—I was impressed as hell. A few seconds passed, neither of us saying anything. We stared at each other, both lost in old memories.

"Do you believe things happen for a reason?" I asked, breaking the silence, and she nodded. "I think everything is the way it's supposed to be now."

"And how are things now? What does that mean?" As she asked the question, I could see the doubt behind her eyes.

She was still unsure about us.

Well, that was going to stop right now.

"It means now that I found you again, I'm not letting you go."

CHAPTER 21

Brielle

"Y ou're just as bossy as you were when we were kids, you know that?" I asked, feeling a smile tug at my lips.

"Probably bossier," he replied, taking off his seatbelt. "But I prefer assertive."

"Incorrigible." I shook my head, amused.

"In charge."

"Stubborn."

"Persistent." Grinning, he lifted the middle console so nothing was separating us. "I see your vocabulary has grown since we were kids," he teased.

"So has your head," I shot back with an overly-sweet smile, and he feigned being offended, putting a hand over his chest like he was wounded. "So, you're just going all alpha-male on me and staking your claim?"

"Hell, yeah." He started prowling toward me. "Are you saying no?"

"No."

He paused. "So that's a yes?"

I laughed lightly. "Yes."

"Good," he grunted before his body came over mine.

He undid my seatbelt, then grabbed me by the hips and dragged me across the bench seat. I let out a squeal as I fell back, but the noise turned to a whimper when Colton lowered himself between my legs and I felt him push against my throbbing center.

"Ellie," he whispered, looking into my eyes, the playful moment turning serious.

"Colton."

"Tell me you want me as badly as I want you." He started rubbing his thumb back and forth over the seam of my jeans, right over my clit.

"More," I moaned. It was both a response to his request and a plea for him to keep touching me.

Grabbing my hand, he placed it over the front of his pants where I could feel he was very hard and very ready. "Do you see what you do to me? I've been like this all night. Hell, I've been like this for days."

"Please," I pleaded as I clumsily tried to undo his belt.

Colton chuckled before leaning back, taking his body away from mine. I whimpered again, this time from the loss of his warmth.

"You don't ever have to beg me, Ellie. Don't get me wrong—I like it when you do." He slid off his belt and tossed it to the side. "But you never have to beg. I'll always be ready for you."

After snapping open the button on his jeans, he pulled down the zipper and pushed his pants and black boxer briefs down far enough for his cock to spring free.

My hands automatically went down to my own pants, wanting to get naked as quickly as possible. In the small space it wasn't an easy feat, but Colton helped peel my jeans and panties all the way off.

I'd never had sex in a vehicle before. The thought of doing it right here on the side of the road had me feeling giddy.

"No one ever comes down this road, right?" I asked,

glancing back and forth, noting that there were no headlights or taillights in either direction.

"Not often," he replied with a grin. "What's the matter? Afraid we'll get caught?"

"Not really." I shrugged, a bit excited by the thought of doing something risky.

Speaking of risky, I needed to be clear about my stance on using protection during sex.

"We have to use condoms. Always," I blurted out, and Colton went still.

"Did someone give you a hard time about this before?" he asked, his eyebrows pinching together.

I nodded. "The only other person I've ever been with," I said, referring to Ava's father. "And we know how that turned out."

"So he refused to use condoms, then left you when he knocked you up," he concluded. I nodded again and he let out an angry sound. "I'm not kidding about kicking this guy's ass. If I ever see him, it's happening."

I huffed at his macho act, even though I knew he was being serious.

"I'm partly to blame," I told him. "I was careless, and I thought making my boyfriend happy was more important than being safe. I just wanted you to know I'm not on anything, and the pull and pray method isn't great for birth control."

Reaching over my body, Colton popped open the glove compartment and pulled out the little square package.

"I've never gone without one," he said as he tore it open. "You're safe with me, Ellie. And I'm clean, in case you were wondering. I haven't been with someone in a long time. We probably should've had this conversation the other night. In fact, there were a couple big things we didn't talk about..."

His lips twisted and he gave me a pointed look, making sure I knew he was talking about how I kept my identity a secret.

I rolled my eyes, even though I knew he was right for calling me out. "I'm sorry, okay?"

"You're forgiven." He placed a soft kiss on my lips.

In one swift movement, he lifted my leg and thrust inside. I was so wet that he slid right in, but being stretched and filled so suddenly caused me to cry out.

"Fuck," he rasped as he pumped into me with long, deep strokes. "You feel so good."

"You feel good, too," I panted.

The gray cloth seats were soft but the seatbelt was poking me in the hip. It was probably going to leave a bruise, but I couldn't bring myself to care. Needing something to hold onto, I grasped the door handle above my head and my other hand went to the back of Colton's neck.

He propped my legs up on his shoulders, practically folding my body in half, and it caused him to go deeper—so deep, I couldn't control the sounds coming out of my mouth.

Slowing his thrusts, Colton locked eyes with me and whispered, "I'm so glad it's you, Ellie."

Covering my mouth with his, he swallowed my whimpers and moans while his tongue tangled with mine.

His hands were everywhere. Brushing over my hard nipples, threading through my hair, rubbing my clit. It was like he couldn't get enough of touching me, and I didn't want him to stop.

Colton rocked into me until the windows steamed up and I was crying out with an orgasm so strong I swore I saw stars.

CHAPTER 22

Colton

"**W**here's a good place to take little kids for fun?"

My dad looked up from his oven-baked pepperoni pizza and thought for a few seconds.

"Well, where did you like going when you were that age?" he asked before taking a bite.

I'd already filled him in on everything about Ellie, minus the sexual details. I told him about how we ran into each other the night of my birthday and that we were dating now. He'd been surprised to hear she had a kid, but my dad wasn't one to judge. In fact, he seemed excited for me when I told him I'd be taking both girls on a day-date tomorrow, since Ellie and I both had Sundays off.

After thinking about his question for a minute, I had my answer. "Anywhere with a giant ball pit was the shit."

He chuckled. "There you go. You just have find one."

Nodding, I took out my phone and decided to look it up. Unfortunately, I got mixed results. Apparently when your internet search contains 'giant balls' you need to be prepared for anything.

Deciding it would be best to leave it up to Ellie, I sent her a text.

Me: Where spank tits tomorrow?

Ellie: Are you talking dirty to me?

I reread the message and cursed under my breath.

Me: Ducking autocorrect has it out for me. I think I need a new phone.
Me: Where do you want to go tomorrow?
Ellie: Omg I'm laughing so hard right now.
Me: Ha ha. Very fumey.
Me: FUCK. Funny.

The phone started ringing in my hand.

"Hey," I answered, and only heard giggling on the other end. Like a love-struck idiot, her laughter caused a warm, happy feeling to spread through my chest—even if she was laughing *at* me.

"I thought I'd put you out of your misery and just call you instead," Ellie said after getting herself under control. "Ava likes to go to the play place at the mall. There's a carousel and a food court, too."

"That sounds fun. I haven't been to the mall in forever. So, what are you up to today?"

"Right now we're doing some crafts. And when I say crafts, I mean I found some crayons and a piece of cardboard for Ava to draw on."

I laughed. Then I heard a little voice mumble something in the background. Ellie said something back but it was too quiet for me to hear.

Snickering, she came back to the phone. "Bug wants me to tell you that she's drawing you a picture." More mumbling. "And she also wants me to tell you that she likes to jump really high. And that she has princess Band-Aids."

Highly amused, I started cracking up at the random facts

she just threw my way. "That's awesome. Tell her I said thank you for the picture and I can't wait to see it. And it's great that she can jump really high and princess Band-Aids are super cool."

After relaying the message, Ellie came back to our conversation. "Anyway, I work tonight, but I'm excited about seeing you tomorrow."

"What if you could see me tonight?"

"I'm working…" she trailed off, not understanding what I was implying.

"I could come to Caged."

"I'd just be dancing the whole time. I wouldn't even get to talk to you."

"I like watching you," I told her. Just thinking about her behind those bars made my cock twitch.

"That's kind of creepy. You know that, right?" she asked, but I could hear the smile in her voice.

I shrugged even though she couldn't see it. "Don't care."

She laughed lightly. "Maybe I'll see you tonight, then."

"You can count on it."

"Okay." She paused. "Three…"

"Two," I responded, smiling.

"One."

"Bye," we said in unison.

When I ended the call, I suddenly realized I'd forgotten my dad was sitting there the whole time.

"What?" I asked as I took in his shit-eating grin.

"Just never seen you like this before," he replied.

"It's different," I explained. "Everything with Ellie is different."

I'd always been a relationship kind of guy. But as I thought back on the two other girls I'd been with, I realized just how different this was. I'd never had these kinds of feelings for anyone before, and Ellie and I were just getting started.

"I can tell. You know, I'm pretty sure your mom had a wedding planned out for the two of you." He chuckled before heading into the kitchen.

His comment caused me to think about the reoccurring dream. Over the years, it happened less frequently, but memories of Ellie had always been in the back of my mind. My mom had said that what we had was special and extraordinary, and I was starting to think she was right.

The surprises and turn of events from the last couple weeks should've left me feeling shocked and confused.

Instead, it felt like everything was falling into place.

CHAPTER 23

Colton

"**S**o this is where the cool kids hang out," I said, taking in the huge circular play area. "It's a lot different than when we were kids. A lot safer."

The brightly-colored asymmetrical structures had kids crawling and climbing all over them. They were made from some kind of foam and plastic, preventing possible injuries. Even the floor was made of a spongy black material. And I was happy that there was a ball pit, which Ava was currently swimming in.

Ellie nodded. "And it's indoors. If we wanted to go to the park during winter when we were little, we just had to freeze our tushies off."

I laughed because she was right. And because she said 'tushy' again. The benches surrounding the outside of the area were filled with parents, and I liked being part of this. I liked sitting here next to Ellie, watching Ava play.

I reached over and slipped my hand into hers, holding it like I had so many times before. As a kid I'd taken every chance I could to hold her hand, but now it was different. Better. Less innocent.

When I looked over at Ellie, happiness was evident on her face.

"I like this part." Lifting my other hand, I gently ran my

thumb down the cleft in her chin. "Right here."

"Ava says it looks like a butt," she deadpanned.

I barked out a laugh. "Well she's got one, too."

"I know." She grinned. "I don't think she's realized that yet, though."

Just then, a boy a little older than Ava came up to her and yanked on her braid, causing her head to jerk to the side. Protectiveness reared up in me and I started to stand. Ellie stopped me by gently putting her hand on my leg.

"That boy is being mean to her," I practically growled, pointing toward the ball pit.

"Just wait a second," she replied, watching the scene play out. "Sometimes it's better to let them work it out."

Disgruntled, I sat back and observed the situation. What happened next impressed the hell out of me.

With rapt fascination, I watched Ava's reaction. She didn't cry or lash out. Instead, she picked up a blue ball and extended it to the boy. A peace offering. The boy looked at it for a second before accepting the gift he didn't deserve. Then he smiled at her and they started playing together, tossing balls into the air.

I relaxed and blew out a breath. "Well, I wasn't expecting that."

Ellie beamed proudly. "She's amazing. She fights with kindness, and it's more powerful than you'd think. I never taught her that—it's just the way she is."

"That *is* amazing," I agreed and we went back to watching Ava play.

After several minutes, she came running over and climbed into Ellie's lap. "Is it time for the ponies yet?"

"Yep," Ellie confirmed as she took out a package of antibacterial wipes from her purse and started cleaning Ava's hands. "I swear I'm not a germaphobe," she told me, continuing to scrub between Ava's fingers. "These places are a cesspool of bacteria. They've done studies where they find actual feces on the surfaces of the playground."

"What's feces?" Ava piped up.

"Poop," Ellie replied and Ava laughed, seeming to find that one of the funniest things in the world.

"Would you like to ride on my shoulders?" I asked her, remembering how much I loved it when my dad let me do that.

"Yeah!" she shouted, doing that tap-dancing thing with her feet that I found so amusing.

Glancing at Ellie, I raised my eyebrows at her in question, wanting to make sure it was okay.

She nodded and mouthed, "Just don't drop her."

"Never," I promised.

As I lifted Ava I caught a whiff of strawberries, and realized she and Ellie must use the same shampoo. Ava's scent didn't have the hint of coconut to it, though. Instead, it was accompanied by the fragrance of baby powder. She had that pleasant, indescribable kid-smell. The kind where she could run, play, and sweat without getting stinky.

Once she was firmly planted on my shoulders, we started walking toward the food court. I held onto her ankles and she held onto my head.

"You have a nice head. It's fuzzy," she told me, running her hands back and forth over my short hair.

Laughing, I raised one of my hands up to ruffle her hair.

"I like your head, too," I said, running my fingers over one of her braids.

"Hey, look! There's an expalator in there," Ava cheered, pointing inside one of the department stores we passed.

"Can we ride on it, Mom?" I teased Ellie, and Ava made a grunting sound.

"She's not your mom. She's my mom." She tried to lean

forward to see my face. "Are you just joking me?"

Amused, I held a hand up in surrender. "Just joking, I promise."

"We can go on the escalator, but only two times. Okay?" Ellie said in her mom-voice, and Ava agreed.

CHAPTER 24

Brielle

We rode the escalator six times.

Then, after nine rides on the carousel, I decided it was time for dinner. If I didn't remind Ava to eat, she simply wouldn't do it. Her doctor advised me that if she got hungry enough, she would want food. He was wrong.

We got dinner from the Chinese place in the food court because the plain chicken and rice was something she never gave me trouble about. Well, most of the time.

Ava stared at her plate with a grumpy look on her face.

"Here's a good bite," I said, handing her the plastic fork after loading it with an acceptable chicken to rice ratio. Reluctantly, she put it in her mouth and chewed. "Look at all the other kids." I pointed to the occupied tables around us. "They're all eating dinner, too."

My mouth watered as all the smells from the different restaurants mingled in the air. The Italian place had been calling to me, but the orange chicken and fried rice I ended up with was a good second choice.

"Are a lot of kids picky eaters?" Colton whispered my way, quiet enough that Ava couldn't hear it, but loud enough for me to make out the words over the whimsical carousel music.

"It's not uncommon. She just takes it to a whole new level." I sighed because it was a source of daily frustration for me.

"I'm pretty sure I ate anything I could get my hands on when I was a kid," he said.

Smirking, I leveled him with a look and took a sip of my Pepsi. "You literally ate dirt."

"You dared me," he pointed out. "I couldn't back down."

I shrugged, still smiling at the memory. "You seemed to like it."

"I lied. I couldn't let you think I was a puss—I mean, a wimp."

"Were you a wimp?" Ava asked while using her plastic fork to push the food around her plate.

"Nope," he told her. "In fact, I'm still the best eater around. I bet you couldn't eat more than me."

"Yes, I can." Ava proved her point by taking a huge bite. Then another. And another.

Colton took a bite of his Lo Mein and made an obnoxious 'Mmm' sound, and Ava responded by shoving more rice into her mouth.

Shocked, I watched them battle it out. At one point, they took a break and had a pretend sword fight with their forks.

Before I knew it she was cleaning her plate, beaming over her accomplishment.

"Okay." Colton shrugged at her, then winked at me. "You're the better eater."

My mouth hung open as I realized he'd just pulled the oldest trick in the book with Ava. And it had worked.

A movie seemed like a good way to end the day. Once we got back to my house, Ava picked out a Winnie the Pooh favorite, and I leaned back against Colton while Ava rested against me.

As the theme song started to play, I thought back to the

night before. Colton had come to Caged to watch me dance, just like he said he would. Knowing he was in the crowd, feeling his eyes roam my body, made me nervous, excited, and very turned on. By the time I was done, I practically threw myself at him in the parking lot where we made out like teenagers in my car.

Eventually I had to go home to bed, but since Ava woke up earlier than usual this morning, I hadn't gotten much sleep.

Now I felt warm and cozy. Being snuggled up with Ava and the warmth of Colton's hard chest behind me had me feeling relaxed. His hand slipped under the blanket and he started softly rubbing his thumb over the palm of my hand.

Yawning, I allowed my eyes to close, promising myself it would only be for a second. I tried to fight it, but eventually sleep won.

∽

When I woke up, I realized I was on the couch alone. The blanket had been tucked around me and a pillow was under my head.

I heard Ava's giggle, then Colton's deep voice, and I followed the sounds to the kitchen. I stood outside the doorway on the other side of the wall, eavesdropping on their conversation.

"Your mom is the best thumb warrior I've ever known," Colton said.

"I'm a good thumb war-er, too," Ava told him.

"Oh, yeah? Okay, let's do this."

There was nothing but silence for about 20 seconds, until I heard Ava's triumphant "Gotcha!"

"What the heck?" Colton sounded bewildered, and I could imagine him looking at his thumb like it had failed him. "Did I seriously just get beaten by a three-year-old?"

"I'm almost four."

"When's your birthday?"

"February 12th."

"You actually know your birthday?" Colton sounded surprised.

"Of course." Ava sighed, clearly exasperated at being underestimated. "Are you gonna come to my party?"

"I wouldn't miss it for the world." His reply was immediate and certain.

"Here, I'll write you an invitation," she said, and I heard a faint scribbling sound. "There you go."

"A smiley-face invite? Now I definitely have to come."

"That's you," she informed him. "See? He doesn't have very much hair."

I tried to suppress my laugh behind my hand, but all I ended up succeeding at was letting out a snort, giving myself away.

Walking into the kitchen, I found them sitting at the breakfast bar. My eyes fell to the 'invitation', which was drawn on a small, yellow notepad.

I dropped a kiss onto the top of Ava's head, then looked at Colton. "I guess you found out she inherited my thumb-war skills."

He frowned down at his hand. "But her thumb is so little."

I shrugged. "Natural talent."

As I absentmindedly braided Ava's hair, Colton came up behind me and whispered in my ear, "I'll show you natural talent."

Rolling my eyes I snickered at his cocky comment, but my body still shivered, knowing that sooner or later he would make good on his promise.

CHAPTER 25

Colton

Business was slow at the shop, so my day was dragging. Because of work and a transport delivery to Wisconsin on Tuesday, I hadn't been able to see Ellie all week.

Even though we talked every day, and it had only been four days since we'd seen each other, I found myself missing her. A lot.

We called and sent texts daily, and I got to FaceTime with Ava every night before she went to bed. If I was being completely honest, I missed her too. Ellie wasn't kidding when she said I'd be getting two for one, and I couldn't have been happier about it.

During my lunch break I decided to make a FaceTime call.

"Hey," Ellie answered, and I noticed the tight expression on her face. She looked stressed.

"Hey, what's going on?"

She blew out a breath and tucked some hair behind her ear. "Chloe was supposed to watch Ava this afternoon but she can't because she caught a virus from the hospital. You know how my first class started Tuesday? Well, the professor told us there would be a quiz today that would count for 25% of our grade. If I miss it, I might as well drop the class."

"A quiz on the second day? That's harsh." I frowned. "What about your parents?"

She shook her head. "Already tried that. They can't get off work this last-minute."

"I can watch her," I offered automatically.

There was a pause and when Ellie responded, she had a skeptical look on her face. "Really?"

"Yeah, really. There's not much going on here today. I bet my dad wouldn't mind if I took off a little early."

A smile broke out on Ellie's face and she let out a relieved sigh. "That would be awesome. Are you sure you don't mind?"

"I'm sure. It'll be good for us to spend some time together."

"Is that Colton?" Ava's voice came from somewhere in the background, followed by thundering footsteps. "I wanna see!"

I was laughing when her little face came up on the screen. How could someone so little sound like a two-ton rhino?

"Hey, Bug. Would you like to hang out with me?"

Her face lit up. "Yeah!"

"Awesome. So, what did you do today?" I asked, looking forward to whatever random answer she was going to have. Ava had an endless supply of interesting things to say.

"I had to pee really, really bad," she started, her arms flailing in animated gestures. "But I just... just swallowed it back into my body. Yeah."

She giggled and I laughed. "I didn't realize that was possible."

Instead of responding to me, Ava started making faces at herself on screen and Ellie tried to nudge her way back into the picture. "Would you be able to get here around 2:00? My test is at 3:00."

"I'll be there," I said, excited.

After hanging up, I told my dad I would be taking off early to babysit. As soon as the words came out of my mouth, he laughed like it was the funniest thing he'd ever heard.

"What?" I asked defensively. "How hard can it be?"

Swiveling to face me in his office chair, he shook his head and chuckled. "Good luck, son."

I walked away feeling confident. My dad didn't know what he was talking about. I was going to rock this shit.

⌣

I watched Ellie rush around her living room. After shoving her books into the backpack, she put on her coat, then almost fell over when trying to step into her boots. I steadied her by putting my hand on her shoulder, and she gave me a grateful look.

"You'll do great. We'll be fine. Stop stressing," I said, rubbing up and down her arm.

"I know." She smiled, throwing her backpack over one shoulder. "Thank you so much for doing this."

Ava tugged on my hand. "Can we go to the mall?"

"Sure," I replied immediately.

A wicked smile spread on Ellie's face. "If you want to take her somewhere, you'll need my car because it has her car seat. Which means you'll have to let me drive your truck to class." She did a 'give me' gesture with her hand and I sighed.

No one drove my truck but me. Ever.

But then I looked down at Ava's big blue eyes and I couldn't say no. If Ava wanted to go to the mall, then we'd go to the mall. I was pretty sure if she said she wanted to go to Fiji, I'd try to find a way to get us there.

I was in serious trouble.

"Okay." I dropped the keys into Ellie's palm. "Be careful with my baby."

"And you be careful with mine," she quipped, raising up on her tiptoes to give me a peck on the lips before leaning down to kiss Ava on her forehead. She headed toward the door while rambling random instructions. "Ava's potty-trained so you don't need to worry about diapers, but if she starts walking around with her legs crossed, it means she has to go pee. No matter how much she insists on it, she can't absorb the pee back into her body. She knows how to buckle herself into the car seat. Just make sure the clips are locked in place. Oh, and the chest clip is called a chest clip for a reason." She made a slashing motion at armpit level. "Don't let her drain your bank account. It's probably best to stay away from the T-O-Y store." She spelled out the word so Ava wouldn't know what we were talking about, and I chuckled.

"We'll be fine," I reassured her again. "Good luck on your test."

With a final wave, she was gone. I glanced down and Ava beamed up at me.

"Okay, Bug. Let's go have some fun."

～

The mall was a blast. After going to the play place, we went for seven rides on the carousel. Each time, Ava chose a different horse to ride. She told me she wanted to be fair. Said she didn't want to hurt anyone's feelings, which was really fucking cute.

We took five round-trips on the escalator, then we hit up the toy store. It would've been so easy to blow an entire paycheck in there, but Ava and I negotiated until we settled on some dragon LEGOs. She was beyond happy and it only set me back fifteen bucks.

With Ava on my shoulders we made a pass through the pet store, then ended our afternoon in the food court for a snack.

I'd just gotten Ava strapped into her car seat when Ellie called.

"Hey," I answered the phone. "How'd your test go?"

"I think it went okay. It was tough but I felt like I knew most of the answers. How are you guys doing?" she asked, and I could hear a hint of anxiousness in her voice.

"We're fine." Walking around to the driver's side of the car, I gave her a brief rundown of everything we did. "And after we went to the pet store—"

"The pet store?" Ellie interrupted. "Please tell me you didn't get her an animal…"

"How mad would you be if I did?" I teased while putting on my seatbelt. There was no way I would get a pet for Ava without Ellie's permission, but I couldn't help giving her a hard time about it.

"Colton…" she warned.

I guffawed. "No, I didn't buy anything. We just looked. That place is like a petting zoo."

"I want a bunny!" Ava cheered from the backseat.

I laughed.

Ellie groaned. "I'm never going to hear the end of this."

"What about a fish?" I lowered my voice so Ava wouldn't hear as I admitted the truth. "I almost bought her a fish."

Ellie gasped. "No fish."

"Why not?" I asked, thinking about how low maintenance it would be.

"Because they always die. Remember that goldfish I won from the county fair? Herbie was belly-up within 24 hours and I was devastated."

"You put him in tap water and fed him Doritos," I deadpanned.

She scoffed. "Details. Besides, fish are gateway pets."

"What's a gateway pet?"

"You know, you get one, it dies, you're crushed, then before you know it you've got five cats, two dogs, and a gerbil."

I started laughing because she wasn't completely wrong, and Ava started laughing, too, even though she had no idea what we were talking about.

"Anyway," I said, starting up the car. "We just got finished up at the ice cream store."

"Ice cream?" Ellie asked, sounding a bit alarmed.

"Yeah… Is that okay?"

She made a frustrated growling noise, and I would've found it really sexy if she hadn't sounded so concerned. "I'm so sorry, Colton. I should've told you. This is all my fault."

"Told me what?" I asked warily.

"Ava's lactose intolerant."

"Oh sh—I mean, shoot," I said quietly into the phone. Damn. I fucked this up. "Is it going to give her a stomachache?"

"That depends. She can handle small amounts," she replied, suddenly sounding more calm than I felt. "How much did she have? A kiddie scoop?" she asked hopefully.

"No." I shook my head even though she couldn't see it. "She had the Double Trouble Sundae."

"Oh shit," Ellie breathed out.

"I'm sorry." Groaning, I let my head fall back and covered my face with my hand.

"No, this is completely my fault. I always tell people before they watch her. I just forgot this time because I was thinking about my test. Listen." Her voice turned serious. "If you come straight here, you might get back in time."

That had me sitting up straight in the seat. "Back in time for what?"

"Don't panic," she said, and those two words had me, in fact, panicking. "You have about 20 minutes until she vomits."

"Gotcha. I'll see you soon." I didn't even wait for her

reply before hanging up and dropping my phone into the cup holder.

I spent the next ten minutes glancing into the rearview mirror at Ava as though she was a ticking time bomb, while also driving very carefully because—precious cargo.

As I watched her, she showed no signs of feeling sick. Happily kicking her feet, she sang along to the radio while looking out the window.

A sigh of relief left me as I pulled the car into Ellie's driveway and I quickly ran around the car to get Ava out.

"Hey, Bug. How are you feeling?" I asked, fumbling with all the buckles and straps that kept her safe.

"Good," she replied as I picked her up.

Then, something extraordinary happened.

Ava made a content humming sound as she hugged me around the neck.

Wrapping my arms around her little body, I returned the embrace.

Stunned, I stood there with her in the driveway for a minute, my heart exploding in my chest.

Getting hugged by Ava was like finding something rare and unexpected.

One time when I went fishing, a Monarch butterfly landed on my hand. I remember watching it, wings slowly flapping, as it found my finger an acceptable place to rest. I barely breathed, too afraid I would scare it away. Finally, the butterfly took off, ready to find the next best thing.

It might've been silly, but I had felt honored and lucky. Like I'd been given some sort of gift.

This moment felt kind of like that, only one hundred times better.

The hug went on for several seconds. The air was getting chilly as the sun sank low on the horizon, painting the clouds a bright orange. I knew we needed to go inside, but I didn't want it to end yet.

When Ava pulled back, we smiled at each other.

Then, without warning, her facial expression changed and vomit sprayed from her mouth, covering my neck, the front of my shirt, and the arms of my coat.

"I'm sorry," she cried, choking out a sob along with more vomit, and some of the foul-smelling chunks landed in her hair.

"Shh, it's okay. It's okay." Trying not to panic, I ran her up to the house as fast as I could while she continued to heave.

The front door swung open and Ellie greeted me, her expression a mixture of apologetic and concerned. She took Ava from my arms, not even seeming bothered by all the puke.

"I'll get her a bath really quick. I'm so sorry, Colton," she said, rushing up the stairs as she tried to talk over Ava's whimpers. "You can take a shower in my parents' bathroom and my dad will get you some clothes."

"It's okay," I called after her, but she had already disappeared around the hall.

Dave appeared from the kitchen and gave me a sympathetic look. "No one ever tells you this, but 70% of parenting is getting thrown up on. Looks like you've been officially initiated."

"I feel really bad about this." I shook my head. "I screwed up."

"Nah. Ava knows she can't have ice cream. Little sneak pulled a fast one on you." Letting out a chuckle, he went to pat me on the shoulder but changed his mind when he noticed the mess he'd be putting his hand in. "I'll show you to the bathroom."

I followed him up the stairs. Taking a right, he showed me to the large master bedroom at the end of the hall and set a spare change of clothes on top of the dresser.

When he turned to me, his face was serious. "Brielle was pretty devastated after you moved away," he stated matter-of-factly. "It was even worse after you lost contact with each other. As a father, it was hard to watch my little girl go through that."

"I know," I said, guiltily looking down at the white shag carpet.

"I don't want to see that happen again," he told me, his voice firm. "You two were just kids back then. I'm not blaming you. But I've seen her heart broken more times than I care to admit."

The Dave I remembered had always been a laid-back guy. Never took things too seriously. But the man in front of me now was a father trying to protect his daughter, and I respected him for confronting me.

Squaring my shoulders, I tried to maintain as much dignity as I could while being covered in barf. "I'm not going anywhere. You have my word on that."

Seeming satisfied with my answer, he nodded once before adding, "She puts on a brave face, but these past few years have been rough."

I nodded, realizing how hard it must've been for Ellie's parents to see her abandoned, to watch her struggle as a single parent.

"I'm pretty sure she couldn't get rid of me if she tried," I promised.

"Good." Dave smiled, his easy-going demeanor back in place. "Go take a shower, Colton. You stink."

Snickering, I headed into the en suite bathroom.

After I was freshly showered and wearing some of Dave's black sweat pants and a blue T-shirt, I found my girls at the other end of the hall.

My girls.

There was no question that this bedroom belonged to Ava. Light purple walls. Disney princess bedspread. At least two laundry baskets full of stuffed animals and dolls. Stacks of books, books, and more books—some of them I recognized.

Ava was sitting on her twin-sized bed dressed in a pink nightgown while Ellie sat behind her, combing out her wet hair. The dim light from the lamp on the nightstand cast a calming yellow glow throughout the room. Ellie ran a towel over her own wet hair and I realized she must've needed a shower, too.

For a few seconds, I watched them and suddenly an image popped into my head. What would be like if we all lived together? If we were a family?

It was just an idea, really. A dream I'd been too afraid to hope for. I'd spent a good part of the last couple years thinking a normal life wasn't in the cards for me.

I wasn't afraid of that anymore.

When things with Travis and Angel had moved so quickly, I thought they were crazy. I didn't think it was possible to fall in love with someone so fast.

Now it was my turn to be the love-struck fool.

My situation was a little bit different, though. Although Ellie and I had spent most of our lives apart, she was still the same person I knew fifteen years ago. She was the girl who held me while I cried the day my mom died. The girl who refused to leave my side that night, no matter how much her parents tried to get her to come home. The one who was there to comfort me every time I woke up and realized it wasn't just a bad dream. And I wasn't even embarrassed about crying in front of her—because she was my best friend.

Ellie was more guarded now than when we were kids, but she had every reason to be. Standing there, I realized that, for the first time in a long time, I was truly happy. And despite how the afternoon ended, today had still been one of the best days of my life.

Glancing my way, Ellie caught me staring. I just smiled. She smiled back. My bare feet padded across the hardwood floors as I went over to the bed.

"How are you feeling?" I asked Ava, sitting down next to her.

She hiked a shoulder. "Good. You wanna play Yegos with me?"

Yegos. So fucking cute.

She looked so content now, you'd never know she just did a remake of *The Exorcist* half an hour ago.

Ellie cut in before I could answer. "Colton might have to go home, sweetie."

"I can stay a while, if that's okay," I insisted, and Ava nodded happily.

"Of course it's okay," Ellie said, pulling me off to the side and lowering her voice. "I don't want you to feel like you have to stick around, especially after what happened. Kids are exhausting sometimes and I can't apologize enough for not telling you about her intolerance—"

"Hey," I softly interrupted. "Seriously, I'm not mad at all. I had a great time. In fact, I'd love to be the one you ask from now on if you need someone to hang with her."

Her expression morphed from shocked to ecstatic in an instant, and I knew I'd do almost anything to put that look on her face.

"You did a really good job today," she said and I scoffed. "Seriously, you did," she insisted, linking her hand with mine. "I can be a little uptight sometimes, but it just comes with the territory of being a mom." She shrugged. "I have the same class every Thursday afternoon at 3:00. It would be awesome if you wanted to watch her."

"Done."

"And for future reference, she can have processed cheeses. American cheese doesn't seem to make her sick and she can have mac and cheese—the boxed kind with the cheese powder, and I substitute the recipe with almond milk. But no cow's milk, yogurt, or ice cream."

"Got it."

Ava let out an impatient sigh. "Did you forget about playing with me?"

I laughed. "Nope. I'm about to dominate these Legos"

Apparently, LEGOs were a lot different than when I was a kid. It came with a million tiny pieces and an instruction manual. After a lot of tinkering, I'd constructed a small dragon and handed it over to the happiest little girl ever.

"Thank you!" she shouted and hugged me around the neck. "I yuv it."

After a bland dinner of chicken noodle soup and toast, I got to witness the bedtime routine in person. There was a lot more to it than what I'd seen over our FaceTime chats.

Ava had to change into another set of PJs because she'd spilled her soup on her nightgown at dinner. I never knew deciding between pink striped pants or polka-dots could be such a debate, but Ellie patiently waited for Ava to choose. She finally settled on the stripes.

Then it was time for brushing teeth. Then Ava had to pee one more time. After getting into bed, she needed ice water in the green sippy cup, not the orange one.

Ellie shot me a look that said 'I'm sorry'. I shook my head and sent one back that said 'I'm having fun'.

Because, honestly, I was. I'd never realized how much hard work it was to have a kid, but it was fascinating and entertaining.

"Will you read me a book?" Ava asked, cuddling up to Ellie while lightly tugging at her earlobe. "That one's my favorite." She pointed at a book about cupcakes.

I cleared my throat as I sat down on the edge of the bed, then I started to read out loud about a little girl who turned pink from eating too much red food coloring. Ava's eyes looked heavy by the end of the story, but she perked up after I closed the book.

"You're supposed to say 'The End,'" she told me seriously.

"Oh." I fought a grin. "The End."

"Again, please," she requested politely, snuggling further into her mom's arms.

"One more time, Bug," Ellie said with a stern edge to her 'mom voice' that even had me wanting to obey.

"Okay," Ava agreed, going back to rubbing Ellie's ear.

Opening to the first page, I started again.

Mid-story, Ava's eyes were closed and her body had gone limp, but I quietly read until the end anyway.

"The End," I whispered at Ellie, and she smiled.

I placed the book on the nightstand, then glanced at her. Our eyes locked and she had a strange look on her face—something I couldn't interpret. She seemed happy, but there was also a little bit of sadness there. I wondered if it had something to do with this being the first time Ava had a dad-type put her to bed. Of course she had Dave, but he was her grandpa, so it was different.

Every kid deserves to have two loving parents. That was what I had for the first seven years of my life. And my mom didn't choose to leave. If it had been up to her, she'd still be here, loving the hell out of me.

There was a picture frame next to the lamp on the nightstand. I picked it up.

It was a photo of Ellie a few years younger and massively

pregnant. Sitting in a rocking chair, her hands were placed over her round stomach. She looked beautiful in gray leggings, rainbow-striped knee-high socks, and a white sweater. A ponytail held her hair away from her face and bright afternoon light from the window lit up her profile. As she gazed outside, the expression on her face broke my heart.

"You looked so…" I trailed off.

"Humongous?"

"Scared," I finished.

She took the frame from me and studied it with narrowed eyes before shrugging. "I guess that's because I was. I had no idea what I was doing, but I knew I was doing it alone. I didn't even realize my mom was snapping the picture at the time. It isn't the best shot, but I didn't have traditional maternity photos done so it's better than nothing."

"What are traditional maternity photos? Is that a thing?"

Wide-eyed, she nodded. "Oh, it's totally a thing. You know, where they have a professional photographer and a cutesy set-up by a meadow with wildflowers or some shit." She waved her hand dismissively like it was the most ridiculous idea ever, but I could tell she wanted that.

Ellie felt like she'd missed out.

"Well, I think you look gorgeous," I said as I took the frame and set it back down.

"Thanks." She smiled. "I can walk you out in just a second."

Ellie started trying to untangle herself from Ava, and I shook my head to stop her.

"Don't worry about it. Thank you for today," I told her, grateful for the opportunity to bond with Ava.

Ava was the most important person in the world to Ellie. Not only had she trusted me to take care of her, but Ellie gave me a glimpse into their lives. She included me, and I knew without a doubt that I wanted this more often.

"No." She shook her head. "Thank *you*, Colton. You saved my A-S-S today." She smirked and I thought it was funny that she still spelled out the bad word, even though Ava was passed out. "How about a date soon? Just you and me?"

"Definitely." I nodded eagerly at the thought of having her alone—preferably naked.

Leaning down, I pressed my mouth to hers. When she swept her tongue past my lips it was hard to pull away, but the sleeping child between us reminded me she was still there when she mumbled something about bunnies in her sleep.

Snickering quietly, I gave Ellie one last chaste kiss. "I'll talk to you later."

"Three," she whispered against my lips.

"Two," I whispered back.

"One."

"Bye," we both mouthed.

At the door, I glanced back at my girls one more time.

My girls.

CHAPTER 26

Brielle

As I pulled up to Colton's apartment, he came out to greet me.

"Hey," he said after I rolled my window down.

"Hey, what's up?" I asked, wondering why he was dressed in his auto shop coveralls. It was Sunday afternoon and we were going on a date. Plus, I thought the shop was closed on the weekends.

Sticking his head through the window, he tilted my chin up before lowering his mouth to mine. I immediately responded by grabbing his collar and pulling him closer as our tongues met. He gently nipped at my lips, causing my breath to hitch and my heart rate to speed up.

He chuckled into my mouth before we could get too out of control. "Do me a favor and pull your car around to the shop. I'll open the garage door and you can just drive in."

"Why?" I asked, confused. There wasn't anything wrong with my car.

"Just do it." He thumped his hand on the hood twice before walking away and I rolled my eyes.

So bossy.

Once my car was inside the shop, I put it in park and turned off the ignition. I got out, taking in the place where Colton spent most of his days.

The first thing I noticed was the smell. It wasn't unpleasant, but like a typical auto shop it had the distinct scent of motor oil and burnt rubber. The concrete floors were clean, except for a few grease stains here and there.

The inside of the large space resembled a warehouse and there were two garage doors at the front of the building, both of which were now closed. Walls made of exposed brick lined the interior, and there were several antique metal signs hanging throughout the shop. Most of them were automobile logos and a few were old expired license plates.

"What's going on?" I smiled at him, narrowing my eyes suspiciously as I waited for him to answer.

"Do you know how to change the oil in your car?" Colton opened the driver's door and hit the hood latch. I shook my head. "How about a flat tire?"

I shook my head again. "I get my oil changed at Walmart. And I guess I've never thought about a flat tire."

"Well, you're gonna learn today," he announced, and I groaned.

Cars were so not my thing. All I knew was that I put gas in it, and it got me from point A to point B. If the check engine light came on, I usually ignored it with the intention of getting it looked at when the car started making weird noises.

"You know, I do get regular maintenance on my car. I just had the tires rotated a few months ago," I told him, hoping that would be enough for him to toss me onto the hood of the car and do dirty things to my body instead.

Ignoring me, Colton propped up the hood on my old Camry and peered down at the engine and all the other doohickeys under there.

He pointed to a little knob. "This is the oil dipstick."

I snorted out a laugh because he said dipstick, and he shot me an amused look before pulling it out. He took a paper towel and wiped off the end of the long metal rod before inserting it back in and taking it out again.

"See here?" He pointed to the end coated in dark oil. "You're a quart low."

"You ever notice how car parts are full of sexual innuendo? Dipstick. Lube. Drive shaft…"

"Nope. Never," Colton replied sarcastically before sending me a knowing grin. "I'd love to teach you how to drive a stick."

"What a great idea," I said with mock seriousness. I ran my hands up his chest and gave his collar a little tug. "How about right now?"

His lips tipped up as he caught on to my plan. "Nice try. Work first, play later."

Grabbing a funnel, he instructed me to put it in the correct place, then had me pour a container of new motor oil into it.

Thinking we were done, I started to wipe my hands on a paper towel and raised up on my tiptoes to give him a kiss. "Thanks for the lesson."

"We're not done yet," he said before walking around to the other side of my car.

"You don't have to do all this. I'm not dating you so you'll fix my car."

"Oh, I know," he said cockily, puffing out his chest, and I rolled my eyes. "But I'm not fixing anything. *You* are."

With his hands on his hips, he stood back and looked at my outfit. I was wearing some comfortable jeggings and an oversized gray sweater—not exactly practical for this kind of work.

"Hang on a sec." Colton disappeared into what looked like a small office off to the right and came back with a pair of gray coveralls that were identical to the ones he was wearing. Even his name tag over the left breast pocket was the same. "I don't want you to get your clothes dirty," he told me as he ruffled my ponytail, causing a few strands to fall out.

Sighing, I slipped on the coveralls and Colton zipped up the front for me, then bent down to roll up the extra material around my ankles.

He stood up and a half-smile appeared on his face. "It's a little big, but it should keep you clean."

"Thanks," I said, sounding a little breathless as I looked up into his eyes.

His finger trailed over the embroidered name tag, which was right over my left nipple. Even through all the layers, I felt his touch. I had to bite my lip to keep the gasp from escaping my mouth.

A heated look crossed Colton's face. "I kind of like the way you look wearing my name."

"Is that why you always wanted me to wear your Little League shirt to your baseball games?" I joked, tilting my head to the side.

"Hell yeah," he replied. "Everyone knew you were there for me. *My* best friend."

"Well, who do we have here?" A voice interrupted our moment and I looked over to see a familiar face poking out of a doorway at the back of the garage.

"Hank!" I smiled, recognizing him right away.

He walked over to stand next to Colton and the resemblance between the two of them was uncanny. Same eyes. Same height and build. Same buzzed haircut. I could see Hank's style hadn't changed. I remembered the denim button-up shirt he was wearing, and from the look of the frayed edges I suspected it was the same one he'd had years ago.

"I thought I heard a commotion out here. Brielle, it's so good to see you two together again." Hank smiled and looked down at my outfit. "Is Colton putting you to work on a Sunday?"

I sighed dramatically. "Yes. Can you believe that?"

Colton grunted. "I'm teaching her how to take care of her car. It's important to know the basics."

"Gotta agree with my boy," Hank said, affectionately dropping a hand onto Colton's shoulder. "If you want something done right, do it yourself—that's what I always say."

"I'm about to show Ellie how to change a tire," Colton told him as he started rummaging through a giant red tool box that looked more like a tall dresser.

"It's a good thing to know." Hank nodded. "I'll leave you kids to it. I just wanted to say hi." He turned to head back to his apartment then stopped. When he looked back at me there was a warmth in his gaze, the skin around his eyes crinkling as he smiled. "I hear you've got a little girl. I'd love to meet her sometime."

I nodded. "I'm sure she'd love that, too."

On that note, Hank disappeared into his apartment and Colton removed the spare tire from my trunk.

"Huh," I said, looking down at the wheel. "So that's where that thing was."

Colton raised his eyebrows at my lack of basic car knowledge. "Everyone should know how to do this. I just want to make sure you're safe, Ellie."

"I know. That's why I love you," I replied, intending for it to be playful, but the statement came out sounding a lot more serious. A lot more real.

Colton's eyes got wide and I sucked in a breath.

Although I was teasing, as soon as I said the words I knew they were true. It was the first time I'd ever said that to any man outside of my family. Those three words could be relationship suicide if they were said too soon, but I didn't want to take it back.

"It's true," I said quietly, feeling vulnerable. I'd spend the last few years completely closed off to the idea of love. Now here I was, pouring my heart out. "I'm in love with you. You don't have to say it back. I just want you to know how I really feel."

The biggest smile ever stretched across Colton's face. "I love you, too, Ellie."

At his words, my stomach swooped—the same sensation I got when riding on a roller coaster. And right then, I understood why they called it falling in love. Because that's what it felt like—falling.

Colton stepped closer to me and my hand scraped over the scruff on his jaw as our lips met. Our tongues stroked each other and our breathing turned into panting. I unzipped the front of his coveralls, running my hand over the white T-shirt he wore underneath, feeling the ridges of his abs. Wetness pooled between my thighs and I started to rub my body against his, needing friction, needing to be closer.

Chuckling, Colton pulled back. "You're still not getting out of this."

I sighed. "You can't blame a girl for trying."

Bending over, he picked up two odd-shaped metal tools and got back to business. "This one is the carjack and this is the lug nut wrench." He walked around the driver's side and opened the door. "First, make sure you put on your parking brake."

Using my foot, I pressed down until the lever was all the way down. "Okay. Now what?"

He led me around to the other side of the car and handed me a brick. "Wedge that in front of the front wheel. It's just a safety measure to keep the car from slipping forward. And never—never—put yourself under a car when it's jacked up."

"Isn't that kind of a given?" I asked, wondering if he

thought I had no common sense.

Shrugging, he picked up a large flashlight. "You'd be surprised how many trained mechanics have made that mistake."

After setting the flashlight on the concrete floor, he pointed it so the light was on the rear wheel.

"Can't we just turn on the lights?" I pointed up to the fluorescent lights hanging from the ceiling.

"We could, but I want you to learn how to do it in the dark. Flat tires happen at night, too."

"I know something else we could do in the dark," I muttered.

"What was that?" he whispered by my ear, causing goosebumps to rise on my neck and arms. "You're really testing my patience today, Ellie."

As he came up behind my body, I could feel his hardness pressed against my lower back. Remembering the way it felt when his thick cock entered my body had more wetness flooding my panties.

"Colton," I practically whined, and he laughed.

He totally knew what he was doing to me.

Crouching down, Colton instructed me on how to loosen the lug nuts and remove the hubcap. Then he had me position the carjack under the vehicle by the back wheel. After cranking the handle until the back of the car was lifted off the ground, I removed the lug nuts first, then the wheel.

"*Oof.*" I made an unattractive sound as the heavy tire almost took me down to the floor.

"Careful," Colton warned, amusement in his eyes. "It's heavier than it looks."

I sent him a glare. As much as I tried not to, the corners of my lips twitched and I couldn't contain my smile.

It took some struggling, but I made it through all the instructions Colton gave me. Once I got the spare tire successfully onto the car, I let out a triumphant sound. Brushing my hands off, I was proud of myself for doing it right. Thinking we were done, I started to stand up.

"Hang on a sec," Colton said, and I gave him a questioning look. "Now you have to change it back. A spare isn't meant to be driven on for long periods of time."

Letting out a resigned sigh, I went back to work.

Colton checked over the tire after I was done, making sure it was secure.

"You did great. It's perfect," he praised, and gave me a quick peck on the forehead. "I'm gonna check your tire pressure, then I promise we're done."

"Oh, good," I said, relieved. Exhausted, I slumped down onto the bench right outside of the office, and Colton finally turned on the lights so he could inspect my car some more. "I don't know how you do this all day."

Colton shrugged as he got down next to the front tire. "I love it."

We were both quiet as he worked. Every now and then, he would glance over at me and smile. I sat back and admired the way his butt looked in his uniform every time he bent over. Finally, he started to put all the tools away and made sure to show me where all the emergency supplies were in my trunk.

"I appreciate all this, Colton. I honestly do. Very thoughtful of you," I told him, wanting him to know it made me happy that he was so concerned for my safety. "But," I paused, unable to resist the urge to tease him a little, "I have to tell you... You might be winning the award for the most boring date in history."

"This is important stuff," he said incredulously. "You'll be thanking me one day."

I grinned wickedly as I ran my finger down his chest. "How about I thank you now?"

CHAPTER 27

Colton

"Lie back on the bed," Ellie demanded playfully.

Who was I to say no? I did as she said.

She started digging around in that giant bag she called a purse before turning back to me. A pair of handcuffs dangled from her fingertips.

"Are those the same handcuffs…?" I trailed off as she bit her lip and nodded, excitement in her eyes and a flush on her cheeks.

Fuck yes.

"You're gonna let me tie you up?" I breathed out, my dick already standing at full attention.

While the handcuffs had been part of an innocent game when we were kids, now they could be used for a completely different reason. The thought of Ellie spread out naked on my bed as I had free rein over her body had me shedding my clothes faster than I ever had before.

She laughed as I kicked off my jeans and dropped them to the floor. "No. *I'm* going to tie *you* up."

"What…?" My hands paused at the waistband of my boxers. For some reason, it never occurred to me that the roles would be reversed like that. But as I considered it, I had to admit the idea wasn't completely unappealing. "Okay, but on one condition."

Her eyebrows shot up. "What's that?"

I grinned. "You're next."

"Fair enough," she responded, and a naughty smile spread over her face as she walked toward me.

After ridding myself of my boxers, I put my hands by the headboard.

As Ellie hovered over me, getting the handcuffs on just right, I raised my head up to bite her breast through her shirt. She squealed and tried to shift away from me but my mouth followed. It wasn't easy, but she managed to get my wrists bound while I continued to playfully nip at her.

She ended up laughing so hard she collapsed onto my face, her breast mashed up against my cheek.

I wasn't complaining.

When she was satisfied with the fact that I was attached to the bed, she sat back on her heels and grinned, her eyes raking over me.

"It's your turn to strip." I nodded my head toward her fully-clothed body and her face fell.

Suddenly, she looked shy and insecure. She looked at the window where bright afternoon light came through my nearly transparent curtains.

"Do you have window blinds? Maybe it would set the mood better if it was dimmer in here…" Glancing everywhere but at me, she started to rub at the skin on her left thumb.

"What's wrong? And don't lie to me, Ellie," I told her gently. "I'll know if you're lying."

Her worried eyes swung back to me and she fidgeted for a second before responding. "This is the first time we've been together when the lights are on. You might not like what you see."

"What do you mean?" I asked, confused. I loved her body.

She sighed. "Having a baby changed me. You probably

didn't notice it in the dark, but I have scars. Stretch marks." She motioned to her lower stomach and hips. "And I had to have a C-section with Ava. There's a pretty ugly scar here." Her hand landed on her lower abdomen over her jeans.

My first reaction was anger. Anger that she could ever think I wouldn't like something about her, just because she didn't think it was beautiful. But that feeling was quickly replaced with the love I felt for her—that was what she needed. What I needed to show her.

"Take off your clothes, Ellie," I ordered softly. "Let me see you."

"Okay." She grimaced. "But don't say I didn't warn you."

First, she started by peeling off those rainbow-striped socks I loved so much. She wore them over her jeans, pulled almost up to her knees. For some reason, I found it sexy as hell. I started to imagine what it would be like if she left them on while I fucked her from behind.

But I was distracted from that thought because she slowly lifted her shirt over her head, then shoved her jeans down to her ankles. With a graceful kick of her foot, the denim was tossed to the side.

Then she took out the band holding her ponytail and shook out her hair.

Bra and panties came next until I was staring at the most magnificent body I'd ever seen. She was soft in the right places and firm in others. Ellie had a dancer's body. I had no idea how she could ever think she was anything other than perfect.

"Turn around," I said huskily.

She cocked an eyebrow and I could almost hear her calling me *bossy* in her head. Pivoting, she turned her back to me. The slope of her back gave way to the perfect flare of her hips. Her ass was round and supple. I knew what it felt like to squeeze the flesh in my hands. But that wasn't what I was focusing on.

On the back of her right thigh, there was a heart-shaped birthmark, no bigger than a quarter. It was smooth, just like the rest of her olive-toned skin, only a few shades darker. If the lights had been on that first night, I would've known who she was right away. She used to hate that mark. Thought it made her weird.

I thought she was beautiful.

"Come here," I said. Now that I was done with my ogling, I needed to feel her. "Straddle me."

After climbing onto the bed, Ellie swung her leg over my hips and I hissed when her slick center rubbed over my throbbing dick. She started to reach over to the drawer to get a condom.

"Wait," I told her. "Scoot up here." I smirked and she looked unsure, but did as I said. "Higher. A little bit closer to my face."

Wiggling, she moved her body up until her pussy was inches away from my mouth, then she looked down at me with heated eyes. She probably thought I was going to lick her, taste her, drive her wild—and I was getting to it. There was nothing I wanted more.

Well, almost nothing.

First, I did something else that had surprise written all over her face. I lifted my head and placed a light kiss over her scar. She sucked in a breath.

"How do you always do that?" she asked, and it came out sounding like an accusation.

"Do what?"

"You always say or do the right thing."

I tried to shrug but it was hard with my hands chained up. "I'm just honest. I need you to know that I love every part of you, Ellie." My mouth curled up at the corners. "Now get that pussy on my face."

CHAPTER 28

Brielle

The first lick made me gasp. The second swipe had me gripping the headboard so hard my knuckles turned white. When he pushed his tongue inside me, I moaned. But when he latched onto my clit and sucked… That's when I completely lost control.

This was my first experience with oral sex. And *holy fuck*.

As I rode Colton's face, my hips bucked uncontrollably and unintelligible sounds fell from my mouth. He hadn't shaved for a couple days and the rough stubble on his face rubbed against the inside of my thighs.

I looked down and found him watching me. At first, I'd been hesitant to be completely bared to him, but the desire and lust in his eyes—I could tell he liked what he saw. That kind of reaction just couldn't be faked.

His lips left my clit and his hands strained against the handcuffs as he tried to reach for my body.

"I wish I could touch you," he murmured, eyeing my breasts. "Touch yourself."

Letting go of the death grip I had on the headboard, I brought my hands up to my nipples and pinched.

I ran my thumbs back and forth over the stiff peaks. "Like this?"

"Fuck yes," Colton rasped before latching back onto me.

Throwing my head back, I let out a long, low moan as he flicked his tongue back and forth over my most sensitive spot.

"Keep doing that," I panted.

"You taste so fucking good," he said against my pussy, his words muffled.

Knowing how much he enjoyed this had my body speeding toward orgasm in record time. He started sucking on my clit in a pulsating rhythm, and my mouth fell open as I felt it building. Fluttering. Tightening.

When the tension finally snapped, I couldn't contain the scream that left my throat. Colton's hands strained against the handcuffs as he tried to reach for me again. He let out a sexy growl of frustration and the vibrations from his mouth spurred on the intense orgasm.

As the clenching of my walls subsided, the motions of my hips slowed.

"Oh, my God, Colton," I breathed out when I finally found my voice again.

When I glanced down, he had a cocky grin on his face, showing off the crooked bottom teeth I loved so much.

"Was that as good for you as it was for me?" he teased, repeating the same words he'd said the first night I went home with him.

I laughed, feeling a little slap-happy from the endorphins flowing through my body.

"Probably better," I said before wiggling back on the bed until my body was lined up with his. As my wet center slid over his cock, he hissed. I kissed him, sweeping my tongue into his mouth, and I tasted myself on his lips. I pulled back enough to look him in the eye. "Hi."

He smiled. "Hi. Can you uncuff me now? I wanna touch you."

"Nope," I replied as I scooted further down his body.

When I reached my destination, I nuzzled my nose at the base of his rock-hard dick, loving his musky scent. I licked up his length, then wrapped my hand around him, stroking up and down a few times.

Taking his tip into my mouth, I went down as far as I could while applying suction. I wasn't super experienced at blow jobs, but I knew the basics.

And judging from Colton's reaction, I was doing it right.

"Fuck, Ellie," he rasped. "I don't know how long I'm gonna last if you keep doing that…" His words turned into a groan as I started bobbing my head up and down.

With my other hand, I started to caress his sac and his balls drew up tight. Salty pre-cum leaked from his tip and I knew he was close.

"Oh, fuck," he whispered, his eyes slamming shut.

I removed him from my mouth and slowed the pumping motion of my hand.

"Wha—what—why are you stopping?" he mumbled.

Lifting an eyebrow, I sent him a naughty smirk and went back to teasing him, running my tongue over his slit.

"Oh, you think this is funny, do you?" he asked between ragged breaths. "Turnabout's fair play, Ellie. Don't forget that you're next."

His threats didn't scare me. If anything, it made me want to see how far I could push him. I brought him to the brink two more times before finally giving him what he wanted.

"Shit… Ellie, please," he begged. "Please… *Fuck*."

As I sucked his dick into my mouth, I glanced up at him and we locked eyes. His hands were fisted, his breathing labored, and there was a sheen of sweat on his forehead. I didn't let up this time as his legs started to tremble, and his cock hardened even more. Just as he let out a moan, jets of cum filled my mouth and I swallowed it down.

Wiping at my face, I propped myself up on my elbows.

"That was fun." I grinned at Colton, and he barked out a laugh.

"Unchain me, and I'll return the favor."

CHAPTER 29

Colton

"Oh no…" Ellie said, still digging through her huge-as-hell bag.

"Oh no, what? What does that mean?" I asked, partially distracted by her naked body. The curve of her ass, the dip in her waist, the slope of her breasts…

"There's a possibility I forgot the key at home." She glanced over at me with remorse in her eyes.

My jaw fell open. "Uhh…" I stuttered while pulling on the handcuffs, realizing they were way too tight for me to slip my hands out.

"I'm so sorry," she rushed out.

"Would you happen to known how to pick a lock?" I asked, grasping at straws.

Shaking her head, she went back to searching her purse. "I'll check again. Maybe it's in here somewhere…"

"Maybe it just got lost in that bottomless pit. What the hell do you even keep in there?"

She shot me a look.

I didn't expect her to answer the question, but she started rattling off a list anyway. "My wallet, lip gloss, granola bars, antibacterial wipes, crackers, tampons…"

And that's where she lost me.

Looking up at the wooden headboard, I tried to think of

a way to dismantle it, but we would need tools for that—tools that were at the shop just a block away. But that meant Ellie would have to go there and ask my dad for the toolbox, and he'd be way too nosy about the reason why.

There was no way in hell I was letting my dad find out about this.

"… Band-Aids, nail clippers, and hair ties," she finished, pulling me out of my thoughts. I was entertained by the fact that she was still talking about all the items in her purse, which made it sound like she was preparing for the apocalypse. "I'll have to go to my house and get the key."

After thinking about it for a few seconds, I realized that was probably the best option. "Okay." I nodded and watched her throw on her jeans and one of my T-shirts, not even bothering to put on a bra.

"I'll be back as soon as I can." She darted for the door.

"Wait!" I shouted and she turned back. "Can I get some boxers at least?"

A giggle burst free from her when she noticed the fact that I was lying there, completely naked, chained to a bed. She quickly grabbed a pair of underwear from the top drawer, but when she pulled them out, the orange pill bottle fell out with them.

The orange pill bottle I'd completely forgotten about.

"What's this?" she asked, narrowing her eyes as she inspected the small container.

"It's Viagra," I stated, kind of wishing I could fall into a dark hole and never come out.

"Oh," she said, looking just as awkward as I felt as she quickly put it back in the drawer.

Inwardly, I groaned. Could this moment be any more embarrassing?

Then I recalled what Ellie said about how she'd already

seen me at my worst, and she was right. This was humiliating, but it wasn't as bad as peeing my pants.

Plus, those pills were worthless with her around. I'd meant to throw them away but being with Ellie made me forget that I ever had a problem in the first place.

She started dragging the boxers up my legs, and I noticed she was avoiding eye contact.

"Ellie." She looked up at me. "I've never taken them. I never needed to with you."

A small smile appeared on her lips as she tugged my underwear all the way up. "I don't want you to be ashamed," she said, sitting on the bed next to me. "There's nothing to be ashamed of. Honestly, I just got embarrassed because I thought you were embarrassed."

"Well, I was a little embarrassed." I laughed. "But then I remembered who you are. You're my best friend, Ellie."

Her eyes softened and she smiled at me. Her hand came up to my face and she lightly ran her thumb over my eyebrow. We stared at each other for a few seconds, seemingly lost in the moment before I rattled the metal binding my wrists.

"The key, Ellie," I reminded her playfully.

"Oh! Right." She shot up from the bed and started rushing toward the door. "I'll be back as soon as I can."

"Wait," I blurted out again and she turned back. "Can I get a TV show?" I pointed to the flat screen on my dresser.

Fumbling with the remote, she turned the channel to the Funniest Home Video show I liked, then set the controller by my head even though I wouldn't be able to reach it.

"Thanks. And I'm a little cold." I pouted.

She bit her lip to keep from laughing as she pulled the covers up and tucked them under my armpits.

"Better?" she asked, sitting on the edge of the bed, and I nodded. "I really am sorry about this."

"I'll forgive you for a kiss," I told her, waggling my eyebrows. "A good one. With tongue."

Ellie didn't even hesitate, and the kiss went from innocent to hot as fuck in about three seconds. I felt myself getting hard again.

"Damn," I whispered against her lips. "You'd better hurry back. It's your turn next."

With a reluctant sigh, she left my side. I winked at her and she grabbed her purse before scurrying out of the bedroom.

"See you soon," she called from somewhere down the hall.

Restlessly shifting my body, I tried to get comfortable because it would be at least 40 minutes until she came back.

The show on TV had an 'epic fail' segment for squirrels, most of which consisted of them trying to get food from a bird feeder. I laughed and tried to ignore the fact that my hands were going numb.

When I heard the front door open and close a few minutes later, I wondered if Ellie had found the key in her car or something. Then I heard Travis's deep voice and Angel's giggle.

Oh no. No no no.

They weren't supposed to be back from the latest haul until tomorrow. Footsteps got closer and I knew they were headed this way. My door was wide open, so there was no way they would miss this mortifying scene.

Squirming, I tried to sit up, but all it did was make the blanket fall further down, fully exposing my body.

Shit.

Panicking, I yelled out, "Don't come down the hallway!"

But it was too late. Angel stepped into view first, followed by a gasp and a squeal as her hands flew up to cover her eyes. Travis wasn't far behind.

"What the fuck?" he asked, his eyes going wide as he stood

next to Angel.

"You weren't supposed to be home yet," I grumped, as if that would adequately explain why I was naked and hand-cuffed to my bed.

"Angel was getting homesick so we decided to come back early. What the hell is going on?"

I sighed. There was no way to sugarcoat this.

"Ellie wanted to get a little kinky but forgot the key." I rattled the handcuffs above my head. "She had to run home to get it."

Travis doubled over, laughing so hard I thought he might pass out, and Angel started giggling, her hands still covering her eyes.

It was starting to get chilly without the blanket on, but the situation was way too uncomfortable for me to ask either of them to come cover me back up.

"I'm glad you guys find it so funny," I huffed. "Now, if you wouldn't mind shutting the door…"

"Oh, hell no. You're lucky I'm not taking pictures right now." Travis started leading Angel away by her shoulders. "We'll be in the living room. Can't wait to meet your girl," he said cheerfully.

Groaning, I let my head fall back on the pillow.

Fuck me.

A minute later, the song 'Pretty Tied Up' by Guns N' Roses started blasting through the apartment, and I heard Travis and Angel cracking up in the living room.

Amused and slightly annoyed, I rolled my eyes and shook my head.

Fuckers.

That wasn't the end of the playlist, though. The next song was 'Unchained Melody' and after that, 'Whip It'.

"You're an asshole, Travis!" I shouted, trying not to laugh.

However, it was the last song that cut my amusement short. It was Rhianna's 'S&M'. It brought back memories of the first night I saw Ellie—before I even knew it was her.

This was the first song we ever danced to. I wasn't familiar with it at the time, but I recognized it now. Just thinking about that night had my cock hardening. Again.

Glancing at the clock, all I could do was count down the minutes until Ellie got back.

CHAPTER 30

Brielle

"I found the key!" I announced as I entered Colton's apartment, but the last word ended with a frightened screech because two people I'd never met before were sitting on the couch, looking at me expectantly and grinning from ear to ear.

"You must be Brielle," the pretty, petite blonde girl said, bouncing up and down with excitement, causing the springs under the cushion to squeak a little.

"You must be Angel." I recognized her from a couple of pictures I'd seen in the living room. Then I looked at the guy sitting next to her. "And you're Travis."

"Yep," he replied, and they both stood up to walk over to me.

"It's so great to finally meet you," Angel gushed. "All my best friends are, like, eighty years old, but it would be so great to hang out with someone close to my own age sometimes."

"It's nice to meet you, too," I said, a little taken aback at how friendly she was. She was *so* happy to see me. Her messy side-braid bounced on her shoulder as she hopped from one foot to the other.

"So, tell us about yourself. Are you hungry? Do you like sloppy joes? They're kind of my specialty," she said without taking a breath, making it all sound like one long sentence.

Chuckling, Travis put his arm around her and kissed the top of her head.

"Don't scare her away, baby," he muttered in her ear.

Not sure which question I was supposed to answer first, I just smiled and shrugged. "I love sloppy joes."

"I can teach you how to make them," Angel said, linking her arm with mine and guiding me into the kitchen. "It's so easy and everyone loves them. So, Colton says you have a daughter?"

Smiling, I nodded and set my purse on the counter. "Ava. She's three."

Looking amused, Travis took a seat on one of the folding chairs at the small table, crossing his arms over his chest. His hair fell into his eyes. He just pushed it back and continued to watch Angel, who I realized was still talking.

"You'll have to let us meet her sometime," she said, opening the fridge and grabbing the hamburger, ketchup, and mustard. She set them next to the stove. "I would totally babysit for you. I know you don't know me or anything, but I would love that. I'm a certified in-home health aide, so I'd say I'm sort of responsible. I mostly care for the elderly, but kids can't be any more cantankerous than my clients." She ended her rambling with a giggle.

I was about to thank her for the offer, because anyone who was willing to babysit had my full appreciation, but Colton's voice echoed through the apartment.

"I'm glad you're all getting along," he called from the bedroom. "But can I get a little help in here?"

All three of us burst out laughing and my face heated up with embarrassment. I covered my burning cheeks, and Angel snorted into her hand. The ambush meeting had caused me to completely forget that Colton was still handcuffed to the bed.

"I'm gonna give him so much shit about this," Travis

muttered while trying to cover his grin.

"And I'm starving so, yes, Angel, sloppy joes would be awesome!" Colton called out again, causing us all to laugh some more.

"I should probably go unchain him." Clutching the key in my hand, I made an awkward exit from the kitchen.

∼

What could have been a really uncomfortable situation for everyone involved ended up being one of the best afternoons I'd had in a long time.

After detaching Colton from the headboard, he'd rolled us until I was pinned underneath him, then kissed me until I was out of breath and wishing we were alone. When he said the handcuffs and the key would be staying at his place for the foreseeable future, I couldn't argue.

My first impression of Travis and Angel? They were unbelievably in love. When Travis smiled at her, dimples popped up on his cheeks and I literally saw her swoon.

Since there were only three chairs, Travis pulled Angel onto his lap as we ate dinner. Every now and then, she would brush his hair off his forehead for him and sometimes he would playfully nip at her fingers, causing her to giggle.

For a second, I was a little bit jealous. But when I glanced over at Colton, the same enamored expression was displayed on his face. And he was looking at *me* that way.

"So," Travis started, "I have to imagine you have some pretty funny stories about this guy," he said to me, and Colton glared at both of us.

"The best," I agreed. "Unfortunately, we pinky swore to keep all our secrets hidden." I mock pouted. "I can't go against the pinky swear."

"Well, I never swore on anything," Travis said, grinning over at Colton. "Did you know this fucker picked a fight with me because of you?"

"The letter," I gasped. "This is the neighbor you punched in the face?" I asked, pointing at Travis.

Laughing, Colton nodded.

From the matching smile on Travis's face, I could tell there were no hard feelings about the scuffle.

"Tell her about that camping trip when we were thirteen." Travis threw a piece of popcorn into his mouth.

Colton guffawed then ran a hand down his face. "We were pretty ornery."

"You don't say," I said sarcastically, imagining all the trouble he could have caused as a teenager.

Ignoring my jab, he playfully pinched my chin before continuing. "My dad took us to Wyoming that summer. The campsite we were staying at had one of those buildings with the big bathrooms. Outside, there were a few vending machines and for some reason, there was this giant stuffed bear—like a real bear." Colton paused. "What's the word for when they take a real animal and make it into a statue?"

"Taxidermy?" I supplied, my lips tipping up because no story could have a good ending when taxidermy was involved.

Colton snapped his fingers. "That's it. Anyway, Travis and I thought it would be really funny if we took it and put it in the women's shower stall."

Angel and I both gasped, a bit horrified to realize how this might have ended for the poor women of that campsite.

Our concerns were confirmed when Travis finished the story. "About 6 o'clock in the morning, we hear all these screams." He laughed. "Woke up everyone within a quarter-mile radius."

"Somehow, my dad knew we did it," Colton chimed in.

"But he was too busy laughing about it to punish us."

"You guys are terrible," Angel scolded while trying to fight a smile.

"It didn't go completely unpunished," Travis told us as his hand absentmindedly ran through Angel's blonde strands.

Colton sent Travis a half-hearted scowl. "That's for sure. During the struggle to get the bear through the doorway, Travis dropped it on my big toe."

"I did not," he argued. "That was all you."

"Either way, that shit hurt. My toenail got all black and blue. Oozed for a week before it finally fell off," he said with a grimace, and Angel and I both scrunched up our faces at the mental image.

"That's disgusting," Travis said as he flicked a piece of popcorn across the table.

Catching it mid-air, Colton threw it back at him and it landed in Angel's hair.

"Hey!" she laughed, picking the kernel out and tossing it into a nearby trash can.

Now that I was seeing Colton and Travis together, I could understand the strong bond they had. Colton was right about them being like brothers.

An almost foreign kind of happiness came over me—something I hadn't felt in a long time. I hadn't been part of a group of friends since high school. As I looked around the flimsy card table and took in the happy faces around me, I started to feel like I was part of the group. Like I belonged.

CHAPTER 31

Colton

T he next couple weeks passed in a blur of work and stolen
moments with my girls.

Ellie and I kept the routine of having dates on
Sundays, but finding time to see each other had been difficult
with her classes and our work schedules. When we got to be
alone, we spent most of the time holed up in my bedroom
playing, teasing, laughing, and fucking.

I couldn't really call it fucking, though.

Because it was so much more than that.

A few nights a week I went to Caged because being
near her, watching her, was better than not seeing her at all.
Sometimes we got carried away after her shift in the parking
lot, which resulted in me dragging ass the next day.

Totally worth it, though.

On Thursday afternoons, I got to hang out with Ava.
Today Ellie dropped her off at my apartment, and it was the
first time she'd been here.

As she sat down in the chair at the kitchen table, I realized
I might have to invest in a booster seat. Her chin barely made
it over the tabletop. The thought of filling my place with kid
stuff made me excited.

She would need toys. And DVDs. Maybe a few changes
of clothes. I would have to ask Ellie what size Ava was so I

could pick up some outfits next time I was at Walmart. And kids liked coloring books, right? Building the list in my head, I made a mental note to pick up some of those awesome little juice boxes.

"What's that?" Ava interrupted my thoughts as she eyed the paper plate I set in front of her.

"It's a ketchup and mustard sandwich," I replied.

Her eyes almost bugged out of her head while her face twisted up like she had smelled something bad.

I laughed at her reaction.

She grinned up at me. "Are you just joking me?"

"Nope. It's the best sandwich ever," I said, and her smile fell. She looked skeptical. "Seriously," I insisted. "Just try it."

Pursing her lips, she picked up one quarter of the sandwich and took the smallest nibble possible. After chewing and swallowing, she glanced at me and took a bigger bite. She made a sound of contentment before plowing through the rest.

Success. The kid devoured it. In fact, she'd eaten it so fast I hadn't even had time to sit down yet.

"That was really good," she said enthusiastically, smiling up at me with her cheeks decorated in red and yellow.

"You mean to tell me your mom has never made you one of those before?" I asked, and Ava shook her head.

Maybe Ellie forgot about our favorite food as kids, but when I tried to think of something Ava might like a ketchup and mustard sandwich had been at the top of the list. Obviously, it'd been a great idea because now Ava sat back and patted her stomach, full and satisfied.

I finished off my own dinner in about three bites, then we settled down on the couch to watch some TV. Flipping through the channels, I passed the news, some sports, and more news. Not exactly the most interesting stuff.

Seeming a little bored and restless, Ava turned to me. "Can we go to the mall?"

I looked at the clock, realizing Ellie was supposed to come pick Ava up in half an hour.

"I don't think we'll have time today, Bug," I said with a frown. I hated saying no to her. "Maybe next time, though."

"Can we go to a biiiig mall someday?" Her hands went out in a wide arc over her head.

I laughed. "What kind of big mall?"

"Yike… Like a new super big mall. Yeah. With lots and lots and lots of new toys and stuff."

I didn't know much about malls but I remembered one over in Indiana that I went to as a kid with my dad after we moved to Tolson. We didn't have a lot of money for family vacations, so our trips usually consisted of either camping, or visiting new places close to home.

"It's definitely a possibility," I told her, causing her face to light up and my heart to swell. "I'll talk to your mom about it."

She snuggled up to me and focused her attention back on the TV. I tried to find some kid shows, but I realized I didn't have any family-based channels in my cable package.

That would have to change.

We ended up deciding on Funniest Home Videos and we both laughed at the wedding bloopers. People fell down while dancing. A bride's skirt got ripped off halfway down the aisle. A flower girl tripped face-first into the cake.

"Are you gonna marry my mom?" Ava's curious question caused my heart to skip a beat.

"I don't know," I told her, having to hold myself back from tell her how much I wanted that. "People usually date for a while before they decide to get married. Get to know each other first."

"Why?"

I shrugged. "That's just the way it is."

She got quiet for a second. "But you already know her."

I looked down at her serious face. "Yeah, I guess I do. Did you know your mom and I used to be best friends when we were kids?"

She nodded. "Yep. Can you tell me a story about it?"

Just then, my phone pinged with an incoming text.

Ellie: Done with class. I'll be heading your way soon.
Me: Awesome. We're just hanging out. By the way, I have a boner pic with you.
Ellie: A dick pic? How romantic.

I reread the message I sent her. Annoyed, I rolled my eyes at my phone's inability to be normal. I seriously needed to get this thing checked out.

Me: Dammit. Autocorrect is a pervert. I have a bone to pick with you.
Ellie: Oh. I liked the original text better.
Me: You've deprived your child of ketchup and mustard sandwiches. How could you?

A minute ticked by and I wondered if she was going to reply. When she did, I was reminded again of just how deep her feelings for me went.

Ellie: The truth is I haven't had one since the day you moved away. It just wasn't the same without you.

A sigh came from next to me on the couch and I glanced down to see an impatient expression on Ava's face.

"Did you forget about my story?" she whispered, as though she didn't want to disturb my phone conversation.

"Nope. Just give me one sec," I told her and typed out a quick message.

Me: Well you have me now.

Setting my phone down on the coffee table, I turned my full attention to Ava. "When your mom was about six years old—"

"Is that really old?" she interrupted.

"Nope. Only a couple years older than you. Do you know how old I am?" I asked, curious about what her answer would be.

She put her hand out and made a shrugging gesture. "Ninety-six?"

I threw my head back and laughed. "I'm twenty-two. Good guess, though. Anyway, we were at the park a couple blocks away from my house. We took our shoes off to play in the sand box and when your mom got out, she stepped on bumblebee—"

"Are bumblebees mean?" she cut in.

"Not all of them, but this one was. He wasn't happy about being stepped on and he stung her." I remembered the way Ellie's foot had swelled, how much she'd cried, and how scared I'd been—but I left the gory details out. "I was really worried about her and I knew we needed to get home. I carried her the whole way."

"You musta been really strong," Ava concluded.

"Well, it wasn't easy. Back then, your mom and I were about the same size."

"Why?"

I shrugged. "Boys and girls are the same size sometimes."

She paused, thinking with narrowed eyes and her lips twisting to the side. I loved the way her mind worked, loved watching her process the information I just gave her.

"You carried her for miles?" she asked, her eyes getting big on the word 'miles'.

I ruffled her hair. "Two blocks. It kind of felt like miles, though. But I did it because I loved her."

"Do you still yuv her?"

I nodded. "Yep. I still love her."

"Your hair is getting kind of long," Ava said, running a hand over the top of my head.

"Hmm, I guess you're right," I agreed, realizing it'd been a couple weeks since I'd buzzed it. "How would you like to help me cut it?"

"Really?!" she asked excitedly, as if I'd just offered to buy her an island. If I'd known cutting my hair was going to make her that happy, I would've suggested it sooner.

She followed me to the bathroom, hopping and skipping the whole way.

After getting out my hair-cutting tools, I put a towel around my shoulders and set Ava up on the bathroom sink so she could reach my head. I held onto her legs to steady her while she clumsily ran the electric clippers over my scalp.

"Am I doing a good job?" she asked, coming dangerously close to one of my eyebrows.

"You sure are." I had no idea what my hair was going to look like after she was done, but I didn't tell her that. Besides, there wasn't any way to mess up a buzz-cut.

"Why do you cut your hair so short?"

"I've done it like this for a long time." I told her, thinking of how it all started with my mom's chemo treatments. "Someone I loved a lot cut her hair this way, so I wanted to do it, too."

Her motions paused. "Should I cut my hair off?"

"No, Bug," I said quickly with a laugh. If I returned a bald Ava, I'm pretty sure Ellie would be pissed. "Your hair is beautiful just the way it is."

CHAPTER 32

Brielle

I knocked on Colton's door, but there was no answer so I let myself in.

"Hello?" I called out, but there was no response.

Following a buzzing sound, I made my way to the bathroom. I stopped, taking in the scene before me. Ava was standing on the sink, her face scrunched up in concentration as she ran electric clippers over Colton's head. Small chunks of hair fell to his shoulders as she made a nonsensical design—some lines were diagonal, some crisscrossed. It even looked like she tried to make some circular, swirly shapes.

Honestly, it looked like shit.

Leaning against the door frame, I watched them. Seeing Ava do this kind of thing with a man—a father figure—wasn't something I ever thought I would get to experience. Neither of them were aware of me yet, and I took advantage of the opportunity to observe their interaction.

"I think I'm almost done," Ava told him.

"I bet it looks great," Colton said, even though I was sure he had to know it was a total hack-job.

"Here you go." She handed him the clippers and he turned them off.

Running a hand over his head, he looked in the mirror, then to Ava. "You're a pro. How much do I owe you for that?"

"The first one was free," she replied, completely serious, and Colton and I both started laughing.

"Mom!" Ava exclaimed, finally noticing me, and she started clamoring down.

"Whoa. Careful, Bug," Colton lifted her off the sink then set her on the floor.

She ran over to give me a hug and I smirked up at Colton. "Nice haircut."

"Thanks." He grinned, running his hand over the uneven mess.

After Colton cleaned up the bathroom, he gave me the summary of the afternoon, including the part where Ava ate an entire sandwich without complaint. I had to admit he was a natural at this. Not that Ava was difficult, but taking care of a kid could be really hard sometimes.

"Can I watch TV for just a few more minutes? Pleeeeaaase," Ava begged as I put her coat on.

"Okay. Two minutes," I told her, and she did some sort of happy dance before running over to the couch. Good thing she didn't realize two minutes wasn't a long time.

I went to the kitchen and Colton followed.

"Thank you for watching her again." I turned to him after grabbing a bottle of water from the fridge.

"You don't have to thank me for hanging out with her. I love it."

"Your hair though…" I started laughing.

With a wicked gleam in his eye, he prowled toward me until I was backed up against the cabinets.

I squeaked as he picked me up and set me on the counter. We both peeked around the wall to make sure Ava was fully occupied. Looking cozy, she was curled up against the arm of the couch, which meant it was a green light for a quick make-out session.

As soon as I turned back to Colton, his mouth came crashing down onto mine. His tongue swept inside and I sucked on it, making him let out a quiet moan. I scraped at his nipples through his gray T-shirt, knowing it was one of his turn-ons, then he did the same to me.

Needless to say, Ava's TV time went from two minutes to ten. And like I said, it was a good thing little kids had no sense of time or else she might've wondered what we were doing for so long.

Breaking the kiss, I pulled back then ran my finger over the scar on Colton's eyebrow.

"I have to go," I whispered breathlessly.

He nodded before going in for one more kiss. "You're working Saturday night, right?"

"Yeah." I nodded.

"It's Travis's 22nd birthday. I think he wanted all of us to come to Caged since it's the only club Angel can get into."

I frowned, thinking about how much I wanted to go with them. Sure, I would be there, but it wouldn't be the same if I was working.

"I'll see if I can get off early," I suggested and Colton smiled, obviously happy with the idea. He gave my ass one last squeeze before helping me down and I grazed his lower lip with my thumb. "By the way… I still love your shy tooth."

He grinned, showing me the very tooth I adored.

CHAPTER 33

Colton

I grunted as I tried to lift the weight of the barbell off my chest.

"Come on. You can do better than that," Travis goaded from a few feet away. "All this time away from the gym and you've gotten soft."

Letting out another grunt, I completed the last rep on the bench press. Sitting up, I glared at Travis. The asshole was supposed to be making sure I didn't drop the bar on my esophagus.

"You suck as a spotter. And you can ask my girlfriend—the last thing I am these days is *soft*."

He barked out a laugh. "Well, as much as it disturbs me to hear about your never-ending hard-on, I'm happy for you."

"And speaking of getting soft, all that driving you've been doing is going to give you trucker butt." I stood up to go do some squats and Travis followed.

"Now you're just making things up," he said while looking self-consciously in the mirror at his back end.

Chuckling, I shook my head. It'd been a while since we went to the gym together. With both of us juggling work at the shop and the transport deliveries, we didn't have time. Plus, the fact that we were both in relationships meant things like working out got shoved back on the priority list.

Surprisingly, being a mechanic was pretty good exercise. The physical aspect of the job was great for staying in shape, but it just wasn't the same as going to the gym with a friend. Travis and I were long overdue for some male bonding time.

"So you and Brielle," Travis began, raising his eyebrows. "You two really hit it off. One might even say you *rushed* into things…" he joked with a pointed look.

"About that," I started, sheepishly glancing down at the blue-speckled linoleum. "I know I gave you some shit back when you and Angel moved so fast with your relationship—"

"Uh-huh." Travis cut me off, crossing his arms with an expectant expression on his face.

"I'm sorry, okay? I just didn't understand it then, but I feel like I'm really eating my words now." I gave him an apologetic look, remembering how I'd given him a hard time, all in good fun of course. He'd taken it all in stride, swearing it would happen to me someday.

I didn't believe him at the time, but I'd never been happier to admit I was wrong.

"I guess I can let it go." He pretended to think it over. "As long as drinks are on you tonight."

"It's your birthday. Drinks were already gonna be on me tonight."

"We're good then." He clapped me on the back before going over to the chin-up bar. "You know, I like Brielle. It's great to finally see you *tied* down."

Shaking my head, I laughed knowing he was referring to the handcuff debacle.

We continued the rest of the workout in companionable silence and I thought that was the end of it.

But I was wrong.

As we walked out of the gym, the puns continued. "It'll be nice to see your girl tonight. The good ol' ball and *chain*."

I scoffed and we climbed into Travis's pickup truck. After fastening my seatbelt, he started it up, then turned to me.

"You up for watching a movie before we go out?"

"Sure." I shrugged. "I'm okay with whatever."

"Good. I was thinking we could watch James *Bondage.*"

"Dude." Trying not to laugh, I rolled my eyes. "I'm never going to live this down, am I?"

"Absolutely not." He looked at me like I was crazy. "Brielle went all *Fifty Shades of Grey* on your ass. That's burned into my mind forever."

"You don't even know what *Fifty Shades of Grey* is," I pointed out.

"No, not really," he admitted as he drove out of the parking lot. "But Angel does."

"Oh, I forgot. You two are like one person now."

"Pretty much, yeah." He shrugged. "You're getting there, too."

I couldn't argue with him, so I just smiled and gazed out the window at all the empty fields we passed on the way back to Tolson.

Once again I had to admit my friend was right, and I couldn't have been happier about that.

CHAPTER 34

Brielle

I t was Saturday night and I was back in the cage. Country night was hopping. Normally, I just got into the zone and did my thing, but tonight I was distracted. Most likely it had to do with the fact that Colton, Travis, and Angel were here having a great time without me.

Colton was in for a surprise, though. I hadn't told him yet, but my boss agreed to let me off at 11 tonight. Just the thought of hanging out with friends—doing something so normal for people my age—had me feeling giddy.

And that wasn't the only surprise I had in store. My parents had agreed to watch Ava the entire night, which meant for the first time, Colton and I were going to get to spend the night together.

When my shift was over, I got down from the cage and went straight to their table. Colton's face lit up with a huge grin.

"Hey," he said, standing up. "What's going on?"

I smiled at him. "I got off early tonight."

"Mmm," he nuzzled my neck while palming my ass, which was barely covered in Daisy Dukes. "You look so sexy in those cowboy boots. Why are you such a sexy cowgirl tonight?"

Laughing, I pulled back and noticed his glassy eyes. "Are you drunk?"

He held up his thumb and forefinger, pinching them together. "A little."

Glancing over at Angel, I realized Travis was probably three sheets to the wind, too. He was leaning his head against her shoulder and sloppily kissing her upper arm. From the entertained expression on her face, I could tell she shared my amusement over their state of inebriation.

"Let me go change really quick, and I'll come hang out," I told Colton, who was still openly groping me.

"Can you leave on the boots?" he requested, his hot breath by my ear causing tingles to spread over my skin. "I fucking love those boots."

"Okay," I agreed and I was rewarded with a huge lopsided grin.

After changing into skinny jeans and a white lacy top, I found Angel sitting alone in the booth.

"Where are the guys?" I asked, taking the seat next to her.

She motioned toward the dance floor and giggled. "Making asses of themselves."

She wasn't kidding about that. Travis and Colton were attempting to line dance to 'Boot Scootin' Boogie' and somehow they had both acquired cowboy hats. Colton hadn't gotten any better at his moves since our first date. Apparently, he thought he had skills because he was trying to show Travis how to do a jig.

While the guys did their thing, Angel and I got to know each other a little better as she sipped at her kiddie cocktail.

She told me about her job as a health aide, which consisted of caring for the elderly by doing housework, cooking, and grocery shopping. I could tell she loved it. When she talked about her clients, it sounded more like telling me about close friends.

I groaned when she asked about my classes, because

nursing school was kicking my ass and I hadn't even gotten to the hard stuff yet. When I told her Ava would be turning four soon, she listened intently while I talked about her upcoming party.

"Okay, so I know this sentence is going to sound weird," Angel began, leaning close so I could hear her over the music, "but I know a balloon animal guy."

"A balloon animal guy?" I repeated, wanting to make sure I heard her right.

She nodded. "Yeah, my friend Ernie. He lives in Tolson. He's, like, 80 years old and he's an expert at balloon animals. He even does parties for free because he loves it so much. I could see if he's available for Ava's birthday."

"Seriously?" I asked, touched by her offer. "She would love that so much. Thank you."

We exchanged numbers and she said she would text me with Ernie's info.

Angel was one of the most likable people I'd ever met. She was so open and optimistic, which was amazing considering the tough life she'd had. Colton had filled me in on a little bit of her history and how she'd ended up in Tolson. I admired her ability to be so resilient.

And she didn't even know me yet here she was, offering to hook me up with balloon animals for a little girl she'd never even met.

I put my phone away, and Angel smiled at me. A real, genuine smile. Completely free of judgment, ulterior motives, or cattiness. I had a feeling that, in time, we would become good friends. Maybe even best friends.

Speaking of good friends, I practically screeched when I caught sight of familiar dark curls.

"Chloe!" Waving excitedly, I flagged her down.

"Hey!" She sat down at our table.

"What are you doing here?" I asked, surprised to see her.

"You think you could tell me you were out tonight and I wouldn't come?" She shook her head. "There was no way I would miss this."

I did a quick introduction between Chloe and Angel, then Colton sat down in the chair next to me. Looping his arm around my shoulder, he planted a big kiss on my cheek.

"So you're the reason she's so perky these days," Chloe said to him while pointing at me.

"Hey," I grumped. "I've always been perky."

Chloe rolled her eyes. "Whatever you say, Cranky Pants. Can I get you a drink? I'm gonna tell Jerry that Tasha told him to give us free drinks, so it's on him." She winked.

I snickered.

"Just a water for me. I think I'm going to have to drive drunkie home tonight," I said, patting Colton on the shoulder.

"You're coming home with me?" he asked in disbelief.

Unable to keep myself from grinning, I nodded. "I'm staying the night. The *whole* night."

"Oh my God," he exclaimed and his arms went around me in a bear-hug, squeezing the breath from my body. "This is the best birthday present ever."

"Dude, it's not your birthday," Travis reminded him from across the table as he clumsily pulled Angel onto his lap.

"Doesn't matter," Colton replied, his voice muffled because his face was buried in my cleavage. "It's a Christmas miracle."

Travis barked out a laugh. "It's not Christmas either."

"Don't care," Colton grunted, running his nose over the skin on my collarbone, sniffing me like he always did before heading back down to my chest.

"Chloe, this is Colton." I giggled as he waved in her general direction without bothering to look up. I glanced down at him. "Can you even breathe in there?"

He lifted his head enough to talk. "If I had to choose a way to go, being smothered by your boobs is at the top of my list."

Selena Gomez's 'Good For You' came on, and Chloe started hopping with excitement. "Let's go dance!"

Colton perked up, obviously happy with the idea, then dragged me out onto the dance floor.

Colton couldn't line dance to save his life, but this kind of dancing? The grind-on-my-ass, have-sex-with-our-clothes-on kind of dancing? He definitely knew what he was doing. Even completely hammered, his rhythm never faltered. Just like the very first night, I found myself melting into his hard chest.

In fact, he was hard *everywhere*.

I started to feel hot and tingly as his hands rubbed up my stomach and grazed my nipples through my shirt. My mouth fell open when his lips landed on my neck, and he sucked at the spot he knew made my knees weak.

"Whew!" Chloe exclaimed, and I opened my eyes to see her fanning herself. "You guys are burning it up out here. I'm going to need a cold drink after that."

She took off in the direction of the bar, and I couldn't blame her for not wanting to watch me get it on.

Laughing, I turned around in Colton's arms. "You know what I really want?"

"Whatever it is, you can have it," he replied with a grin.

"I want to go back to your place." I rubbed my front against his. "Now."

"Dance one more with me?" he asked as a slow song came on. "I promise not to step on your feet."

Nodding, I put my arms around his neck and we started to sway to 'H.O.L.Y' by Florida Georgia Line.

Colton dropped his forehead to mine and ran his thumb

over my chin.

"I love you so much," he said close to my ear. Maybe it would've been more correct to say he slurred it, but it was still sweet.

Rubbing my hand over the short hair on his head, I said it back.

We kissed through most of the song and the world around me fell away.

～

Drunk-Colton was extremely entertaining. And very affectionate. After we said our goodbyes to everyone, he practically mauled me in the parking lot. It took some convincing but I finally talked him into getting in the car so we could go back to his place.

"Baby, I'm shameless!" he hollered along with the music on the radio, completely off-key, as he serenaded me with the old Garth Brooks song.

I just smiled as I tried to concentrate on the road. The car-karaoke went on for most of the drive and if he didn't know the words to a song, he would just make them up.

"Hold me closer, Tony Danzaaaa," he sang and I laughed.

"Colton, this is 'Tiny Dancer'," I informed him. "By Elton John."

"No, no. Listen to the words, Ellie. He says Tony Danza." He planted a sloppy kiss on the back of my hand.

Amused, I went back to letting him sing it however he wanted, making a mental note to get Colton drunk more often. He was hilarious.

Once we got to his apartment, he tried to convince me to have sex in the car, but I insisted on going inside where no one would see us.

It wasn't like Tolson had a ton of traffic, but it wouldn't have been completely out of left field for Champ to stumble home from the tavern. I didn't feel like giving Colton's neighbor a show. It took some bribing, but when I told him I had a surprise for him he gave in.

Steering Colton through his front door, I led him to the bedroom. I dug through his drawers until I found a gray T-shirt and his favorite sweatpants, then I started to unbutton his shirt.

"Oh, you want tickets to the gun show?" he asked while flexing his arms, which made it difficult for me to get his shirt off. It also made him lose his balance and he tipped to the side before leaning against the bed.

"You did not just say that." Laughing at him, I gave up on trying to change his clothes.

"All you had to do was ask," he slurred, and fell back on the bed. He reached for me, but I moved out of the way.

"Now for your surprise," I said while digging through my overnight bag. "But you can't peek."

"I'm not peeking," he promised, flinging an arm over his face.

Quickly, I changed into the new lacy white bra and panty set, then decided to up my game and wear the cowboy boots, too.

"Okay," I breathed out. Fluffing my hair, I leaned against the wall and tried to strike a sexy pose. "You can look now."

I was met with silence.

"Colton?" As I peered closer, I noticed his parted lips and the slow rise and fall of his chest. He was completely passed out.

Suppressing a giggle, I quietly changed into my pink flannel pajama pants and an oversized white T-shirt I got out of Colton's drawer. Pulling back the covers, I climbed in next to him.

Feeling content I snuggled close, soaking up the warmth of his body. Lifting my hand to his face, I traced his lips and ran a finger down his nose.

A month ago, I never could have predicted this would be my life.

In such a short amount of time, I had fallen head over heels in love with Colton. I had friends and I was happy.

As I closed my eyes, I let out a content sigh.

I felt like I was finally getting everything I'd ever wanted.

CHAPTER 35

Brielle

When Colton told me he wanted to take Ava and me on a day-trip, I was really excited. I had to leave his place early in the morning to get back home, but before I left I set a couple Advil and a bottle of water on his nightstand. I had a feeling he was going to be dealing with one hell of a hangover.

Part of me wondered if he would want to reschedule our outing, but he showed up at my house, bright-eyed and ready to go at noon, just as planned.

Ava used to hate riding in the car for long periods of time, so I had never taken her anywhere far from home, but she did great for the two-hour drive. After she got tired of the 'Frozen' soundtrack being on repeat, Colton handed her his phone because he'd downloaded a couple coloring book apps.

"Are you sure you want to let her play with that?" I asked, feeling warm and mushy over the fact that he took the time to put kid games on his phone. "She might drop it or something."

He smirked, looking good behind the wheel of my car. "If she breaks it, I'm pretty sure she'd be doing me a favor."

Reaching across the middle console, Colton took my hand in his. The last 20-minute stretch of the ride was quiet and peaceful.

After we made it to our destination, the first thing Ava

wanted to do was find the indoor park. The play structure at this mall was way better than the one we were used to. It was basically a huge foam pirate ship and the whole area was brightly lit by a high-dome skylight ceiling.

Ava squealed and giggled as Colton tried to grab at her through the netted sides of the bridge connecting the ship to a dock.

Running to the other side of the ship, she hid behind one of the cartoonish pirate statues and Colton pretended to look for her. I smiled, remembering the way he and I used to play just like that.

Thirty minutes later, they started to lose steam. Looking worn out, Ava climbed into my lap and Colton sat down next to me on the bench.

"There's a cellphone store over there." He pointed down one of the corridors, then frowned down at his phone. "It's been acting weird."

"You mean weirder than usual?" I asked, raising an eyebrow. If they turned off his autocorrect, I was really going to miss his perverted texts.

Shaking his head, he slipped it back into his pocket. "It's been turning itself off." He shrugged. "Maybe there's something wrong with the battery."

"We might go get a snack while you're doing that." I discreetly gestured toward the frozen yogurt store. "I thought I saw a sign for lactose-free I-C-E C-R-E-A-M." I spelled out the word so I wouldn't get Ava's hopes up in case she couldn't have it.

Colton and I made a plan to meet back at the ship in 30 minutes. With Ava's hand in mine, we made a pass by the ice cream counter.

We were in luck. The store had soft-serve vanilla frozen yogurt that was, in fact, lactose-free. Put some sprinkles on top, and I had one happy little girl.

Smiling, I watched her devour the dessert. As she shoveled spoonful after spoonful into her mouth, her snack started to dribble down her chin but she didn't seem to notice.

After finishing up, her face was a hot mess. I wiped at her mouth with a few napkins. When I got too aggressive with it, she started sputtering in protest.

"Sorry, Bug," I apologized, sneaking in a couple more swipes. "There. All done."

"That's okay. I yuv you forty-five point six cents."

Leaning down, I kissed her slightly sticky cheek. "I love you, too."

Our hands swung between us as we passed a few clothing stores. This mall had most of the same stores we were used to back home. Express. Victoria's Secret. The place with the cinnamon rolls. That didn't stop Ava from marveling at them like they were brand new, though.

"I kind of have to pee," she said, her footsteps staggering because she was trying to walk with her legs crossed.

"We'd better go to the bathroom then," I told her while searching for signs to point the way.

"No, that's okay," she said. "I can just swallow it back into my body."

I laughed. "It still doesn't work that way."

Spotting the restrooms, I pulled Ava along at a quick pace. Since getting rid of pull-ups completely eight months ago she'd only had one nighttime accident, but I didn't want to take the chance of that happening here. Lately, Ava had been waiting until the last minute to tell me she needed to go.

Luckily, we made it in time.

After washing our hands and having way too much fun with the automatic hand dryers, we were headed back out.

Ava tugged on my hand. "Can we go on the expalator?"

I glanced down at her to tell her we needed to meet back up with Colton first, but we almost ran straight into someone in the hallway.

"Sorry, I wasn't looking where I was—" My apology was cut short, the breath leaving my body as I looked into familiar blue eyes.

They were the same eyes I had looked into every day for the past four years. Only these eyes didn't look back at me with love—his shock mirrored my own.

"Josh," I gasped, an array of unpleasant emotions hitting me all at once.

What the hell was he doing here? Honestly, I thought I would never see him again—and that was the way I preferred it. Then I recalled the college he ended up going to was in Indiana, so I could only assume it was close by.

"Bree," he said, seeming just as surprised as I was.

He looked a lot different than I remembered. No longer was he the gangly boy with curly brown hair and a sweet smile.

Cocky and entitled were the words that came to mind as I took in his attire and the smug expression that seemed to be permanently etched onto his face. His pants were some kind of pastel plaid and the pink polo shirt he was wearing had the collar popped.

He actually had the collar popped. That alone screamed douchebag.

"How are you?" I said cordially, still in shock. I really didn't care about how he was doing, but it seemed like the polite thing to say.

"I'm great. So great. Got accepted into law school," he boasted, rocking back on his heels and adjusting the brand-new suit he had slung over his shoulder. "I've got big things ahead."

Got big things ahead?

Inwardly, I scoffed. What a douche-y thing to say. Then again, I shouldn't be surprised. This was Josh. The man who turned his back on the most special person in the world.

"Good for you," I said, trying to keep the bite out of my voice but I didn't do a very good job.

"It *is* good. I'm very happy with my life, Bree," he insisted, his eyes flaring with anger. "The best thing I ever did was leave that white-trash town and everyone in it behind."

"Tell me how you really feel," I said sarcastically, trying to hide how much his statement hurt my feelings.

When he said *everyone*, that included the little girl at my side who was currently clinging to my leg.

As if my thoughts brought attention to Ava, he glanced down at her. His eyes widened a bit like it was the first time he was noticing her presence. I didn't like the way he was looking at her. Instead of love or affection, I only saw disinterest and possibly a hint of disgust on his face.

"People back home have been calling me a deadbeat," he scoffed, as if the very idea of it was ridiculous. "I don't appreciate that kind of slander, you know. I never even took a paternity test, so I don't even know if she's mine."

Judging by the venom in his voice, I could assume these were things he'd wanted to say to me for a long time. I put my palms over Ava's ears so she wouldn't hear what I was about to tell him.

"You wouldn't even have to, Josh. All you have to do is look at her," I hissed. "Plus, it would be impossible for her to belong to anyone else. You were the only person I was with."

"You were just trying to trap me," he insisted, as though he didn't hear me. "But you just would've been holding me back. I never wanted to be saddled down with a kid that isn't even mine."

Appalled, I couldn't believe Josh had convinced himself he wasn't Ava's biological father. People always said she looked just like me, but that was only because they hadn't seen him. There was no denying that he contributed to 50% of Ava's DNA.

"If people are calling you a deadbeat, that's their own opinion," I said. "Anyway, I wouldn't know what people are saying in Hemswell. I haven't lived there for years."

Swatting at my hands, it was obvious Ava didn't like being left out of the conversation. I picked her up, feeling the need to protect her from his scrutiny. Ava leaned her head onto my shoulder and started sucking on her thumb—a sure sign that she was uncomfortable. She'd kicked that habit six months ago.

I wasn't kidding when I'd told Colton that she was a good judge of character. Somehow she sensed that Josh wasn't a good guy and my heart broke for her. She had no idea that he was the reason she was created, and I wasn't about to tell her either. Not yet, anyway. Maybe someday I would explain the situation when she was old enough to understand that some people just suck.

"Can she talk?" he asked, and the question pissed me off.

"She's almost four. Of course she can talk."

Anger bubbled up inside me. I'd spent years telling myself his absence didn't matter until I convinced myself it was true. And I still believed we were better off without him, but seeing his smug, asshole face made something inside me snap.

What I really wanted to do was to tell him to fuck off, but little ears were listening. Grudgingly, I decided to be the bigger person.

"I've never asked you for anything. The least you can do is show me some respect." I turned, ready to throw a final good-bye over my shoulder, but he let out another rude scoff.

"Respect? Speaking of respect, I also heard from someone back home that you're stripping these days. Really classy, Bree. Can't say I'm surprised, though."

Outraged, my mouth fell open. He had no right to judge me for the way I lived my life.

Josh and I had never been a match made in heaven, but there was a point when I thought he cared about me. He'd just proven that I had been delusional.

Maybe he was just an asshole who wanted to hurt my feelings. Maybe insulting me was his way of making himself feel better about the choices he'd made.

Either way, it wasn't okay.

Not only could Ava talk, but she could also hear. If he had nasty things to say to me, fine. But the fact that he was doing it in front of her made my blood boil.

I believed there was a right time and a place for the F-word. If Ava was going to learn that, now was as good a time and place as any. Just as I was about to tell him to *fuck off*, her thumb left her mouth with an audible pop.

"My mom is a dancer and she's beautiful." Her little voice came out strong as she stood up for me.

Josh's eyes flew to her and he looked a little shocked at her declaration.

My throat got tight, my nostrils flared, and my eyes stung—all the tell-tale signs that I was about to cry.

Crying wasn't something I did often and the tears filling my eyes had nothing to do with Josh's cruel words. It had everything to do with how quickly Ava came to my defense.

I had never been more proud of her.

Turning my head, I nuzzled her cheek and tried to hide my tears because I didn't want her to think I was sad.

"Thank you, Bug," I whispered. "And you're beautiful, too."

"Just like you?" she asked, pronouncing her 'L' correctly. My heart squeezed with a feeling of nostalgia because her speech impediment improved every day.

I nodded. "Just like me."

Now that I'd blinked away the moisture in my eyes, I pulled back to smile at her. Setting her down I turned to face Josh, still intent on giving him a few choice words.

But he was gone.

Letting out a sigh of relief, I had to admit I was glad he didn't choose to stick around to hear what I wanted to say. If I never saw him again, it would still be too soon.

"Who was that guy?" Ava asked as we walked back to meet Colton.

"That was no one," I told her, hoping she would drop the subject.

"He looked like an Easter egg."

Despite the bad mood I was in, I laughed at her comment. "You're completely right about that."

Feeling shaken up and distracted, I pulled Ava in the direction of the play area. Leaning up against a pillar by the pirate ship, Colton was waiting for us while fiddling with his phone.

An easygoing smile spread over his face as he saw us approaching. "Well, apparently, there isn't anything wrong with my phone." He frowned down at the device. "But somehow they talked me into buying a new battery, a car charger, and a new case. Go figure, right?"

"Oh," I said dumbly, still trying to come to terms with what just happened.

"Are you hungry?" he asked. "The food court has that Chinese place Ava likes."

"With chicken and rice?" she asked.

"Yep." Colton nodded and lifted Ava onto his shoulders.

We took a few detours into the familiar shops Ava insisted

on visiting before heading to the food court, and I tried my best to seem cheerful.

The conversation with Josh left me feeling uneasy. I knew I shouldn't let his words bother me, but they did. It was like he had brought my biggest insecurities to the surface. In just a few short minutes, he'd managed to make me feel two inches tall.

I tried to tell myself it didn't matter, but I was upset. And, apparently, I wasn't very good at hiding it.

"Hey, are you okay?" Colton asked, glancing in my direction as we sat down at a wobbly table with our food trays.

"Yeah." I tried to smile, but it didn't feel very convincing.

His lips pressed into a thin line because he knew I was lying, but I was glad that he didn't call me out on it. Instead, he turned his attention to Ava and they had their eating contest while I picked at the orange chicken in front of me.

Although this mall didn't have a carousel, Ava was happy to compromise on riding up and down the escalator a few times. Since it was getting close to Valentine's Day, the department stores were decked out in pinks and reds. Hearts and balloons were everywhere.

"Oh!" Ava pointed to a display of Valentine's Day-themed gifts. "Can I have that?"

"This one?" Colton picked up the fluffy white bear. Ava hugged it and looked up at him with the biggest puppy-dog eyes I'd ever seen.

Covering my smile, I watched as she totally played him.

He barely even took a second to consider it before nodding. "Sure. Why don't you pick out one for your mom, too?"

Being very careful with her selection, she finally decided on a matching pink bear. After that, we bundled up in our coats and went back to the car.

"You want me to drive?" Colton asked, seeming concerned

as I buckled Ava in.

Absentmindedly, I made a sound of agreement and handed him the keys.

As we got on the highway I gazed out the window, still thinking about the unexpected run-in with Josh. The trees outside became an unfocused blur as the conversation played over and over in my mind.

"Hey, look at that," Colton said, snapping me out of my inner thoughts. "Little bug got worn out."

I glanced back at Ava who was passed out in her car seat, hugging both bears.

Smiling a little, I looked at Colton. "I think that's the first nap she's taken in like a year."

A minute of silence passed between us before he spoke again. "What's wrong, Ellie? And don't say it's nothing because I know it's something. Did I do something wrong? Because whatever it is, I'm sorry."

"No." I sighed and decided to spill it now that Ava wouldn't hear me. "I ran into my ex at the mall."

Colton's hands tightened on the wheel. "Your ex, as in Ava's father?"

I nodded, rubbing at the skin on my thumb. "That's the one."

The car started to slow and he flipped on the turn signal like he was going to get off at the next exit. "We're going back."

"What?" I gasped. "Why?"

"Because I'm going to find that motherfucker," he growled. "What did he say to you? Was he mean to Ava?"

"Colton, don't. She didn't even know who he was and he's probably gone by now anyway," I reasoned. "It doesn't matter. Don't let him ruin this day any more than he already has. Please?"

Colton's lips pressed together as he seemed to debate what to do, and my tense shoulders sagged in relief when he bypassed the exit and kept driving.

The last thing I needed was for him to go on a rampage, punching any guy wearing pastel.

"What did he say to you?" Colton asked again, his voice low and tense.

"Not much," I replied honestly. "It was a short conversation and I'm not really interested in reliving it. He made a dig at me for being an exotic dancer." I winced because it was a little painful to say it out loud.

"That son of a bitch," Colton muttered, his jaw so tense I could see the muscles working in his face.

Over the past few years, I'd been okay with my occupation. Sure, it wasn't the most respected profession, but it had never directly affected anyone else. Now that Colton and I were dating, would he be ashamed of me? How many times would he have to sugarcoat the truth when people asked him what I did for a living?

"Ava told him I was beautiful," I whispered, swallowing hard as I remembered how brave she was.

"You are," he said, reaching over to hold my hand. "You're the most beautiful thing I've ever seen. Ava, too."

Colton was trying to reassure me. I knew he was trying to make me feel better, but I couldn't stop thinking about what Josh had said.

You just would've been holding me back. I never wanted to be saddled down with a kid that isn't even mine.

So far Colton had been great with Ava, but would there be a time when he felt like we were holding him back? Was he really ready to be an insta-dad?

I glanced down at our intertwined fingers, wishing this afternoon had gone differently.

Everything had been going so great lately, so perfect.

Almost too perfect.

And now, an unpleasant sense of foreboding hung over me. I couldn't help feeling like I was just waiting for the other shoe to drop.

Colton said before that he thought everything happened for a reason. Running into Josh was one hell of a coincidence, and the worst kind of reality check.

Maybe it was meant to remind me that I'd been living in a fantasy world.

The first night at Colton's apartment had happened because I'd wanted to pretend. Maybe I'd been pretending this whole time, fooling myself into thinking I could have it all.

Colton squeezed my hand. "Are you sure you're okay?"

"Yeah," I lied, trying to force a smile. "I'm fine."

CHAPTER 36

Colton

Ellie wasn't fine.

I didn't consider myself an expert when it came to dating, but I knew enough to know that when a woman says she's fine it usually means the opposite.

When I dropped Ellie and Ava off at their house I could tell she was trying to hide it, but it was obvious that whatever went down with her ex bothered her.

Pestering her about it proved to be unhelpful. The more I asked, the more she said that word—*fine*.

Over the past couple days, it hadn't gotten much better. Since we'd started dating, we hadn't gone a full day without talking in some way. Lately her texts had been short, and we seemed to be stuck in a game of phone tag when we called each other.

I could almost feel her pulling away from me. Nothing she'd said indicated she was unhappy about anything, but her demeanor had been different.

Me: Hoes your day?

I typed out 'hoes' on purpose. I wanted to see if I could get her to use the opportunity to make fun of me. Crack a joke. Call me a pervert.

But nothing.

It was after-hours at the shop, but I needed something to do. To keep myself busy, I worked on the semi because I had a haul to make in the morning. I'd just gotten done checking the tires when my phone pinged with an incoming text.

Ellie: Fine.

There was that word again.

Frustrated, I blew out a breath. If I didn't have to be up so early for the delivery, I would've been tempted to go to Ellie's house to see what was going on with her. But one of my dad's top rules about driving? Don't do it if you haven't had enough sleep.

While I hated following it right now, I knew it was a good rule. Falling asleep behind the wheel wasn't something I was interested in doing, so Operation Hunt-Ellie-Down would have to wait.

CHAPTER 37

Brielle

That other shoe I was so worried about? It finally dropped. Because I was late.

Not in the sense that I was running behind for work.

I mean, I was *late*. Four days late, to be exact. And I was *never* late.

The only other time I ever missed my period ended with me crying on the bathroom floor staring at two pink lines.

I had spent the last two days alternating between stressing and doing my best to live in denial.

But I couldn't put it off any longer—now it was time to find out for sure.

With shaking hands, I tore open the package of pregnancy tests. Not wanting to leave any room for error, I'd gotten the double pack of digital early detection tests.

I surveyed my arsenal of supplies. On the bathroom counter, there were two tests, a cup, and an instruction pamphlet. I read the directions very carefully, then peed into the cup, foregoing the option to pee directly onto the sticks, which was way more difficult than it sounded.

Then all I could do was wait.

As I paced around the bathroom, I prayed the results were negative. Colton and I were careful—we'd used condoms every time. But I knew that careful wasn't always 100%.

I lifted my hands to my breasts, testing their weight and noting the tenderness when I squeezed. Sore boobs could be a sure sign that I was about to start my period.

Or…

A symptom of pregnancy.

Dropping my arms, I decided to stop fondling myself. Either I was pregnant or I wasn't. No amount of groping was going to change that.

Tears pricked my eyes as I found myself reliving old memories. Almost four years ago, I'd been in this exact same position.

For a few terrifying minutes, I felt like I was in a lose-lose situation.

I imagined what it would be like if I was carrying Colton's child. He was an honorable guy and I knew he would want to do the right thing, even if it wasn't what he wanted.

At first, he would act happy and supportive.

But my heart hurt when I thought about watching him go from loving, to resentful, to eventually leaving me.

If Colton stayed with me, I would always wonder if it was out of obligation. And if he left… I would be crushed.

I wasn't sure if my heart would ever recover from that.

My mind went back to those first lonely nights in the hospital after I had Ava. My mom had wanted to stay with me, but I insisted that she didn't need to. It wasn't because I didn't want her help. I just didn't want her to see me lose my shit—and I did lose my shit. I cried for hours, rocking the tiny pink bundle in my arms. At one point, the nurses became so concerned over my breakdown that they'd insisted on giving me a sedative while they took Ava to the nursery. Reluctantly, I'd agreed because I knew I needed to rest.

When I woke up, I called Josh over and over again, getting his voicemail every time. After two days of leaving tearful messages and pathetic texts, I left the hospital with a baby girl and the resolve that I was going to have to raise her on my own.

The weeks that followed were the darkest times of my life. Struggling to care for a newborn while dealing with a broken heart had left me feeling lost and depressed. If it hadn't been for my parents, I'm not sure how I would've coped.

But I knew one thing—I never wanted to go through that again. Honestly, I wasn't sure I could survive it a second time. I wanted to have more kids someday, but not right now. Not in a relationship that was new and fragile.

Nervously rubbing at my thumb, I stopped pacing. It'd been enough time for the test results to show, so I took a deep breath and looked down at the sticks next to the sink.

Not pregnant. Not pregnant.

Relief slammed through me and a hysterical laugh burst from my mouth. I leaned back against the tiled wall and sagged down on to the floor.

Burying my face in my hands, I cried happy tears.

My moment of respite was short-lived, though, because I heard Ava scream from somewhere in the house. Quickly shoving all the evidence into the trash, I ran from the bathroom. As I was rushing down the stairs I could tell her wailing was more than just her being upset—she was hurt.

I followed her cries into the kitchen where she sat on the counter and my dad stood next to her, holding a towel over her face.

"What happened?" I asked, breathless from speeding through the house.

"We were eating breakfast in the living room. She tripped and hit her face on the coffee table. I tried to catch her but it just happened so fast," he explained, his tone distressed.

My dad was usually cool as a cucumber, so his reaction

made me worry.

Ava's wailing became louder as he removed the towel from her mouth and I sucked in a breath when I saw the damage.

"Oh, Bug. It's okay. It's not that bad," I lied, trying to soothe her.

It really was that bad. There was a lot of blood and I could see an ugly-looking gash below her lower lip. After I asked her to open her mouth wider so I could look inside, I could tell that her teeth had pierced through her cheek from the impact. I wasn't a nurse yet, but it didn't take a medical expert to see she was going to need stitches.

"Am I gonna be okay?" she sobbed as blood dripped down her chin. I gently brought the towel back up to her face.

"Yep, you're going to be just fine," I told her, trying to inject some cheerfulness into my voice. "But I think we need to go see the doctor."

She whimpered. "My lip feels funny."

"I know. But they'll put some good medicine on it so it won't hurt anymore," I told her. "Just trust me, okay?"

"Okay." She nodded, her cries subsiding.

As I got our coats and shoes, not even bothering to change out of our pajamas, it took everything I had to hold myself together. Ava had never been to the emergency room before and I didn't want her to be scared. Seeing me panic or cry would definitely freak her out.

On the outside I was the picture of calm, but on the inside I was an emotional wreck. In a matter of minutes, I went from thinking I might be pregnant to rushing out the door holding a bag of ice to my little girl's swelling face.

On the way out to the car I called Colton, needing someone to talk to. It rang four times before going to voicemail.

"Hey," I started, my voice shaking. "Um, I know you're

on a delivery today, so I hate to bother you. Ava got hurt and we're on our way to the ER now. Just… please call me back?"

After buckling my seatbelt, I glanced in the rearview mirror to find Ava puffy-eyed and still holding the cold pack up to her lip. "How are you doing, Bug?"

She muffled something that sounded like, "I'm okay."

"Here, I'll put on the *Frozen* CD. We'll be at the hospital in less than two songs," I said, trying to sound as reassuring as possible.

Ava nodded and looked out the window.

Before Anna was done singing about building a snowman, we were pulling into the ER parking lot.

∽

"This is the last stitch, Miss Ava," the doctor told her as he looped the curved needle through her skin with steady hands. "You've been a great patient."

She didn't even look away from my phone, which was playing an episode of Doc McStuffins on YouTube. Thank God for wi-fi.

The hospital staff had been so amazing I was seriously considering buying them a fruit basket or something as a thank-you gift. The nurses made Ava laugh, despite the circumstances, and the numbing process had been painless. All she had to do was sit with some ointment over the injured area for fifteen minutes, and she couldn't feel a thing as the doctor did his magic.

After explaining the stitches could come out in five to seven days and that she might have a small scar, the nurse had me fill out some paperwork, then we were on our way.

Still shaken from the events of the day, I sat for a minute behind the wheel of my car before starting it up. Closing my eyes, I took a few deep breaths.

"Where's Colton? I want to talk to him." Ava's words came out sounding a little off because a good portion of her mouth was still numb.

I frowned when I looked at my phone to see no missed calls or texts.

Forcing a smile, I glanced back at her. "I don't know, Bug. I'll try calling him again." This time it went straight to voicemail, but I didn't want to leave another message so I hung up. "He must be busy," I told her, my voice rising an octave as a feeling of irrational panic squeezed my chest.

Colton would never ignore me on purpose.

But that wasn't quite true, was it?

Old feelings resurfaced as I remembered all the afternoons I spent staring at my mailbox and the disappointment that followed every time I sorted through the envelopes.

It was well into the afternoon now, and even though Colton was on the road he should've stopped and gotten my messages.

The rational part of me knew he would call back when he could, but that didn't stop me from mentally flipping the fuck out.

By the time we walked through the front door, Ava was running to the bathroom to inspect the badge of courage on her face, and I was in the middle of a mind-fuck of my own creation.

I called again. Straight to voicemail—again. I left a message this time.

"Hey, we're back from the hospital now." I paused awkwardly. "It's not like you to not call me back... Please call me back? Bye."

When dinner time came and I still hadn't heard from him, I officially felt like I had crossed over into 'crazy girlfriend' mode. I'd sent a couple of texts, basically saying the same things I did in the voicemails, and checked my phone about every five minutes.

My dad could tell I was having a hard time, but he didn't pry, which I appreciated. When he offered to put Ava to bed for me, I got the feeling he felt guilty because she got hurt under his watch.

"You know it's not your fault, right? Kids get hurt," I told him as I helped load the dishwasher.

"Oh, I know. You forget this ain't my first rodeo," he said in a bad accent while miming throwing a lasso.

It made me smile a little. "You're such a goofball, Dad."

His face got serious. "It's been a long day. I can tell you need a break," he made a shooing motion with his hand. "I've got this."

"Thank you," I breathed out before drying my hands and heading to the living room to find Ava watching *Tangled*. "Hey, Bug." I sat next to her on the couch. "How you feeling?"

"Good," she replied cheerfully, and I smiled at her ability to be unaffected by what could have been a traumatic day.

"Grandpa wants to put you to bed tonight. Is that okay with you?"

"Of course! Do I get to stay up yate?" she asked, jumping to the floor and doing a ballerina twirl.

I pinched my fingers together. "A little bit late." Leaning down, I kissed her cheek. "Goodnight, baby."

After leaving another pathetic voicemail on Colton's phone, I went to the bathroom and was relieved when I saw the smear of red on the toilet paper. Even though the tests confirmed I wasn't pregnant, it was still good to see the evidence.

I put on some black leggings and a gray hoodie, then I went to the closet to get the memory box.

I was looking for something specific.

My fingers closed around the faded, somewhat wrinkled picture.

Holding it up, I studied it. A six-year-old Colton and I stood together, arms looped around each other as I proudly displayed a mason jar full of lightning bugs we had caught. Colton was grinning at the camera, but my face was turned, smiling at him like he'd hung the moon.

Was this an honest representation of us?

I remembered hearing someone say that in every relationship, there was a 'reacher' and a 'settler'. I couldn't help feeling like I was the former. I wasn't even close to being at Colton's level, which meant he was settling for a life with me.

Instead of romantic dates, he settled for coming to watch me work at Caged. Instead of adult conversation or hot phone sex, he settled for watching me read bedtime stories to Ava.

He had his shit together. A career he loved. His own apartment.

In comparison, my life was a hot mess.

What if he changed his mind about us? How long would it take for him to realize he was getting the shitty end of the deal?

Clutching the picture in my hand I collapsed into my bed, feeling exhausted, confused, and overwhelmed.

I checked my phone one more time. Still nothing from Colton.

Then the emotional dam broke and I cried.

CHAPTER 38

Colton

s I finished up the delivery, I still couldn't get my mind off things with Ellie. I pulled the semi over at a rest stop just before the Missouri state line to check my phone. No texts, no missed calls.

It made me worry. Even when I was off on a haul, I usually heard from her.

I tried to bring up her number to call, but something was wrong with the screen. It was frozen. I turned it off then started it back up, thinking that would help. No such luck. In fact, the screen started flashing at me and I had no idea what that meant.

However, it was clear that my phone had finally met its untimely death.

New battery my ass.

When I finally made it back to Champaign that evening, I stopped at Best Buy and went through the process of getting a new phone. It took for-fucking-ever, but luckily they were able to recover all my pictures, videos, and even the missed voice-mails and texts from the day. I checked them as soon as I got back out to the semi.

Hearing Ellie's panicked voice as I listened to her messages had my heart hammering in my chest and, suddenly, I felt like I couldn't breathe.

Ava had to go to the hospital?

It'd been a long time since I'd experienced real fear. The thought of Ava scared and in pain had me afraid. Terrified.

After starting up the truck, I drove straight to Ellie's house. I pulled the rig up out front and noted that all the lights inside were off. It was almost 10pm, so it wouldn't surprise me if everyone was asleep.

Still, I needed to talk to Ellie and make sure Ava was okay.

I dialed her number and after it rang several times, I almost thought she wasn't going to pick up.

"Hello?" she answered, sounding sleepy.

"Hey. Sorry. I didn't mean to wake you up. I got your messages. Is everything okay?"

"Um, yeah." I heard rustling like she was sitting up in bed. "Ava had to go to the hospital—"

"Yeah, I know," interrupted impatiently. "Can you come down to talk?"

"You're here?" she asked, sounding surprised and much more alert.

"I'm outside," I told her as I hopped down from the truck. "Can you meet me on the porch?"

"I'll be there in a minute." She hung up and I waited, hopping up and down to warm myself from the cold night air.

When Ellie came out, she was bundled up in a gray oversized hoodie and her hair was thrown up into a messy bun. Those rainbow socks were pulled up to her knees. Her eyes were red-rimmed. She'd been crying.

I wanted to go to her—hold her and tell her everything would be okay—but everything about her body language was closed off. She wrapped her arms around herself and stood firmly planted by the door.

I broke the silence first. "What happened?"

"Ava tripped and hit her face on the coffee table," she told me, rubbing her hands up and down her arms in an attempt to stay warm. "Her teeth went through her lip and she had to have stitches."

I made a sound of frustration because I wasn't here when she'd needed me. "I'm sorry. My phone died. Like, really died. I had to go get a new one." I held up the phone, inwardly cursing at the one that let me down. "I got your messages and I came straight here. Is Ava okay?"

"Yeah, she's okay now. She was amazing at the ER. I just let her watch cartoons on my phone while they sewed her up and she didn't move an inch."

I smiled, feeling proud. "She's brave," I said, then I noticed how tired Ellie looked. She didn't just look exhausted, though. She looked beat-down. Sad. "Are you okay?"

"It's just been a really hard day." Her voice cracked, and it sounded like she was going to cry.

"Hey," I said softly, moving forward and wrapping my arms around her. "Everything's okay now."

For a second she melted into me, laying her head on my chest. Her face rested in the hollow of my neck and she inhaled, running the tip of her nose over my skin. Her fingers curled into my shirt and she clung to me like she was trying to soak up all the warmth and comfort she could.

Then she pulled away and took a step back, putting distance between us.

"I don't feel okay." She rubbed at the skin on her thumb and even in the darkness, I could see the red, angry-looking blister she'd created.

A bad feeling came over me. "Why?"

She shook her head and sighed. "I think we need to talk, Colton."

"Don't," I pleaded, already knowing where this conversation was headed. "Don't do to this to me. Don't do this to us."

"We just really rushed into things. Maybe it was a bad idea for us to get romantically involved."

I barked out a humorless laugh. "Too fucking late. Give me one good reason that we shouldn't be together."

"I can give you several reasons. One, I'm not good enough for you," she stated, and I could tell she really believed that.

"That's bullshit," I grunted. "How can you say that?"

"This relationship started because I lied to you."

"We forgave each other, remember? You forgave me because I stopped writing and I forgave you for lying. I'm not gonna hold that over your head—that's how forgiveness works," I told her. "And I don't care how it started. We're together now. That's what matters."

"Sometimes I'm selfish," she said, continuing the list of complete nonsense. "And when you didn't answer the phone today... I kind of freaked." She grimaced. "I guess I didn't realize until recently how deep my trust issues went—how messed up in the head I am. I mean, I went bat-shit. I think I left you, like, four voicemails."

"Six," I corrected her, and she made an exasperated sound as her hands flew up to her face.

"Oh, my God," she breathed out, obviously embarrassed by the excessive messages. "You deserve to be with someone who trusts you. I'm too needy."

Counting off on my fingers, I began my rebuttal. "You don't trust me? I haven't given you any reason not to. You're a stage-five clinger? Bring it on. I don't want you to change. You think you're selfish? Well, sometimes I'm bossy as fuck. We all have our faults, Ellie."

"I come with a lot of baggage. You're basically dating a single-mom-stripper. I'm a real winner," she said with a huff, and seeing Ellie tear herself down like that was starting to piss me off.

"Let's get one thing straight—Ava is not baggage. I would never see her like that," I said, my hand slashing through the air as the anger I was trying to contain came to the surface. I knew the things that asshole said to her the other day got under her skin, and I would say whatever I could to erase it. "You're beautiful. You make me laugh. You make me happy." I ran a hand over my head in frustration. "And, for the record, I don't give a fuck about your job. Hell, that's how we got together in the first place."

I looked at Ellie, arms crossed over her chest and a stubborn glint in her eyes. I wasn't sure what else I could say to get through to her. We stared at each other for a few seconds before she spoke again.

"You haven't done anything wrong," she said quietly, hanging her head. "This isn't your issue, Colton. It's mine."

"It's not you, it's me?" I asked with disbelief. "Are you seriously using that line on me right now?" With my hands on my hips, I let out a humorless laugh. "What's next? You'll tell me you think we should still be friends?"

"I do want to keep being friends…" she said weakly, and I scoffed.

"It's not a bad thing to need someone as long as they're willing to be there for you. I'm here," I said vehemently, spreading my arms wide. "Be selfish. Be needy. Be bat-shit crazy. Whatever you are, I'll still want you."

She made a frustrated noise and turned away from me. "I thought I could do this. I thought I could be with you, but I can't."

"Where is this coming from?" I asked, knowing there was something she wasn't telling me. "I'm so fucking confused right now. All these excuses you're giving me? I'm not buying it. What's this really about, Ellie?"

She took a deep breath and I knew she was preparing to

tell me the real reason for whatever the hell was happening right now.

"I started my period today," she said, and the random statement caught me off-guard. I raised my eyebrows, because that was the last thing I expected her to say. Was this some kind of raging episode of PMS? Ellie turned to face me and she continued. "I know that might seem like a weird thing to tell you. But I was four days late and I thought I was pregnant."

I stood there stunned and speechless, because the image of her with a swollen belly—a belly that held my child— flashed through my mind. And I wanted that. I wanted that more than I'd ever wanted anything.

Suddenly, it made sense why she was losing it. As I looked at Ellie, I saw the fear in her eyes and I knew the reason why she was so scared.

"I'm not an asshole," I told her, my voice raspy from emotion. "I would never leave you the way he did. You deserve happiness and I want to be the one to give it to you."

"And you deserve to be with someone who believes you," she said in a whisper and looked up at me with tears in her eyes.

Seconds of silence ticked by, neither of us knowing what to say.

"What do you want?" I asked, feeling helpless. "I don't know what else I can do."

Tears spilled down her cheeks. "I just need some time to think. Maybe we should take a break."

Oh, hell no. She'd just pulled out every excuse and cliché in the book. Those words guaranteed a swift death to any relationship. Not gonna happen.

"I'm not letting you break up with me," I said stubbornly. "You know that Seinfeld episode where the woman refuses to let George end their relationship? Well, this is kind of like that."

Ellie's face scrunched up in confusion, causing a tear to glide to the side of her nose. "What do you mean you're not letting me break up with you?"

I stepped forward until I had her pinned against the side of the house. "I love you and I'm not letting you go."

Another tear fell. "It doesn't work like that."

"It does for me. I'll give you some space. Give you a few days to think about it. But just know that this isn't over."

Using my thumbs, I wiped away the wetness on her face before gently pressing my mouth to her trembling lips.

Pushing away from the blue siding I backed away from Ellie, hating the way we were leaving things up in the air. I turned to walk away but stopped.

Looking over my shoulder, I had one last thing to say. "Tell Ava I'm proud of her for being brave today."

Snow started to fall as I made my way across the front lawn, and my heart actually hurt. It felt like someone took a sledge hammer to my chest. I took deep breath, trying to relieve the tightness around my ribcage.

"Colton, wait," Ellie sobbed and I stopped. "Three…"

I whipped back around. "Fuck that, Ellie. I'm not saying goodbye to you."

"Three," she insisted with a huff, stomping a rainbow-colored foot. More tears fell down her face and it was killing me to see her so upset.

"We'll say goodnight," I compromised, because I could see she was hanging by a thread, "but I'm not saying bye. Okay?" I asked and she nodded. "Two."

"One," she whispered.

"Goodnight," we both said quietly.

And then I walked away.

CHAPTER 39

Brielle

T he next few days kept me busy. Between work, classes, and taking care of Ava, I didn't have time to think about much else. And I was thankful for that.

Unfortunately, *thinking* was exactly what I was supposed to be doing. That was the whole point of telling Colton we needed to take a step back from our relationship, but every time I pictured my life without him in it, it was too painful to bear.

During work, I got lost in the music. At class I buried myself in papers and tests. And at home, I soaked up every snuggle, hug, and 'I love you.'

Nighttime was the hardest. In those quiet minutes before I slipped into sleep, my thoughts and feelings wanted to take over. I did my best to push them away.

Staying true to his word, Colton gave me space. I was both relieved and disappointed by that. Even though I didn't hear from him all day, each night I couldn't resist sending him a goodnight text. And he always responded.

Through a blur of tears, I typed out the message on the glowing screen.

Me: Three
Colton: Two

Me: One
Colton: Goodnight
Me: Goodnight

CHAPTER 40

Colton

Bright sunlight came through the open window and the white curtains blew in the steady breeze. A butterfly flew into the room, fluttering around before it decided to land on the bouquet of daisies on the nightstand.

"Don't you just love butterflies?" Mom said softly as she stared at the orange and black pattern on its wings.

"Yeah." I nodded. "I really do."

I didn't have to look around to know where I was, but my eyes wandered over the room anyway. Wooden desk shoved into the corner. Hospital bed on the far right wall. And my mom—fragile and weak, with bright blue eyes.

In the back of my mind I knew this was a dream, but I didn't want to wake up.

Not yet.

"Come on over, baby." Mom patted the place beside her. "What's got you looking so down?"

I closed the distance to the bed and, when I sat down, I realized I wasn't a kid in this dream—my body barely fit on the edge of the mattress. As I glanced down, I realized I was wearing my auto shop coveralls.

Meeting my mom's eyes again, I realized she was still waiting for my answer.

"Girl troubles," I told her with a half-smile and a shrug.

"Ah," she said, nodding her head in understanding. "Brielle beat you at thumb war again, huh?"

Being careful not to jar the IV, I covered her hand with mine and gave her a rueful smile. "It's a little more complicated than that."

"The most popular relationship cliché in history." She smirked, adjusting the pink stocking cap on her head.

I shrugged, not knowing where to start or how to explain. "I'm in love. It's not just Ellie, though. I've got two girls who own me right now."

"A love triangle? That sounds scandalous," she teased. "I thought you were a one-woman kind of guy."

"I am." I huffed out a laugh. "Ava is Ellie's daughter. She's so awesome, Mom. You'd love her."

Reaching out, she ran her hand over my short hair. "My handsome boy. All grown up. What you and Brielle have is special," she said, repeating the words she'd said in this dream so many times before. "Something really extraordinary."

I smiled, finally understanding what she meant. She knew all along that Ellie and I would end up together. "Tell me what to do. Tell me how to fix it."

"Don't ever give up on something just because it's hard." She sighed as another spring breeze came through the window. "I think I could use a nap. Would you like to lie down with me? I haven't had my little-man cuddles yet today."

This wasn't how the dream was supposed to go. She was supposed to give me advice, tell me the meaning of life. I wanted to keep asking questions, keep pressing for answers.

But she looked tired so I just nodded, deciding to take comfort in my mom for as long as I could.

When I swung my legs up onto the bed, I realized I was six years old again. Being smaller allowed me to lie next to her, and I rested my head on her stomach.

"And she loved a little boy very much..." Trailing off, she

struggled to take a breath. "Even more than she loved herself."

I recognized the paraphrased line. It was from 'The Giving Tree'
by Shel Silverstein, Mom's favorite children's book.

"I love you, too, Mom," I whispered against her soft floral
nightgown.

Waking up with a start, realization hit me hard and fast.
That was it—those were the words I never got to hear her say
in the dream, the words I couldn't remember. They weren't
profound or life-changing. It had nothing to do with my current predicament.

She was simply telling me that she loved me.

And it was enough. After all these years, it felt so good
to finally remember some of my mom's last words. While it
made me happy, I'd never missed her more than I did right
now.

Sighing, I checked my phone, hoping to see something
from Ellie, but there was nothing new.

Ellie: Goodnight

I stared at her last text, fighting the emotions warring inside my body. Throughout the day, I had to physically restrain
myself from calling her, texting her, going to her.

And now, I wanted nothing more than to hear her voice.
My thumb hovered over the call button for a few seconds, but
I decided against it. Waking her up in the middle of the night
wasn't going to do me any favors, and I needed all the help I
could get.

I was serious when I told her I refused to let her go.

Ellie was it for me.

Every single part of my body recognized her as my other
half. My mind. My heart. Hell, even my dick.

I rubbed at my sternum, trying to ease the hollow ache in

my chest as I thought about the other night.

The fact that Ellie thought she wasn't good enough for me blew my mind. She'd given me the longest list of break-up reasons ever, and all of them were complete bullshit. Well, all except the pregnancy thing. Given her past experience, her fear about that was legit.

I hated that she was so scared, that life taught her to be this way. Even more, I hated the fact that I had anything to do with it in the first place. I couldn't change the past, couldn't take back what happened when we were kids.

Childhood-Ellie had been fearless. I never would've admitted it to her then, but she was way braver than me.

Trying to stay optimistic, I told myself that maybe tomorrow would be the day she changed her mind.

I exited my texts, and the little coloring book apps stared back at me. On a whim, I went to my pictures. I had no idea what made me do it—I never used my camera—but what I saw had me grinning. Apparently, Ava had figured out how to use it.

Selfies. Dozens of them.

Smiling. Tongue sticking out. Fish face.

I could see the straps of the car seat over her shoulders and I recognized the blue Disney shirt she had on. It was the same shirt she'd been wearing the day we went to Indiana. Apparently, she'd been taking pictures instead of coloring.

No wonder she was so quiet back there.

Swiping my finger across the screen, I went from one to the next. Some of them were off-center. A close-up of her eye. A mass of light brown hair.

Then she flipped the camera around. Pink and white Velcro shoes. The door handle. A car next to us on the highway.

I was smiling so wide my face hurt. I loved seeing the world through Ava's eyes.

The last picture made my heart skip a beat. It was a perfect shot of Ellie and me in the front seat. Our heads were turned toward each other, and genuine smiles lit up our profiles as we locked eyes for that second in time. Between us, our hands were clasped together over the middle console.

Maybe giving her space wasn't the best thing to do. As much as Ellie claimed to be annoyed by how pushy I was, sometimes I thought it was one of the things she loved the most.

Blowing out a sigh, I set my background to one of Ava's silly selfies.

Then, I tried to formulate a new plan.

CHAPTER 41

Brielle

J ust as I stuck four candles on the rectangular vanilla-frosted cake, the doorbell rang, causing the tune of 'Happy Birthday' to ring through the house. Ava ran past me but stopped short when she reached for the doorknob.

"Can I open it?" she asked excitedly.

"Go ahead," I told her. It was her party, after all.

Chloe was on the other side, a big purple bag in one hand and a bouquet of balloons in the other. "Hey, birthday girl!"

"Um, actually, I'm not a birthday girl. I'm a Band-aid girl." Ava laughed maniacally and held up her thumb. "Yeah, because I'm wearing a Band-aid! See?"

"What kind is that?" Chloe humored her by inspecting the bandage. "Is that Belle? She's my favorite princess."

"You wanna come see my toys?" Ava jumped up and down before grabbing Chloe's hand and dragging her toward the stairs.

Chloe gave me a quick hug before being pulled away.

"I guess I'm going to Ava's room now." She laughed.

"Okay. Don't stay up there too long, Bug. You don't want to miss cake and presents."

"Okaaaay," Ava sang, then started chattering to Chloe about Barbies.

Before I could close the door, I saw a familiar blue truck

pull up onto the street in front of the house.

Crap.

My heart started to pound because I hadn't expected to see Colton today. Immediately, I straightened my ponytail and started to smooth some messy strands away from my face.

I walked across the lawn, meeting him at the curb. He held a Spider-Man bag with pink tissue paper coming out the top.

As I took in the sight of Colton, I tried to rein in my out-of-control libido. How was it possible for someone to look so good in worn jeans and a simple gray button-up?

"What are you doing here?" I asked, breathless from surprise.

"I'm here for the party," he said curtly. He lifted the present up and I couldn't read his expression. I wasn't used to him being closed off from me and I didn't like it.

"I just thought since…" I trailed off, and he finished the sentence for me.

"You thought since we were taking a 'break' I wouldn't come," he said, putting air quotes around the word *break*.

I shrugged. "Well, yeah."

"No offense, but I'm not here for you. I promised Ava I'd come to her party. You might not trust me to follow through, but *she* does."

Ouch. Double ouch. I guess I deserved that.

Taking out his wallet, Colton pulled out a small yellow piece of paper and unfolded it. Something squeezed inside my chest when I saw that he'd kept the little drawing Ava made him.

"You can't kick me out. I have a personal invite from the birthday girl herself." He held out the picture, then slipped it back into his wallet.

He started walking toward the house and the distance both literally and figuratively was killing me. "Colton."

When he turned back, the look in his eyes almost broke me. He looked so defeated. The Colton I knew didn't accept defeat, and I hated myself for being the one to put that look on his face.

"I promise to stay out of your way," he said softly and disappeared into the house, leaving me on the front lawn trying desperately to get my emotions together.

I needed to suck it up. This was Ava's special day and I refused to let my love-life drama ruin it.

CHAPTER 42

Colton

Today wasn't going as planned. I didn't know what I'd been expecting, but it wasn't the cold greeting Ellie gave me. Part of me had hoped she would take one look at me and throw herself into my arms.

Not even close.

She'd been surprised that I even showed up. Ellie wasn't kidding about having trust issues. The fact that she thought I wouldn't come to Ava's birthday party? That stung.

But I wasn't going to let that deter me. I told Ellie I wanted all of her, and I meant it.

At least Ava was having a great time. The party was in full swing and I could hear her giggles floating through the air in the backyard. The weather was unseasonably warm at almost seventy degrees, so Dave decided to grill out. Half of the people in attendance were outside on the deck.

Angel's friend, Ernie, was there wowing the guests with his balloon animal skills. Everyone clapped as he twisted two blue balloons together and made an elephant. I didn't know the old man well, but I was glad he was willing to come to the party today.

As he smiled down at a cheering Ava, the wrinkles in his weathered face deepened. Removing his ball cap, he took a bow. Obviously, he was having just as much fun as everyone else.

I felt a little out of place sitting off to the side in a lawn chair—not because I didn't know anyone, but because I felt like the outsider.

If Ellie and I weren't together anymore, what did that make me? The creepy guy who wouldn't quit coming around?

A throat cleared next to me and glanced up to see Ellie's friend, Chloe. Memories of Travis's birthday at Caged were fuzzy, but I still recognized her.

"Chloe. Good to see you again," I told her, leaning back in the chair.

"So you remember me, huh?" She smirked.

"Hey, I wasn't that drunk the night I met you," I claimed, and she raised a skeptical eyebrow. I huffed out a laugh. "Okay. Maybe I was that drunk. Even if I hadn't met you before, I'd still know who you are. Ellie talks about you all the time."

"Ellie," she said, a small smile on her lips. "You know you're the only one who calls her that?"

I nodded. "Called her that since we were kids."

"I'll be honest with you right now. That night... I've never seen her so happy. I'm gonna give you some advice," she said quietly as she adjusted the sunglasses on her face. She moved over to a nearby tree, putting her back to me and fiddling with the branches.

I found it highly amusing that she was trying to act all covert about our conversation.

I cracked a smile. "I'm all ears. I could definitely use some advice right now."

Sighing, she glanced at me over her shoulder. "Bree's had a rough time when it comes to dating. I guess I probably don't need to tell you that." She turned back to the tree but I could still hear her. "Just don't give up on my girl, okay?"

"Okay," I agreed, even though I felt like I was running out

of options.

"And if you tell her I said this, and I will hunt you down," she warned, her voice low. "but I'm on your side. Hashtag team Colton." She gave a little fist pump and I chuckled.

"Thanks," I told her. "I appreciate that."

"Now if you'll excuse me, I need to go talk some sense into my friend."

I watched Chloe go back up to the house, then I gazed at the windows, hoping to catch a glimpse of Ellie—I knew the second-story window closest to me belonged to her bedroom. Shaking my head, I mentally scolded myself for being such a creep. I was one step away from being a Peeping Tom.

That self-deprecating thought vanished as I caught a flash of a pink tutu and wild brown hair.

Ava came barreling toward me, fairy wand in one hand and a red balloon animal in the other. Opening my arms wide, I caught her as she jumped into my lap.

"You having a fun party?" I asked, even though I knew the answer was yes.

"Of course!" she said, then pointed to her face. "See my stitches? See??"

Inspecting the black threads under her lip, I made a sound like I was impressed. "They did a great job and I heard you were really brave."

She nodded, then looked at me for long seconds. Her eyes roamed my face as she twisted her mouth to the side, and I started to feel a little uncomfortable. It kind of felt like she was peering into my soul, like she was able to see something I was desperately trying to hide.

Finally, after she seemed done with her assessment, she spoke. "Are you frustrated?"

I shook my head a little. "No, not frustrated."

"Are you sad?"

Damn. Maybe she really could see into my soul. I didn't want to lie to her, so I just decided to be honest.

"Yeah. I guess I am," I replied.

Ava picked up my hand, placed a kiss on my palm, then looked up at me with teary eyes and a shaky smile. "There. I gave you a kiss. Now you can be so happy?"

Well, shit.

Although Ellie had warned me about Ava's sensitivity to other people's feelings, this was the first time I'd seen her react that way on my behalf.

If my heart hadn't been broken before, it definitely was now.

But instead of admitting that, I smiled and lied through my teeth. "Yep. Now I can be so happy."

As she snuggled deeper into my arms, I realized Dave was finished grilling and everyone had gone inside to eat. I didn't want my time with Ava to end yet, so I made no move to get up.

I had no idea what would happen after today.

As much as I wanted her to be, Ava wasn't mine. When would I get to see her again? If Ellie didn't want me in their lives anymore, there wasn't anything I could do about it.

The thought of losing not one, but two people I loved gave me a tight, unfamiliar feeling in my throat. I swallowed hard.

Then I felt Ava's little hand come up by the side of my face. When her fingers closed around my earlobe, I sucked in a breath and tried not to move.

It was the butterfly moment all over again.

She only did the ear thing to special people—people she loved and had a bond with. The fact that she was doing this with me? I never thought I could feel so happy and so devastated at the same time.

As her thumb slowly rubbed back and forth, my heart cracked open and I did something I hadn't done since my mother died—I cried.

A lone tear glided down my right cheek as I blinked quickly, trying to get my eyes to dry up before anyone could witness it.

Oblivious to my emotional meltdown, Ava sighed wistfully. "I yuv you sixty-seven pounds."

The first tear that fell was quickly followed by another, and I discreetly wiped them away and cleared my throat. "I love you, too, Bug."

Gazing out at the backyard, we sat that way for several minutes while I regained my composure. I knew it was time for me to leave. This was a happy occasion and I didn't want to bring anyone down.

Squeezing Ava one more time, I put her back on the ground as I stood up. I bent down to plant a kiss on the top of her strawberry-scented head.

"I bet there's cake inside. You'd better get in there before it's all gone," I told her, doing my best to sound upbeat.

She gasped dramatically and ran up to the house, motivated by the threat that everyone might eat all the cake without her. I watched her disappear into the house.

Reaching into the pocket of my jeans, I palmed the keys to my truck. I had no reason to go back inside. No reason to stay. I'd already left Ava's gift—a My Little Pony house—amongst the other presents on the dining room table. I would've liked to watch her open it, but it was better this way.

For the second time in a week, I forced myself to walk away from the girls who owned my heart.

CHAPTER 43

Brielle

My dad came through the sliding glass door with a giant platter of hotdogs and hamburgers.

"Lunch is ready," he announced, putting the food down on the kitchen island between the potato salad and baked beans.

Setting up the spread buffet-style, I placed a stack of paper plates and plastic silverware at the end next to the buns.

Everyone started crowding around the food, and Aunt Tess literally started smacking her lips as she eyed the potato salad, so I moved out of the way. No one got between Aunt Tess and her potato salad.

I found my mom standing by the window in the dining room, watching something through the glass.

"What's going on?" I asked, joining her.

"That boy," she started, pointing out at Colton who had Ava on his lap. "He's a keeper."

I swallowed around the lump in my throat. She knew our relationship wasn't on solid ground right now, but I hadn't clued her in on the details.

"I know," I whispered.

Because she was right. He was the keeper. I just wasn't so sure about myself.

As if she read my mind she turned to me, her expression

soft. "And so are you." Leaving my side, she patted me on the shoulder. "Aunt Tess is liable to eat up all the potato salad," she muttered quietly, causing me to smile. "Don't take too long to get in line."

Nodding, I went back to watching Colton and Ava. Just then, her hand came up to the side of his head and her fingers started rubbing at his ear.

Gasping, my hands flew up to my face and my heart jumped in my chest. I'd never seen her do that to anyone but my dad and me.

I knew that meant she loved Colton. That she felt safe with him. He was right—Ava did trust him to follow through.

So why couldn't I?

CHAPTER 44

Colton

Like always, Monday morning was slow at the shop. Usually, working on cars made me feel calm and content. But that wasn't how I felt right now.

Around noon, my dad told me he was closing up early and I could take off once I got my tools cleaned up. Maybe he could tell I was having a hard time. I hadn't told him much about what was going on with Ellie—just that we were taking some time apart. The sympathetic look in his eyes told me I wasn't doing a very good job of hiding my feelings.

After I got off work I walked home, looking forward to popping open a beer and wallowing in self-pity once again. I had come full-circle from the day before my birthday.

Frustrated. Defeated. Discouraged. I hated having a problem with no solution in sight.

Unfortunately, when I opened the fridge, there was no beer to be found.

Closing the door, I stood up and found myself face to face with Ava's cardboard drawing. I had it taped to the front of the freezer door, proud to display my gift.

Sadness weighed down on me as I looked at the stick figures she'd drawn with red and black crayon. Ava barely knew me at the time, but she'd included me in her picture.

Suddenly, I felt like I couldn't be here. I couldn't sit around feeling sorry for myself in my apartment.

So I did something I'd never done before—I walked across the street to the tavern for a drink. Alone.

Since it was just past 1:00 in the afternoon, the place was pretty empty. I chose a seat in front of the bar and ordered a Coors Light. A throat cleared next to me and I saw Champ sitting two stools away, peering down at the glass of brown liquor in his hand.

"Hey, Champ."

"Hey, Colton," he replied without looking up. A minute of silence stretched between us before he spoke again. "Love troubles?"

I let out a snort. "Actually, yeah. How'd you guess?"

He smiled a little. "Young men, such as yourself, don't come here alone during the day unless there's trouble in paradise."

No one really knew Champ's story, and I wondered if he was speaking from personal experience. He'd been labeled the town drunk for years. Everyone loved him but no one took him seriously.

"It's complicated," I said, cringing at how lame that sounded.

"It always is." He swirled the glass in his hand before finishing it off.

The bartender must have known the routine well because he quickly replaced his empty glass with a full one. Champ nodded his thanks before turning slightly in his seat to face me.

"Did I ever tell you about Larry?"

I smirked because I'd heard the name so many times, but I had no idea who he was. "Not directly, no."

"He was the love of my life," he stated, and my eyes widened in shock.

There was nothing wrong with being gay, but I was .

surprised he was coming right out and telling me that. Small-town people didn't always have open minds.

"It's a modern world," he said defensively, as if he knew my thought process. "And I'm too old to give a fuck what people think anymore."

I held my hands up.

"No judgement here," I told him honestly.

He seemed to believe me and nodded his head before continuing. "We fought like cats and dogs, but he was my person. Thirty years ago, things weren't so easy. Hiding our relationship was difficult. Things got tough and, instead of fighting through it, we gave up."

"I'm sorry," I said, understanding how hard it must have been for him.

He shrugged and tipped back his head, emptying the glass again. "I always thought we'd find a way back to each other, but he moved away. Then about a year after that, he went missing. Just *poof.*"

He made a wild hand gesture in the air and he almost fell off the barstool before catching himself. His slurred words came out nonchalant, like it didn't matter. But, of course, I knew better.

"I'm sorry," I apologized again, not knowing what else to say.

"He ended up on one of those shows…" He trailed off like he was having trouble finishing his thought. I had no idea how much he'd had to drink but his inability to pronounce words correctly suggested it was a lot. Snapping his fingers, he turned to me. "Unsolved missing persons. I think it was something like that." Staring down at his empty glass, he started sliding it from one palm to the other, like he needed something to do with his hands. "I like to think he's living it up on a beach somewhere, sipping on a Piña colada with his toes in the sand. But sometimes... Sometimes I let myself believe he might come back to me someday."

Champ's story was really fucking sad. Now I felt bad for finding his midnight rantings amusing. He wasn't crazy—he was heartbroken. Although, I guess sometimes the two went hand in hand.

I lifted my beer to take a drink.

He glanced over at me with bloodshot eyes. "If you want my advice? Don't ever give up on something just because it's hard."

My head turned to look at him so quickly I thought I heard something crack in my neck. He'd just said the exact same words my mom always said in my dream. That couldn't be a coincidence.

"Thanks, Champ," I said, hopping down off the stool and abandoning my drink.

I needed to get to Ellie. Make her listen to me. Make her realize I wasn't giving up.

But first, I had to make a stop and talk to the guy with all the wisdom.

∿

"I need some advice," I told my dad as I sat down on his couch, not bothering with small talk. "Relationship advice."

"The squeaky wheel gets the grease," he spouted off one of his wise sayings, leaning back in the recliner.

My lips tipped up because he was ridiculous. "That doesn't exactly apply to the situation, Dad."

"Measure twice, cut once?"

Still smiling, I shook my head. "Still not working. I don't understand a lot about women, but I know Ellie's scared. She's afraid I won't stick around, just like her asshole ex."

His face lit up as he thought of the next line. "You're damned if you do and you're damned if you don't."

I chuckled. "Okay, you might be getting warmer with that one. But seriously. I don't know what else I can do to show Ellie that I'm in this, that she can trust me."

Pausing, something a lot like regret filled his eyes. "I think I need to apologize to you, son. I'm sorry I didn't help you stay in touch with Brielle."

"It's not your fault, Dad. I'm the one who decided to stop writing to her."

"I'm the parent. You were just a kid. It was my responsibility to help you keep the friendship going. I could've driven you there. I could've encouraged you to call her." He sighed and looked away. "I have a confession to make."

"What confession?" I asked, confused.

"Brielle's parents called a couple times after we moved... She wanted to talk to you but I told them you weren't home. I didn't lie about that—you really were out and about, probably raising hell with Travis, but I didn't tell you to call her back on purpose." I stared at him, speechless. But he wasn't finished. "That's not all. The spring after we moved... They called me again. Brielle wanted to see you and they offered to drive her here for a day." He took a breath, as if what he was about to say was difficult. "I asked them not to. I told them not to come."

"What?" My voice came out in a harsh whisper. "Why?"

"After we moved, I was happier. I felt better here. New town. New house. New friends. And you seemed happy, too. To tell you the truth, I wanted to cut all ties to the life we had before," he said, staring down at his clasped hands. "Your mother would've been so disappointed in me."

"Dad," I said, feeling shocked and betrayed.

"I made a bad judgment call, based on my own selfish reasons. I've felt guilty about it for a long time. I'm so sorry, son."

Both of us were quiet for a minute as my dad hung his head in shame. As I looked at him—my hero, the man who had provided for me, the man who beat the odds by building a successful business in this town—the feelings of betrayal were quickly replaced with empathy.

He'd lost his wife—his high school sweetheart, the woman he'd made a life with, the mother of his child. I couldn't imagine what it would be like go through that.

Looking over at the wall that displayed all our pictures, I took in the sight of the life he'd given me. Camping trips. Fishing at Elmer Lake. Blowing out ten candles on a birthday cake. Travis and me standing in front of the shop when we were teenagers, proudly wearing our new uniforms.

"You did the best you could. I really believe that," I told my dad, wanting him to know how grateful I was, regardless of his mistakes. "I'm not unhappy with the way things turned out. I just need to figure out how to get things back on track with Ellie."

Nodding, he scratched at his temple while he seemed lost in thought. "Well, I guess I'm pretty out of practice when it comes to love." He shrugged. "If your mom were still here, she'd know what to do."

"You're the most determined person I know," I told him. "You never give up and I admire that about you. I think I'm a lot like you. What is it you always say? The apple doesn't fall far from the tree?"

"You think I was always this way?" He huffed out a laugh and shook his head. "Absolutely not. Your mother gave me one hell of a talking to before she passed away. She could tell I was going to have trouble picking up the pieces after she was gone. Said I couldn't let you down like that. She taught me how to be driven to succeed. But you? You were born that way. You got that from her, not me. If you're the apple, then she was the tree."

"I didn't know that," I said quietly, feeling like I was seeing my dad through new eyes. When my mom died, I'd been too young to remember much about her other than how she made me feel—safe and loved. "I remember the smell of her cooking and that she used to cry when she read me that book *The Giving Tree*. Sunflowers were her favorite and she hated the smell of roses. She was the best mom. I guess she would've had to be to raise someone as stubborn as me."

Smirking at my dad, I noticed his eyes looked misty.

"Remember that time I said a swear word and she washed my mouth out with soap?" I asked, wanting to bring up a funny memory we could both laugh at. "That was some nasty shit, but I convinced her I liked the taste. Like it was some sort of treat or something. She never washed my mouth out again."

Dad guffawed. "That was quite the act you put on. I tried to tell her you were pulling her leg, but she was convinced you loved the taste of soap. You even went as far as asking for it after dinner for dessert."

We both laughed again, and it felt good to be able to talk about Mom this way.

"If I could convince Mom that I wanted to eat soap, there's gotta be a way to get Ellie to believe I won't leave her," I half-joked.

"You're going to need some kind of grand gesture, I suppose," he suggested. "Something to show her you want to be with her forever."

"Forever…" I trailed off as the best idea ever came to me. Standing abruptly, I grabbed my truck keys from my pocket and rushed toward the door. "You're a genius, Dad."

"I do what I can." He was chuckling as I closed the door behind me.

CHAPTER 45

Colton

E llie's ex hadn't been hard to track down. It was amazing what you could find out on the internet.

Joshua Harrington—originally from Hemswell, Illinois—was now a resident of Frankford, Indiana. In high school, he was the second-string quarterback, runner-up for homecoming king, and almost valedictorian of his graduating class.

That was the thing about Joshy-boy—everything about him was *almost.*

Just like he'd almost ended up with the hottest woman ever. Just like he'd almost been a father to the coolest little girl in the world.

He was the epitome of potential gone to waste.

Snickering from behind some bushes, I watched as that sack of shit tried to put out the flaming sack of shit that was currently beneath the soles of his fancy-ass Sperrys. He rapidly stomped his feet to put out the fire while choking on the foul-smelling smoke. It was safe to say his shoes were ruined.

That was confirmed when the whiny asshole practically shrieked, "Whoever did this, I'm going to find you! I just bought these shoes!" He angrily waved his fist in the air before going back to trying to scrape the burnt crap onto his front stoop. "Dammit," he muttered before giving up, kicking off the shoes, and going back inside his upscale townhouse.

Honestly, the trip to Frankford wasn't necessary, but I was pissed and needed to take it out on someone. Things with Ellie had been great until she ran into her ex. He'd made her sad, made her question her self-worth, made her have doubts about our relationship.

The fiery bag-o-poo prank was classic.

Was it original?

No.

Was it juvenile? Immature? Petty?

Yeah.

Was it worth the two-hour drive?

Hell yeah.

The prank hadn't been my original plan, though. At first, I'd wanted to confront him face to face. Have a nice little chat. Okay, maybe that wasn't quite true. Maybe I wanted to punch him in the face a few times.

But just as I had pulled up to the curb down the block, I saw him leave his house to go on a run with his Rottweiler. Not more than 20 feet away from my truck, the dog took a giant crap in the grass, and guess who didn't bother to pick it up?

That's right—Joshy-boy.

I just happened to have a paper bag and some matches in my truck.

Coincidence? Fate was more like it. The asshole was destined to meet a burning pile of shit on his doorstep.

All I had to do was wait for him to get back, then I made my move.

Since it was still daylight, I risked someone catching me in the act. No one stopped me, though. Either I wasn't spotted, or his neighbors thought he deserved it just as much as I did.

I stared at Josh's door for a few minutes, knowing how easy it would be to go up there and pound his face in. The motherfucker deserved it. My hands itched with the urge and I had to clench my fists to fight it off.

The only thing stopping me was Ellie. I knew it wasn't what she would want.

Plus, I wouldn't put it past the asshole to press charges and the last thing I needed was to get arrested.

I needed to keep my eyes on the prize.

Ellie and Ava.

After hopping back into my truck, I drove out of Frankford with a smile on my face.

~

Two hours later, I parked my truck in front of a house I never thought I'd see again. I knew things about this house that the current residents probably didn't. Like the fact that there was a dead cat named Tootles buried in the backyard. And in the attic there was a loose floorboard where hidden treasures used to be kept.

I took a deep breath as I made my way up to the white two-story house.

As I walked up the driveway, I searched the concrete pavement for what I knew I'd see. Kneeling down, I placed my hand over the much smaller handprint, noticing the massive size difference. Right next to my handprint was another— only that one belonged to Ellie.

Memories assaulted me as I stepped onto the familiar porch and knocked on the yellow front door. I could've sworn it used to be blue.

When it opened, a tall elderly man looked back at me.

"One of those handprints in your driveway is mine," I blurted out, awkwardly pointing over my shoulder.

He smiled a little, his laugh lines deepening. "Can we

help you?"

The door opened a little wider and a small old woman appeared at his side.

Another 'we' couple. It gave me hope that they might understand my predicament and take pity on me.

"Yes. Yes, you can. You don't know me, but I have a really huge favor to ask."

CHAPTER 46

Brielle

he morning after Ava's birthday I had a moment of clarity. All night long I had tossed and turned as memories of Colton flashed through my mind.

Happy memories. All the good times we'd had as kids. The way he'd barged into my life and refused to leave. His eagerness to include Ava and the bond they effortlessly formed. I thought about the hot nights we had together, the way he lit my body up like no one else could.

Also, Chloe had given me one hell of a talking to at Ava's party. When she pointed out that my concerns just sounded like a bunch of crappy excuses, I told her that Colton had said the same thing. I tried to find him to talk, but he'd already left.

As I rubbed my eyes, I picked up my phone to check the time and saw that I had a new text. When I opened it, I smiled.

Sometime in the middle of the night, Colton had sent me a picture. We were in my car and it was obvious Ava had taken it from the backseat. Colton and I were looking at each other, but it wasn't my face I was drawn to—it was his. The expression on his face while he looked at me took my breath away. So much love. Unmitigated happiness.

This. This was an honest representation of us.

When it came down to it, I wasn't scared of Colton. I was just afraid of history repeating itself. There was still a chance he could hurt me, but I decided to stop being a coward. I loved him enough to risk it.

The crippling fear and anxiety was gone. Now I felt peace.

And guilt. So much guilt for what I had put Colton through over the last week. I thought about calling him or sending a text, but it didn't seem good enough.

A simple apology over the phone wasn't going to cut it. Adequate groveling was in order. So, after making sure my parents could watch Ava this evening, I went to the store to get my groveling supplies.

~

On my way to Colton's apartment, I mentally rehearsed what I would say to him. There were only so many ways to apologize, and 'I'm sorry for basically ripping your heart out' didn't quite have the ring to it I was hoping for.

Suddenly, my thoughts were interrupted by a loud pop and my car started bouncing unevenly. Pulling over to the side of the road, I got out of the car to confirm my suspicions.

I looked down at the flat tire. It wasn't just flat—the rubber was completely shredded, as if the whole thing blew up.

"You've got to be kidding me," I muttered.

I'd never had a flat before. This was horrible timing. Of course, there was never a good time to get a blowout.

I was only 10 minutes outside of Tolson. I could call Colton and ask him to come help me, but that would ruin the surprise. Besides, I knew how to change a tire now, thanks to him.

Smiling, I imagined his smug face when I would have to admit that he was right—tire changing was a skill that came in handy.

After popping the trunk, I took out the spare tire and gathered the tools I would need, then set them down by my car.

As I dropped down to the ground, I cringed at how muddy it was on the side of the road. There was no getting around it—I was going to be a mess by the time I got done.

I went through all the steps, just like Colton taught me. Much to my surprise, three people stopped to offer their assistance during the process.

"Do you need us to call someone for you?"

"Want some help?"

"Do you need a ride?"

I politely declined all their offers, but now I could see why people loved Tolson so much. Everyone was so friendly.

I grew up in a small town, but in all those years I'd never had people offer to help me unless it was for their own personal gain. In Hemswell, no one offered to make balloon animals for a kid's birthday party, just because they loved doing it. People didn't stop to ask a stranger if they needed help on the side of the road.

In the past several weeks, I'd been shown what it was like to be accepted. To be loved. And I wanted it all—the man, the town, the friends. If I was being completely honest I wanted the balloon animals, too. I just needed to be brave enough to believe I could have it.

After twenty minutes and some unattractive grunting, I had successfully attached the spare to my car and I was back on the road.

Now I stood on Colton's doorstep with sweaty palms, a speeding heart rate, and muddy jeans. I adjusted the paper sack on my hip and when the door swung open, Angel's surprised face stared back at me. But then her surprise gave way to a big, genuine smile.

"Come in," she said, sounding excited to see me. "I didn't realize you were coming over."

"Well, I didn't really let Colton know." I shrugged. "I

thought I would surprise him."

"Oh." Angel's face fell and, for a second, I was afraid she was going to tell me he didn't want to see me. "Colton isn't home right now. But you can hang out and wait if you want."

I glanced at the clock on the stove and noted that it was after 5pm.

"I thought he would've been home by now," I said awkwardly as I started to doubt my plan.

Travis's voice came from the hallway as he appeared. "He usually is but he got off early today. Said he had something he needed to do but he should be home by this evening."

"Oh, okay." I tried to hide the disappointment in my voice. "Well, I can just come back later—"

"Don't be silly," Angel cut me off. "You can stick around until he gets back. Travis and I were supposed to go out tonight, but we can stay."

I shook my head, surprised that she would consider cancelling her plans to accommodate me. "I don't want to impose on your date. Really," I insisted.

Angel's face scrunched up as she thought for a second. "Well, I think you should wait for him. I know he'll be happy to see you."

"You think?" I asked, hopeful.

She nodded her head enthusiastically. "Definitely. Just make yourself at home."

Travis stepped up behind Angel.

"I'm pretty sure if I let you leave, Colton would kill me." He chuckled. "Since I enjoy living, I'm gonna have to insist."

Grinning, I set my bags down on the kitchen counter. "Okay."

After Travis and Angel said goodbye, I prepared dinner and lit a candle to set the mood. Then all I could do was wait.

CHAPTER 47

Colton

When I got home I toed off my boots, and the only source of light in the apartment was the dim glow from a candle on the table.

I flipped on the kitchen light. Two paper plates with sandwiches and Cheetos sat untouched, and I wondered if I'd interrupted one of Travis and Angel's romantic dinners.

"Hi." Ellie's soft voice startled me, and I turned to see her stand up from the couch, rubbing her eyes like she'd just woken up.

Immediately, I hid the object I was holding behind my back.

"Ellie," I breathed out, happy to see her, but also wondering what she was doing here. My curiosity would have to wait. "I have some things to say."

She shook her head. "Let me talk first."

"Nope," I argued. "If you're going to break things off with me for good, the least you can do is let me say my piece." I took a deep breath. "I know you. You're my best friend. Hell, we can even finish each other's sentences. I know what it's like to be loved by you, and it's so fucking awesome. I know you do that when you're anxious." I pointed down at the abused skin on her thumb. "But most of all, I know you're the person I want to be with. Always. I want a family with you, Ava included. You might think you're selfish, but what you've done with Ava? The way you've built your life around her… Ellie, you're the most selfless person I know. But if you need someone to be selfish with, let it be me." The last words left me in a raspy plea.

"I'm not breaking up with you," she said, her voice soft.

"Oh." I paused as pure happiness buzzed through my entire body. "Well, in that case, go ahead." I motioned for her to continue with my free hand, and the corners of her lips tipped up.

"So bossy," she teased, then her face got serious. "When we were kids I thought I was in love with you, and I still believe it was real. But the love I felt for you then is nothing compared to what I feel now." She took a breath. "One of my biggest fears is that I'll lose my best friend a second time. But if you want me, then you have me."

"I do want you," I said firmly. "I want you more than anything."

We moved toward each other, meeting in the middle of the living room. As she rose up on her toes to kiss me, her arms went around my waist and her hand grazed the object I was still holding behind my back.

Our faces inches apart, her eyes flew up to mine.

"What are you hiding?" she asked as she tried to peek around my body.

I turned so she couldn't see what it was. "It was supposed to be a surprise."

Her eyes lit up with interest as she tried to circle around me again. "What surprise?"

I huffed. "Well, I guess I might as well show you. I wanted to have it framed…" My words faded as I presented her with the block of old wood.

Ellie gasped as she took it from my hands. Trailing her

finger over the grooves in the surface, she traced the letters and the heart.

"Colt and Ellie forever," she whispered, her eyes wide. "How did you get this?"

I smirked. "Went to your old house. After I told them our story, they agreed to let me take the plank from their porch as long as I replaced it with a new one."

"I can't believe you did this," she said, smiling down at the 6-inch square. "Thank you, Colton. I love it." She stared at it for a few seconds, and when her eyes came up to mine, tears spilled over. "I'm so sorry."

"I hate it when you cry," I whispered as I wiped at her cheeks with my thumbs. "I'm not mad at you, Ellie. Just don't try to break up with me again. It won't work," I teased, even though I was completely serious. "And for the record… If you had been pregnant, I would've been the happiest guy in the world."

"Yeah?" she asked, a smile tugging at her lips.

"Yeah. Boy Scout's honor." I held up a hand.

She raised a skeptical brow. "Were you even a Boy Scout?"

"Fuck no." I laughed.

"I still can't believe you went all the way to Hemswell," she said, shaking her head.

"Well, I was kind of banking on the fact that you'd have to stay with me after a grand gesture like this. Six hours of driving and some manual labor goes a long way, right?"

"In this case, yes, it does." She beamed. Then her head cocked to the side and I could see her mind working, mentally calculating the driving time. "Wait. *Six* hours? Why were you driving for six hours?"

"I, ah… I went to pay your ex a visit," I confessed, scratching at my jaw.

"You did what?" she asked, sounding alarmed.

Grinning, I took out my phone and pulled up my videos. "Don't worry. No one got hurt."

When I turned the screen toward her, it showed Josh answering his door, finding the gift I left for him.

"Is that—?"

"Your ex, yes."

"And is that...?"

"A flaming bag of dog poop," I finished for her.

His high-pitch shrieking came through the speakers and Ellie covered her mouth while she laughed, watching the scene play out. She shifted closer to me, putting her head next to mine, and I caught a whiff of her intoxicating scent.

Strawberries, coconuts, and happiness. Pure fucking happiness.

After the video was over, I hit delete and set my phone down on the counter.

"I have two questions," I told her and she raised her eyebrows. "Why are you covered in mud?" I pointed down at her jeans, then pointed at the table. "And what's for dinner?"

Sheepishly, she shrugged. "I sort of had a flat on the way here. I changed it, no problem." She waved her hand like it wasn't a big deal, but the thought of her on her knees with a carjack made my dick twitch.

"Hang on a sec. You knew how to change a tire by yourself? Where did you learn that?" I asked sarcastically.

She sighed. "You're going to make me say it, aren't you?"

I stood back and gave her a 'give me' gesture with my hand.

"You were right," she muttered quietly at her feet.

"I'm sorry, what was that?" I cupped a hand around my ear.

Her lips twitched. "I said, you were right."

"Maybe I should get that on video," I joked, reaching for

my phone, and Ellie made an adorable scoffing sound.

"Let's talk about dinner instead." Pulling me over to the kitchen table, she made a sweeping motion with her arm. "Ketchup and mustard sandwiches, of course."

"You made me our favorite dinner?"

"Well, I'm not sure how good it'll taste as adults, but, yeah. My attempt at groveling doesn't even compare to what you've done." She glanced at our sign, then frowned down at the plates.

"Ellie, the fact that you're here is enough. Plus, you can make it up to me in a different way."

Cocking an eyebrow, she looked intrigued. "Oh, yeah? What did you have in mind?"

I sent her a wicked smirk. "You'll see."

CHAPTER 48

Brielle

rustrated, I yanked at the metal chaining me to the headboard. Colton let out a low chuckle, his breath fanning over my swollen clit.

He wasn't kidding when he said turnabout was fair play in this game. I let out a pathetic whine as he denied my release for the fifth time. He kept bringing me to the brink of orgasm over and over again, but then he would back off.

I had no idea how long it had been going on because I'd lost all sense of time. All I knew was that it was sometime in the middle of the night and I'd been reduced to shameless begging.

"Shiiiiit. Oh, my God. *Please…*" I pulled at the handcuffs again.

"You're not gonna do that to me again, right?" Colton asked, referring to my freak-out that resulted in us almost breaking up.

"No," I moaned, digging my heels into the mattress.

"You're mine for good?" He slipped two fingers into me and started rubbing my g-spot again.

"Yes," I panted. It was the truth, but honestly I would have told him anything he wanted to hear at that point. "Please, Colton. *Please.*"

My mind was fuzzy. I couldn't feel my toes. My face felt

tingly. I couldn't concentrate on anything other than the fact that I *needed* to come.

He gave my center another lick before reaching over to the nightstand and taking out a condom.

"I'd like to keep torturing you," he said, rolling it on. "But." He sucked one of my nipples into his mouth. "I don't think I can hold out any longer."

"Oh, good," I breathed out, feeling disoriented. "That's really good."

"I want you to come on my dick, Ellie."

I made some unintelligible sound of agreement and, with one powerful thrust, he buried himself to the hilt. He pumped his thick cock into me, hard and deep while rubbing his thumb over my clit.

"Shit," I gasped, spreading my legs wider as I felt my walls start to clench around him. I was already so close.

His mouth claimed mine in a possessive kiss and his fingers threaded through my hair. Thrusting harder, he tightened the grip he had on my strands, causing my head to tilt back. His lips left mine and he scraped his teeth over my chin before sucking at a sensitive spot on my neck.

"Tell me you love me," he ordered, grinding his pelvis against mine.

"You know I do."

He pinched my right nipple. "Tell me. Say the words."

One thumb started circling my nipple while the other went back to my clit.

"I love you." My voice came out in a squeak because I was coming. So hard.

The breath was stolen from my lungs and my mouth fell open with a silent scream. My inner muscles spasmed as Colton continued to rock into me.

Toes curling and back arched, I heard him groan as he

came with me.

Colton rested his forehead against mine as we tried to catch our breath, and he sweetly kissed the tip of my nose.

"I love you, Ellie," he whispered, not bothering to leave my body just yet.

Our eyes locked—my brown to his gray—and even in the darkness I could see the love I felt for him reflected at me.

The intensity of the moment, both physically and emotionally, was so overwhelming. The full weight of the mistake I made by pushing Colton away crashed down on me. Because of my fears, I almost made the worst decision of my life.

I almost lost my best friend.

But he wouldn't give up on me.

I felt a tear slip from my eye and slide down my temple.

I tried to reach for him, but I was reminded yet again that I was attached to the headboard. The metal clanked, and I let out a little growl. My frustration didn't last long, though, because Colton brought his hands up to mine and linked our fingers, giving me the extra contact I needed.

"I really do love you," I said quietly, my lips brushing against his.

I was rewarded with his signature cocky grin.

"I know," he said confidently. "Be right back."

He gave me a quick kiss before leaving the bed. Immediately, I shivered from the loss of his warmth. I thought he was going to get the key and unlock the handcuffs, but instead, he cleaned himself off and then hopped up next to me.

"What are you doing?" I asked, still feeling dazed.

He tilted his head to the side. "You didn't think you were getting off that easy, did you? No pun intended."

"Easy?!" I huffed out a laugh and tugged at my restraints. "You're kidding, right?"

Slowly, he shook his head from side to side before

positioning his face inches away from my pussy. "Nope."

"My butt's going numb." I pouted before squirming on the mattress.

"That's an easy fix."

Grabbing me by the hips, he flipped my body over.

Startled, I squealed at the sudden change, my shackled arms now crossed by the headboard. Out of the corner of my eye, I saw Colton reach over to get another condom from the nightstand.

"Oh, my God," I breathed out in disbelief. "Seriously?"

"Yup." Chuckling, he gave my ass a light slap. "It's gonna be a long night."

CHAPTER 49

Two Weeks Later

Colton

"I'm here! I'm here!" I heard Ava call out after the front door slammed shut.

Wanting everything to be perfect, I smoothed out the Disney princess throw blanket, then set the pink and white bears next to the pillow on the toddler-sized bed in the corner of my room. Next, I placed a copy of *The Giving Tree* between the bears.

It took some rearranging, but I'd managed to create a special space just for Ava. I'd already gotten permission from Ellie because they were going to start spending a few nights a month at my apartment. This was going to be a complete surprise to Ava, though.

There was a stack of coloring books on my bed. Next to that, a pile of DVDs. A few frilly outfits hung in my closet and Spider-Man PJs were folded up on the dresser.

The best part? I'd gotten a beta fish. He was blue and totally badass. The small one-gallon tank sat on top of my nightstand and the bubbling sound of the filter filled the room.

Ava appeared in my doorway and her eyes flitted around at the changes I'd made. A gasp and a huge smile later, she started doing that tap-dancing thing she did whenever she got really excited.

274 | JAMIE SCHLOSSER

Giggling, she ran down the hall to find Ellie. "Mom, are we gonna live here now?"

"No, but we get to sleep over." I heard Ellie laugh and I followed the sound while carrying an armful of blankets and pillows.

I dumped them on the couch and crouched down in front of Ava. "My new fish needs a name. Think you could help me out with that?"

"Goober!" she replied immediately, as if she had the name on standby.

I laughed. "Goober it is."

"Yay yay yay!" More giggling. More tap-dancing.

"Why don't you go pick out the movie you want to watch and I'll make some popcorn."

"And ketchup and mustard sandwiches?" Ava requested before taking off down the hall.

"And sandwiches," I agreed, turning to see Ellie looking at me with wide eyes.

"Goober is a dead fish swimming," she hissed dramatically. "He's floating down the green mile right now."

Shrugging, I started to set up the couch for movie night. "If he dies, I'll just go get another one. There were ten more just like him at the pet store." I fluffed the pillows and stood up. "Besides, I bought premium fish food. No Doritos for Goober."

Shaking her head, Ellie tried not to smile and Ava came out with her movie choice—*The Good Dinosaur*. I didn't really know what it was about, but when I went to Walmart, it was on display with a bunch of other new kids' movies. Wanting to be thorough, I'd grabbed one of everything.

With Ellie on my right side and Ava on the left, we snuggled up on the couch. I surveyed the damage we'd done. Sandwich crusts, juice boxes, and several kernels of popcorn littered the coffee table.

A box of crayons had been dumped on the floor and I had a few new pictures to hang on my refrigerator.

Instead of concentrating on the movie, I thought about the plans we had the next day. My dad was going to meet Ava for the first time, and we were supposed to go over to his place in the morning for breakfast.

I hadn't seen my old man so excited in a long time.

After Ellie and I made up, he'd made it a point to apologize to her for his wrong-doing when we were kids. Said he wanted to bury the hatchet. Start off on the right foot. At first I'd been afraid that Ellie would be hurt or angry at him, but she looked at him with understanding and forgave him, no questions asked.

Ava gasped at something that happened in the movie, bringing my thoughts back to Arlo the dinosaur, and I held her a little tighter.

By the time the end credits were rolling across the screen, both girls were asleep. I woke Ellie—because I couldn't carry them both—and she sleepily followed me to the bedroom.

Laying Ava down, I made sure she was tucked in, and I noticed she was almost too big for the toddler-sized mattress. It would do for now.

Joining a much more awake-looking Ellie in the bed, I lay down to face her.

"I think I know why I can never win thumb war," I whispered to her in the darkness.

Our faces were so close that her nose brushed mine when she propped herself up on an elbow.

"Oh yeah?" She smirked, the blue glow from the fish tank illuminating her features. "Please, enlighten me."

"Clearly, your right hand has some kind of supernatural defect," I explained in hushed tones. "We've never done it left-handed."

She scoffed and held out her left hand.

After whispering the chant, our thumbs danced together and she put up a good fight. I fought harder. For the first time ever, I pinned her thumb underneath mine.

"Fuck yes!" I hissed quietly, giving a fist pump. My victory had to be toned down because I didn't want to wake Ava, but nothing could stop the triumphant smile on my face.

Well, almost nothing.

"Good job. Congratulations." Ellie patronized while rubbing my shoulder.

"Wait a second. Did you—did you *let* me win?" I asked incredulously.

She gave a mock gasp. "Of course not."

"You did," I accused, outraged.

Ellie's quiet giggle turned into a snort and Ava stirred on her little bed. We both froze, afraid that we might've woken her up, but after a few seconds she rolled over and let out a sleepy sigh.

"We'll talk about this later," I mouthed as went back to lying down.

Ellie bit her lip to keep from laughing. I gently rubbed at her chin with my thumb and she ran a finger over my eyebrow.

"I love you," I whispered.

"I love you, too," she whispered back. "Three…"

"Two."

"One."

We grinned at each other. "Goodnight."

∽

Sometime in the middle of the night, the end of the mattress dipped and I felt Ava crawl up the bed. She wedged her little body between us. I helped her get under the covers and she turned to face me. Letting out a contented sigh, she closed her eyes before lightly gripping my ear.

I loved this. Loved having my girls stay the night.

A few times a month wasn't enough, though. I wanted more. I wanted it *every* night.

It was too soon to bring that up to Ellie, but one way or another I was determined to make it happen.

EPILOGUE

Three Months Later

Brielle

I stared down at the address Colton sent in a text.

Colton: Meet me here in 30 minutes.
Me: Oookay. Why?
Colton: Just do it.

Although he couldn't see it, I rolled my eyes and shook my head.

So bossy.

Twenty-five minutes later, I was pulling up to an old white farmhouse in the middle of nowhere. The surrounding cornfields were filled with spring crops, the green rows seeming to stretch for miles. At the back of the property, there was an older-looking metal machine shed along with a two-car garage.

Since it was such a nice day my window was rolled down, and the air breezing through smelled clean and almost sweet. Nothing like the air I was used to in town. Out here, with no other houses or buildings in the way, I could see the whole expanse of the sky. Bright blue and decorated with a few fluffy clouds. It made the scene even more beautiful.

Parking my car next to Colton's truck, I got out and he

met me by my door.

"Hey," I said. "What's going on?"

"Come on." He linked his fingers with mine. "I want to show you something."

Tugging on my hand, he led me over to a patch of tulips and daffodils next to a garden with big leafy plants. "There's a rhubarb patch here." He pointed to one section before motioning toward another. "And that's asparagus."

Confused, I continued to stay silent, letting him drag me around while being my tour guide.

"And back there—those are fruit trees. Two apple and a peach."

"Well, it's beautiful," I told him. "But why are you showing me this?"

"Because the house is for sale and I want to buy it. Travis and Angel are moving out of the apartment next month…" Nervously tapping his fingers on his jeans, he took a deep breath, then blew it out. "And I want you and Ava to move in with me." He didn't wait for me to say anything before continuing. "I know it hasn't been that long, but I know what I want. I think you'd be happy here. Ava, too. The house is old, but I don't mind fixing it up. You can even pick out the color when I redo the siding."

"Yellow?" I asked, my heart pounding with excitement.

"Any color you want."

"And we're in the town of Daywood?" I spun in a circle, searching the horizon for a town.

"About a mile outside of it actually," Colton replied. "It's about 10 minutes to Tolson, and 15 minutes to your parents' house. Daywood has a grocery store and a couple restaurants. And if you're still not convinced, the shed has a horse stall."

I gasped. "You can't buy Ava a horse."

"Well, she can ride it, too, but it's for you. Didn't you tell me when we were kids that every girl wants a horse? If you want it, then I want to give it to you."

"Colton," I breathed out, feeling my eyes sting with happy tears.

"But that's not all," he said, dropping down to one knee, and my breath caught in my throat. He opened his hand. In the middle of his palm sat a white-gold ring with a princess-cut solitaire diamond. "Marry me."

All the air left me with a whoosh and I blinked rapidly. I refused to be one of those people who cried on their engagement day.

"Are you asking me or telling me?" I joked, unable to resist giving him a hard time.

He gave me a cocky grin. "Telling you."

There was only one word that popped up in my mind. "Yes."

A brilliant smile spread over Colton's face, crooked bottom teeth and all. Grabbing my hand, he started to put the ring onto my finger but paused. "So that's a yes, you'll move in with me? Or yes, you'll marry me...? Because you only get the ring if you agree to all of it."

I laughed. "Yes to both."

"Good." He finished sliding the sparkling object on. I sighed as I looked at it, wondering how much it cost him.

Speaking of cost... "We should probably talk about the price of the house."

"I'm getting a good deal on it," he replied, aloof.

"Colton, you're going to have to let me help with the payments."

"That's not what I was going for when I asked you to move in. All you have to do is live here."

"And I will live here, while making payments," I said stubbornly.

His lips quirked up and he ran his thumb over my chin. "We'll talk about it later."

I huffed because that was Colton's code-talk for 'end of discussion'. My irritation didn't last long, though, because the sun peeked around the clouds, causing an almost blinding light from my ring. I went back to admiring it.

"One last thing," Colton told me, looking even more nervous than before.

"You're very demanding today," I teased, knowing my answer was going to be yes.

Yes to everything.

"When you take my last name I want Ava to have it, too. I want to legally adopt her, if she'll have me."

Crap.

Maybe I really was going to cry.

I tried to hold it back, but the tears welled up and ran down my cheeks anyway. Drawing my lip between my teeth, I tried to keep it from trembling. My throat was so tight that all I could do was nod, and he wrapped his arms around me. I returned the embrace, running my hands down the muscles of his back.

"Thank you," I whispered shakily.

"Thank you for saying yes." He huffed out a laugh as he squeezed me tighter.

"As if you would've taken no for answer," I retorted with a smile, then the reality set in. "Oh, my God," I gasped, pulling back to look at his face. "We're getting married!"

Smiling, he leaned down to give me a kiss.

"And we're going to do those traditional engagement photos. You know, by a meadow with wild flowers or some shit," he said, repeating my words from months before about the maternity pics I'd wanted so badly.

I launched myself at Colton, wrapping my legs around

his waist. He laughed as I rested my forehead against his.

"How do you feel about a little outdoor sex?" he asked, eyeing the shady area under a nearby maple tree. "I fucking love this dress." His hand traveled up the back of my thigh until it reached the edge of my panties.

Giggling, I released my hold on his body and shook my head. "We're going to be late to the picnic. My parents are already there with Ava."

"You're right," he agreed with a sigh. "My dad and everyone else is there, too."

"I'll follow you there," I told him because I had never been to Elmer Lake before.

Colton gave me another toe-curling kiss before hopping into his truck.

Colton

My family and friends had unknowingly ruined my plans. I'd wanted to bring both Ellie and Ava to the house, then I was going to ask them to move in with me along with the proposal.

But then Travis sent me a text letting me know that we were having a spontaneous picnic at Elmer Lake. He'd already gotten the plans hashed out with my dad and his mom. Angel invited her friends, Beverly and Ernie. She also told Ellie, then Ellie invited her parents.

So before I knew it, I was scrambling to change the agenda and asked her to meet me at the house beforehand.

After getting Ellie to accept my proposal, you'd think it would be smooth sailing.

Nope.

As I touched the second, much smaller ring in my pocket, I felt like I had to remind myself to breathe. The thought of asking Ava to let me be her dad was scary as fuck.

What if she didn't want that?

Sometimes Ava was brutally honest, and I'd learned over the past few months that it was pretty fucking difficult to make a little kid do something they were hell-bent on *not* doing. Plus, I didn't want to *make* her accept me as her dad—I wanted her to want that on her own.

As I stood there, heart racing, I tried to distract myself from my anxiety by listening to the conversations happening around us.

Beverly, the elderly woman Angel had befriended when she first came to Tolson, was cheerfully talking about her summer plans. "My grandson, Jimmy—he's such a sweetheart. You remember him, right?"

"Of course," Travis replied, and I gave an absentminded nod.

We'd all met him at Christmas last year, although I wouldn't have described the guy as sweet. Jimmy was a tattooed, whiskey-drinking hellion.

"Anyway," Beverly went on, "He's going to be staying with me for two months, and I'm going to play matchmaker."

"With who?" Angel asked, confused, because Tolson wasn't exactly overrun with single women.

A mischievous grin spread over the old woman's face. "A lovely young lady from Daywood just moved in next door. She's skittish as all get out. I'm trying to make friends with her, but the poor thing is scared of her own shadow." Her smile turned confident. "Jimmy will know how to bring her out of her shell."

Well, that sounded like a disaster waiting to happen. But Beverly was almost four times my age and probably four times as wise, so what did I know?

Ava's voice pulled my attention away.

"...Four, five, six." She counted the pieces of bologna on the wooden dock by the tackle box. "That means we'll catch six fish?" she asked, glancing up at my dad.

"Don't count your chickens before they're hatched— that's what I always say. Or, in this case, don't count your fish before they're caught." He chuckled, seeming proud of himself, like he'd just given Ava the greatest words of wisdom ever, but she just looked downright confused. From the baffled expression on her face, it was obvious she had no idea what he was talking about.

"Don't mind him," I told her, sending a smirk in my dad's direction. "He's getting senile in his old age."

Dad guffawed and went back to digging around in the tackle box.

Still feeling jittery, I went over to Ellie and whispered by her ear, "I'm really nervous."

She scraped her fingernails over the scruff on my jaw in a comforting gesture, and I was momentarily distracted by how good she looked in her sundress. The yellow cotton stretched over her breasts and the hem fell to about mid-thigh. It was pretty innocent-looking, but I knew what was *under* that dress.

"You weren't this nervous when you asked me," she pointed out.

"That's because I knew you wouldn't turn me down," I said, causing her to smile and roll her eyes. I wasn't wrong, though. And if she'd said no, I was fully prepared to pester her until I turned it into a yes.

"Do you want me to talk to her about it first?" she asked, concern etched on her face.

I shook my head. "I want to do it. Hey, Bug," I called over

to Ava. "Want to go exploring?"

Nodding, she wiped her dirty hands on her own sundress—white with pink flowers—and ran over to me.

After placing her on my shoulders, I started walking around the lake. I held onto her ankles while she lovingly rubbed my earlobes. As the warm breeze caused ripples over the water, I remembered a tall tale my dad used to tell me.

"Have I ever told you the story of Elmer the fish?" I asked Ava, knowing that I hadn't.

"No," she responded, her interest piqued.

"He was the biggest bass ever caught from this lake. He was so magnificent that no one could bear the thought of eating him, so they threw him back. More people started catching him, and each time they would tag him with a mark, then let him go back home." Ava's silence let me know that she was listening intently, so I continued. "He just kept getting bigger and bigger until no one could catch him anymore. Every time someone's fishing line breaks, they say it's Elmer. He's a legend in these parts. Some people think he's named after the lake and others say the lake was named after him."

Finishing the story and reaching our destination, I set Ava down on a big rock slab.

"Where is he now?" she asked.

I shrugged. "No one knows. He's probably swimming around out there, eating everyone's fishing hooks."

I took a seat on the rock and Ava plopped down onto my lap.

"If we catch Elmer, can we let him live with Goober?"

The fish currently living in my room was Goober the 3rd, but Ava didn't know that. Ellie hadn't been wrong about the fish dying. Or the fact that they were gateway pets. I was seriously tempted to give up and just get a ferret or something.

"I don't think Elmer would fit in that tank."

"Oh. Well, maybe we could just put him in the bathtub at my house," Ava said, looking out at the water.

Snickering, I ruffled her hair and I took a few seconds to gather my courage. Taking a deep breath, I decided to just bite the bullet before I chickened out.

"Ava... What would you think about me marrying your mom?" I started, going for direct.

Her eyes got wide as she glanced my way. "Would she get to wear a princess dress?"

I laughed. "Yeah, she could wear any dress she wanted to."

"What about me? Can I wear a princess dress?"

There it was. My opening.

I took the tiny ring from my pocket and held it up for her to see. "You'd get to wear a dress, too. And if you want..." I swallowed hard. "I could be your dad."

"Like a real dad? A really really dad?" she asked, her voice full of hope and her eyes shining with happiness.

I felt my own eyes start to get misty. "Yeah, Bug. A really really dad. Do you want that?"

"Yeah!" She nodded and hugged me around the neck.

Just then, a yellow butterfly fluttered around us and landed on a nearby dandelion. I watched it as I held my daughter—*my daughter*—and the bright wings flapped a few times before it flew away.

"Can I have my ring now?" Ava asked, her words muffled because her face was still pressed against my shirt.

I barked out a laugh. "Sure."

After she pulled back, I put the ring her on right pointer finger. Just like her mom's, it was white-gold, but hers had a pink heart-shaped diamond framed by smaller white gems. Okay, they were actually cubic zirconia, but she was four and the possibility that she would lose it at some point was highly likely.

"Let's go show Mom!" she said before climbing my body like a jungle gym and taking a seat upon my shoulders once again.

As we got closer to our gathering, Ava's excitement couldn't be contained. Scrambling down, she practically jumped to the ground, then broke out in a sprint toward an anxious-looking Ellie, who was worrying the skin on her left thumb.

"Mom!" Ava squealed. "We're getting married!"

All eyes swung to us as I reached my girls, expressions ranging from shocked to ecstatic. The cat was out of the bag. Now that everyone knew, I took Ellie's ring out of my pocket and slipped it onto her finger.

With a laugh, she held her hand out for everyone to see and Ava did the same.

A chorus of "Oohs" and "Congratulations" came from our family and friends. The men clapped me on the back and the women flocked around Ellie.

Angel started chattering about wedding details at 100 miles a minute and Travis sent me a knowing smirk. I didn't know anything about wedding shit, but I had a feeling Ellie would have tons of help in that department.

Dave sent me a wink because he'd already known about my plan. I might've been a demanding guy, but I was still a gentleman. I wouldn't have dared to ask Ellie to marry me without her dad's permission.

Ellie glanced over at me and we locked eyes. I'd seen her happy before but through all the memories, I had never seen her look like this.

Elated. Glowing. Stunning.

I'd had to jump through so many hoops for this moment, which only made it better. As I looked back on our relationship, I realized there was no limit to the things I would do for Ellie.

I would've paid more to learn her name.

I would've chased her down at Caged night after night.

And I would spend the rest of my life proving to her that she could count on me over and over again.

The End

DANCER PLAYLIST

"Vacation" by The Go-Go's

"Girls Just Want to Have Fun" by Cyndi Lauper

"Thunderstruck" by AC/DC

"S&M" by Rihanna

"Don't Let Me Down" by The Chainsmokers

"She's Like the Wind" by Patrick Swayze

"Head Over Boots" by Jon Pardi

"Why Don't We Just Dance" by Josh Turner

"Middle of a Memory" by Cole Swindell

"Pretty Tied Up" by Guns N' Roses

"Unchained Melody" by The Righteous Brothers

"Whip It" by Devo

"Boot Scootin' Boogie" by Brooks & Dunn

"Good For You" by Selena Gomez

"H.O.L.Y." by Florida Georgia Line

"Shameless" by Garth Brooks

"Tiny Dancer" by Elton John

OTHER BOOKS

ACKNOWLEDGEMENTS

First, I want to give a huge thank-you to my entire support system. I couldn't do this without my family and friends who have been my cheerleaders every step of the way. Drew—Thanks for being Super Dad to our crazy kids. Kim—He's not a yeti! Brittaney—Tits giggled. Melissa—Thanks for being my day drinking partner and listening to me talk about my characters for hours.

To the wonderful bloggers who have reviewed and/or promoted my books—I appreciate you so much! Book world wouldn't be the same without romance-lovers like you.

To my betas Kate, Brittaney, Liz, Allison E., Allison M., and Carole. You ladies rock!

My Newbs—Thank you for never judging me when I have a really stupid question, and for offering your knowledge and support when I need it most.

And to my readers, the lovers of the good guys of romance—YOU have made my dream come true. Your reviews mean the world to me and your kind messages motivate me to keep writing. Thank you!

ABOUT THE AUTHOR

Jamie Schlosser grew up on a farm in Illinois, surrounded by cornfields. Although she no longer lives in the country, her dream is to return to rural living someday. As a stay-at-home mom, she spends most of her days running back and forth between her two wonderful kids and her laptop. She loves her family, iced coffee, and happily-ever-afters. You can find out more about Jamie and her books by visiting these links:

Facebook: www.facebook.com/authorjamieschlosser
Amazon: amzn.to/2mzCQkQ
Twitter: twitter.com/SchlosserJamie
Bookbub: www.bookbub.com/authors/jamie-schlosser
Newsletter: eepurl.com/cANmI9

Also, do you like being the first to get sneak peeks on upcoming books? Do you like exclusive giveaways? Most importantly, do you like otters?

If you answered yes to any of these questions, you should consider joining Jamie Schlosser's Significant Otters! www.facebook.com/groups/1738944743038479